# LOST IN A HOMELAND

**Ann Bowyer**

Lost in a Homeland © 2015 Ann Bowyer

All rights reserved in all media. No part of this book may be reproduced or transmitted in any form by any means, electronic or mechanical (including but not limited to the internet, photocopying, recording or by any information storage or retrieval system) without prior permission in writing of the copyright holder.

This book is a work of fiction. The names, characters, places and incidents are products of the writer's imagination and are not to be construed as real. Any resemblance to persons living or dead or actual events is entirely coincidental.

Cover design: Richard Bowyer

# Other Books by the Author

A Token of Love

(The first book in this series)

Visit www.annbowyer.com to find out more about the author or follow her on Facebook or Twitter

*Thanks to my family, especially my husband, for their patience and encouragement to keep on writing. Also a big thank you to all those wonderful people who assisted in its production*

# Lost in a Homeland

## Chapter One

## October 1932

George gazed across the ocean. After the stormy weather of the previous few days, the sea was calm but its intense cobalt told of its depth. Tiny waves broke on the surface and plumes of smoke trailed high in the sky as the ship's engines throbbed below his feet. Anybody scrutinising the deck would assume George, like any other traveller, was taking the opportunity to get away from the cramped quarters below. But George hadn't noticed the restricted conditions, or the number of his fellow passengers who had been sick and were now glad of more tranquil conditions. His focus was inwards - memories churning over and over – bodies in trenches, men without limbs, their blooded faces looming large … Why did these flash backs come now? Now, when the trauma of more recent weeks was so fresh? Was it because it was perverse to relive the nightmare of a drought whilst sailing across the ocean?

He tried to think of a future – their future but his mind was blank. They left all those years ago because there was no work, so why should there be any now? England hadn't escaped the grip of the depression any more than Canada.

'Freddie will look after us,' Amy had argued so many times.

But a man needed his independence, needed to look after his own family, earn his own way in the world. And he had failed. On every count, he had failed. He thought of Archie and the trenches. Maybe it would have been better if it had ended with the sniper's bullet which had got Archie. What had he got to show for all his efforts?

As the ship's propellers pushed them onwards across the Atlantic, nearer and nearer to England, his mood became blacker and gloomier. What was there to look forward to? To live for even?

\* \* \* \* \*

Amy, followed by the three children, climbed the steps which led to the deck. At the top she paused, scanning the passengers, knowing George would be among them. Since the ship had departed, sailing first along the St Lawrence Seaway and now across the Atlantic, each day was the same. After a silent breakfast, he would leave the table without a word. She shared his despair but they had three children and there was no time for self-pity. Bobbie was too young to understand the immensity of it all and Sam didn't care. It was only Will who was resentful and disobedient and blamed her for everything. But the drought and the tornado weren't of her creation. She had only done what any sane woman would have in the circumstances - gone for help. George was so proud, so independent, so determined, so obstinate. No one could ever say he hadn't given his all - they both had, but the force of nature was something no man would ever tame. If they had had savings to fall back on, maybe they could have stayed. If her mother had found it in her heart to help them ... but they had nothing and she couldn't bear to see them starve when help was a letter away.

She stared at George's back. How could she cheer him up – make things better for him? Someone once told her that every cloud had a silver lining but so far she hadn't been able to see one nor did it make the black hole in which George had sunk any less. She knew she was struggling to reach him.

\* \* \* \* \*

Freddie shouted his 'good-byes' to Jonathan through the open window and drove out of the drive and onto the road. The Vauxhall was a dream to handle after his last car and, wherever he drove it, its sleek red body with its black roof and running boards always caused a stir. He enjoyed the sensation of owning such a vehicle, revelling in the stares and dismissing the fact that he owed his mother an awful lot of money. The garage would come right, he was certain of that and if not, well, his inheritance would settle it - one day.

The day was fresh and sunny and lifted his spirits. He forgot about the row he'd had with Enid that morning. How could he not meet his sister after all these years? It was unreasonable of Enid to suggest otherwise. He dismissed the whole episode from his mind. He'd enjoy the long drive from Buckinghamshire to Southampton but it would have been so much fun if Beth had been able to come - a night away together was what he needed to cope with the problems of his domestic life. She understood him, fulfilled his needs. From the moment he had looked into her blue eyes he knew she was the woman for him but he was trapped - trapped in a marriage arranged by his mother - a marriage which satisfied appearances. Enid was the right class, unlike Beth who ran the White Hart public house, which she had inherited from her parents.

But it would never do to turn up to meet his sister with his mistress and he dreaded to think what his mother would have said if he had. In fact, judging from comments she had made at various times, he questioned if it was possible his mother already had her suspicions. Or was it him being over-sensitive? One or two pointed remarks had been made recently about the number of visits he was making to the White Hart. Did she disapprove of his drinking habits or was it that she objected to the company he kept? He had cast these thoughts aside, saying that Enid's pregnancy made life intolerable and sometimes he needed to get out of the house and he had reminded his mother how difficult life had been when Jonathan was on his way.

As he negotiated a series of tight bends, he concentrated on his driving technique before reliving the numerous conversations he'd had with his mother. Amy's letter sounded desperate but, even after reading it, his mother was reluctant to help.

'She chose to marry that man in spite of being betrothed to Charles. He would have given her everything - wealth and position,' his mother had grumbled and he knew she was only thinking of how marrying into aristocracy would benefit herself. 'There's an old saying - he who makes the bed must lie in it. Why should I help?'

He had tried to explain that the severe weather in the Prairies was not of George's making but she would have none of it, so he tried another tack.

'Mother, you can't allow your daughter and grandchildren to starve and if you don't help, they surely will.'

'Hmmm.'

'If I had the money I'd send it, but, with the garage only beginning to come on stream, you know I haven't got any. Anyway, just think. It would never do if it came out that you allowed Amy to die of starvation.'

She had relented then. The cheque was written. A letter composed setting out the conditions under which the tickets - not money – were being sent - that they all returned to England. He was charged with the task of purchasing the tickets - not easy with the Olympics in Los Angeles and the state of the world's economy which had resulted in fewer ships making the crossing. He had posted the letter with the tickets, knowing George would not willingly accept his mother-in-law's condition but it was the best he could do.

Now he questioned if he would have been able to sway her if she had known of his involvement with Beth. He was also unsure what sort of reception Amy and George would receive when he took them to 'Hazeldene'. He hadn't told Amy in his last letter that Enid refused, when she was seven months pregnant, to cope with five extra people in her household. He'd only told Amy the good news about possible employment for George. There was a house with the job but George still had the interview to attend and they all had to live somewhere in the meantime. 'Hazeldene' would accommodate them all but his mother wasn't too happy about them staying with her either.

\* \* \* \* \*

Violet cast her eyes round the cramped front room of the London Victorian terraced house in which she had grown up. Her eyes rested on the photograph of her father in a dark wooden frame on the mantelshelf. It was taken shortly before he died of the flu. In this room, Harold had asked her mother's permission to marry her – their small reception had been here. She studied the large aspidistra in its ochre pot, resplendent in the window and thought of the time she had been asked to water it and the mess she had made. Then she glanced up at the picture rail upon which hung the brown framed "Laughing Cavalier". He stared back at her. No matter where she was in the room, she was certain he was always looking at her. Finally she admired the smart new rag rug which her mother had spent months making and which lay in front of the hearth, covering only a small portion of the stained floorboards. Yes, she had been happy here.

It was October and cool in the evenings but with so many of them huddled together on extra chairs retrieved from the dining room, the fire wasn't necessary and, in any case, her mother was always frugal - a case of having to be with such a big family. Ted was dispensing the sherry. She glanced at her mother who, she thought, looked almost regal on her 70th birthday.

They were all here - except her father and George, of course. She had grown used to not having her father around but she still missed George. He was the one brother with whom she could identify but George had married Amy and taken her off to Canada. Their last letter had been months and months ago and was chirpy enough. Amy was always cheerful, though now she thought about it, that letter had been different. There was an undertone and she had detected something wasn't right. She thought back over the recent years. There were those letters between Ma and the local MP something to do with asking questions in parliament. She hadn't paid much attention. Ma's politics bored her. But Amy's first letter from their new address had been so upbeat. Surely things were going well now they were settled on another farm?

Ted handed her a glass of sherry and, as the eldest, was about to offer a toast but he was prevented by one of her sisters, Phoebe.

'I'm glad you're all here, there's something important I want to tell you. Richard and I ... well, Richard's proposed,' she paused and glanced at her mother, who smiled her approval. 'And I've accepted.' She beamed at them as they all voiced their congratulations.

Trust Phoebe to steal the limelight, Violet thought, and on the very day she had wanted to tell everyone she was pregnant. She hugged the news to herself. Maybe she would wait until another day.

## Chapter Two

'How will we ever fit on one of those?' Will demanded in a disparaging tone. He pointed to the trains lined up at the dockside. A steam engine chuffed huge curls of steam as it heaved its wagons away from the port. 'Sure are small. They look like toys.'

Amy had been scrutinizing the people – or more particularly, the women – waiting on the dockside for those on board to disembark. Fashions out in the Prairies hadn't changed much in years and she was mesmerized by the long and sleek style, often topped with cloche hats and worn with matching gloves and shoes. She followed Will's pointed finger wondering if there was anything he would find acceptable in England. He was scathing about almost everything, but, when she caught sight of the train, even she had to agree, he was right. From where they were standing on the deck of the Montcalm, it did look minute, especially after the ones in Canada. She could see several trucks and motor cars and she was in no doubt he would disapprove of those, too.

'We're very high up, Will. They only seem small. They'll be bigger when we disembark. You'll see.' She tried to sound positive but knew when they got to stand closer he would still criticize. Ever since they had left the farm, he had done little else. There was no pleasing him. As if matters weren't hard enough with George. Was it something to do with the male sex? Or was it herself? She reached out to both of them – wanted to offer them comfort, but no matter what she said, they were each tucked inside their own world way beyond her reach. Of course, on giving the matter proper consideration, she realised the two of them, her husband and son, had lost the most. Will had grown up knowing his place in life was to run the farm and, in the absence of his father, to take over as man about the place. When the farm was sold, he had seen it through with George – and it was heart breaking for them both. Life was going to be so different for them all but more especially for Will, who, at such a tender age, had been robbed, not only of his dog which they had been forced to re-home, but of his position in life. It would mean a huge adjustment – for all of them.

She squeezed Bobbie's hand - he was the only normal member of her family right now. Maybe because, as a five year old he didn't comprehend the difficulties ahead or realise what they had left behind. Maybe. She glanced at Sam, her middle son, who was his usual awkward self. She had read once that being a middle child was difficult - being neither the oldest nor the youngest. She could understand that but, Sam, always into mischief, never seemed to have a care in the world and she didn't believe he was too concerned whether he was the oldest or youngest.

'Freddie did say he would meet us,' she said to George who stood behind her, watching as the crew secured the ship to the dockside with huge hawsers. She hoped she was right because, in spite of George not sharing all the facts, she was only too well aware they had spent most of their few dollars on the journey. In fact, if Freddie didn't meet them, she wasn't sure if they had enough even for the rail fare.

She glanced up at George, who was staring straight ahead. He didn't reply. His expression was vacant, as it had been for most of the voyage, and she was left wondering what he was thinking. His silence left her feeling locked out. It was like the war all over again but this time, she had been part of the nightmare. His loss was hers, too, and she needed to talk about it and plan for the future, as well as laugh, cry, hug - but above all, share their troubles.

It was hours later before they disembarked. To her relief, as they walked down the gangway, she spotted Freddie. He stood head and shoulders above those around him and doffed his hat when he saw them. For the first time since leaving Canada, she was conscious of their shabbiness. Freddie was wearing a crisp white shirt and a very smart suit, the trousers having what she thought might be referred to as turn-ups. He even wore a waistcoat. He looked so dapper and so … successful. She was interested to see he had only acquired a few grey hairs in the years since they had last been together, whereas she had sprouted lots. She tried not to feel bitter but it was impossible not to make comparisons. There was George's depression, Will's misbehaviour, their destitute state not to mention the previous months in which there had been so little to eat, whereas their mother had bankrolled Freddie's business and helped him buy the mansion of a place in which he and Enid now resided. If only she had found it in her heart to lend them a few pounds, they might have made a go of things in Canada. But, she reminded herself, she had married for love - completely against her mother's wishes, and in spite of all his faults she still loved George. Her mother had found it in her heart to pay for their fares back to England, but if only she had found it in her heart to lend them the money to stay.

After all the hugs and shaking of hands and introductions of the children, Freddie guided them to where the car was parked.

'Well, what you do think?' he turned to George. 'I'm really pleased with its performance - drives like a dream.'

'Is that all you can talk about when there's so many other things we need to know.' Amy frowned in disgust. Freddie hadn't changed. He was as besotted with motor cars as he was when they left for Canada over seven years ago.

'This is important, sis. To me at any rate - after all, it is my business. Or have you forgotten? Motor cars are my living.' He turned to George. 'What do you think? Didn't you have a car in Canada?'

George avoided answering and bent to peer inside.

Amy changed the subject. The fact that George had abandoned their one luxury because he hadn't realised the oil needed replenishing and the engine had seized up still rankled and continued to be the source of arguments.

'How will we all fit in?' she asked, peering inside.

'It'll be a tight squeeze, I'm afraid but I thought you and the boys could sit in the back.' He scrutinized his nephews. 'Will's quite tall, but I think you'll be fine. We can stop and have a rest half way. It's as well your trunks are coming later.'

'There isn't much. How's mother?' Amy asked and felt her stomach churn.

'She's looking forward to having you all.'

'Having us all ...' her voice trailed off. Surely, they would be staying with Freddie - at least until they got their own place? 'You don't – surely we're ... We're not staying with mother, are we, Freddie?' She glanced at George who had given up his inspection of the car to prevent Bobbie from stepping into the road. 'Please don't say we are.'

A guilty look crossed Freddie's face. 'Enid's seven months pregnant and wouldn't ... well, let's say, the five of you would be rather a lot in our small house. I'm sorry, sis. Marital peace and all that. Take my word, it'll be better this way.

Better for whom, she wondered. 'But, Freddie ...' she began in a low voice, hoping George hadn't heard. The voyage home had been difficult enough - the last thing she wanted was a difficult car journey.

'It won't be for long. As soon as George has met Reginald, you'll be able to move into your new home.'

'Did I hear that right?' George, now holding Bobbie by the hand, scowled at her and immediately knew by their faces that he had. 'We're not staying at your mother's,' he said in a firm tone.

'It's not for long,' she tried to soothe him.

He took a deep breath, exhaling slowly. 'Godamn it, Amy. You can't expect ...' He looked at Freddie.

'Don't look at me, old man. You know what women are like, especially when they're pregnant. Mother'll be no trouble - just avoid her. It's a big enough house.'

'Just till we get our own place.' Amy said but knew by his expression whatever she said would be useless. How could she blame him? She still found it hard to forgive her mother for burning his letters all those years ago and, though she had written regularly to her, there were never any replies and they hadn't spoken since their marriage more than twelve years ago. If she said it was going to be difficult, it would be an understatement. It was going to be horrendous but there was no other choice.

'No,' George said in a firm voice. 'No. Not even for a short while and, be realistic, how can I avoid her?'

Freddie turned away but not before he had given Amy a look which told her he expected her to sort her husband out.

'Enid's in the last months of her pregnancy. The last thing she wants is three extra children running about,' she said and placed her hand on his arm and gave it a slight squeeze.

'Then the answer's obvious.' George ignored her hand. 'At least it is to me. We'll go to my mother's.'

'But – how can we? The house isn't big enough for us all. When we got married, we had one room and now there are five of us. Where would we all sleep?' They should have sorted the matter out during their voyage across the Atlantic but George wouldn't talk and now they were rowing and in front of Freddie of all people. 'Anyway, we have to face my mother sometime. It's not fair to leave me to do it alone.'

'Not fair?' George said in a raised voice. He glanced at Freddie's back and lowered his voice. 'You're asking too much if you expect me to live under the same roof as your mother.' George's face was set.

'She did pay for our tickets home,' she said and immediately wished she could take the words back.

'Godamn it, Amy, don't you think I know it and don't you think she'll rub my nose in it. I never was good enough for you and now as sure as hell I've proved it.'

'Don't be so silly. It wasn't your fault there was a drought. Nobody could ever overcome what we faced.'

'She wasn't there and anyway, she won't see it that way.'

'Hey, you two. No arguments on your first day in England,' Freddie interrupted from the other side of the car. 'We should be setting off. It's a long journey, you know.'

George took the hint and opened the rear passenger door. 'In you get, boys.'

The three hushed children climbed into the back seat but when Amy tried to follow, George's iron grip held her. 'You sit in the front.'

'But you'd be more comfy there,' she said, then seeing the expression on his face sat in the car.

'I'm not coming.'

'What!' She got out of the car again and stared into his face in disbelief.

'Go, see your mother and say thank you if you want but sure as hell I prefer to stay with my own family.'

'But, George …'

'No, Amy. I'm not staying at your mother's – not ever.'

'But what about the job …' Amy looked at Freddie for help. 'Isn't there an interview or something?'

'Oh, a formality - to be arranged,' Freddie said.

'Sure thing, Freddie. I remember Violet writing there was a new telephone box at the end of the street. I'll call in a day or two.'

She felt herself bundled back into the front of the car, anything she might have said, dying on her lips. There was no arguing with George when his mind was made up.

'No cheeking your Mom or your Uncle for that matter,' George said to the boys as he closed the door.

Freddie didn't wait for further squabbles. He slid into the driving seat in an instant, banged the door closed and slipped the car into gear.

'Freddie, please. Stop! I can't leave George like this.'

The car jerked to a standstill and she got out again and ran back up the road.

'George, please. I can't bear this.'

'Amy, no matter what you say, I am not sleeping under the same roof as your mother. No, not ever. Now you're holding Freddie up.' He walked her back to the car. 'It's better this way.'

She sat back in the car, tears springing to her eyes.

'George, please,' she started to say but he had closed the door and her last image was of him standing with a set expression on his face, watching the car drive away. She beat back the tears not quite believing what had happened. Since their marriage, they had never been apart - except, that is, for the short time she had spent in hospital having Bobbie. Now it felt as though, in pushing her into the car, he had pushed her out of his life. Everything felt unreal. Had she lost George for ever? She felt as though she was drowning in her misery.

There was a howl of protest from Sam and for a moment her thoughts were drawn back to the children. Will had stuck his elbow in Sam's side, apparently in retaliation for some earlier misdemeanour. An argument ensued and she found herself forever intervening trying to keep the peace.

They stopped for a break at Farnborough when Amy made Will sit beside Freddie and she sat between the other two. The rest of the drive was completed in a fair amount of silence. Will had the sulks, the other two looked out of the window, and Freddie concentrated on the road with the occasional comment while Amy went over and over in her mind, the words which had passed between her and George.

As the journey progressed, she was already regretting she hadn't gone to London with George. He was right her mother was insufferable and he had every reason to feel resentful. But wherever they resided, they were going to be reliant on whoever it was for financial support until George got work and, too late, she'd realised George would never be able to accept anything more from her mother. It had hurt enough to accept the tickets for the journey back to England. He saw himself as a failure and stupidly, she now realised, he would regard any further help as humiliating.

But if George didn't have any English currency, how would he purchase a railway ticket? Then more doubts crept in … supposing, supposing he never came back … Whatever would she do? She had never doubted George in all their married life, whatever was thrown at them; she had felt safe because he was there. She shut her mind to the thought. She had broken off an engagement approved by her mother, one which would have led to wealth and position, to run off to London and marry the man of her dreams. That must have been difficult enough for her mother to live down - a divorce would be unthinkable. George *would* come back, she told herself - he *had* to.

\* \* \* \* \*

George stared after the car until it disappeared into the distance. It felt as if he was looking through a camera - everything was detached, far away - not happening to him. He was already regretting his impulsive refusal to stay under Mrs Attwood's roof. It was enough they were in debt to her and probably would be for the rest of his days, he reminded himself, but he hadn't come all the thousands of miles across Canada and the Atlantic Ocean only to abandon Amy and his family. This was the very reason he had come. Originally, he'd wanted to stay and get the farm up and running again but it would have meant years of separation and missing his children growing up. Amy was still the only woman for him and he'd never leave her, yet this was pretty well what he'd done. Would it improve his reputation in the eyes of Mrs Attwood? Probably not.

'Hey,' a firm hand grabbed him as he was about to step off the pavement. A car sped past him. He allowed himself to be pulled back from the edge, realising he'd looked the wrong way. He'd contemplated the sea enough times - thought long and hard about leaping over but had always known he couldn't do it. He'd survived the Great War - seen sights he'd rather not recall. No, he was not a coward.

He turned to thank his saviour.

'You didn't want to be doing that, now did you, sir,' the lofty policeman said, making sure he was steady on his feet before letting go of his arm. 'You look lost. Can I help you?'

He sighed and stared down at his feet. How could he explain? Anyway what was the point of telling a complete stranger?

'I need to get to London.'

'Railway station's that way, sir,' the officer said pointing.

'Thanks,' he muttered and turned away.

## Chapter Three

'He's a little darling,' Mrs Attwood declared as Bobbie, small for his years, sat on her lap. 'He reminds me so much of you at that age.'

'Does he, mother?' Amy took a sip of tea and prayed the other two were not up to some mischief. She was grateful Bobbie, at least, had charmed his grandmother. From the moment they arrived, he was the only one of the three children who was not intimidated by her mother's air of authority, her obvious aloofness or by the size of the house.

She thought back to the moment she climbed out of Freddie's car and her feet crunched on the drive. Everything was so green – and damp. The variety of leaves caught in the last light of a vanishing sun fascinated her as did the puddles which had appeared in the drive following a recent shower of rain. It was a shock after the dryness of Manitoba where everything was shrivelled – even her own skin, she reflected. There had been no money for the luxury of skin cream.

She gazed up at the imposing Georgian house with its tall, red brick chimneys and large sash windows which were a stark contrast to the humble timber house they had left in Canada. She spotted the small windows on the third floor – the servants' quarters. When she was a child, there had been a cook and a series of servants. Now that was a word to conjure with and one which she hadn't heard in years. Nobody had maids in the Prairies. True, some had hired help but not servants.

She climbed the steps to the front door, noticing in its deep black gloss her own reflection. The door had equally shiny brass furniture - as her memory told her there would be. She turned to inspect the garden again, hardly believing its beauty, still lush with late summer growth and sighed with an ache of despair for what might have been. She brought herself up short, stifling an unexpected pang of wistfulness. She must think of England as home now.

Freddie had been anxious to get away, so once the door was opened by the maid, he had waved good-bye and driven away. She regretted they hadn't had the chance to talk but what she wanted to discuss wasn't something for the children to hear.

She didn't recognise the maid but she seemed to be expecting them and Amy shepherded the boys up the steps and into the hall. It was vast after weeks of travel, first by train and then by boat and their voices echoed as though in a cavern. Everything else was much as she recalled – the large hall cupboard with its elaborate oval mirror, the umbrella rack complete with two black brollies, the tiled floor and the table where she used to put her mail for posting.

Her mother was waiting for them in the drawing room and stood to greet them, a little unsteadily on her feet, and Amy was alarmed at how much she had aged. Her hair, now quite white and thinning slightly was pulled back into a tight bun as it always had been.

The leather topped desk, where her mother dealt with correspondence, still stood in the bay window. On the opposite wall was the oil painting of a woman holding a posy of roses - Lady Margaret. It brought a horrid recollection. Had she married Charles, this woman would have been her mother-in-law. Irritated by this thought, she stared at the ornate clock on the mantel shelf, its brass pendulum swinging to and fro. It would soon strike the quarter hour. Yes – nothing here had changed yet she - she had. She no longer belonged and without George she felt naked and vulnerable.

Her mother ordered tea, the maid disappeared and she introduced each of the boys. There was an uncomfortable silence in which Amy wanted to embrace her mother but her coolness made her hesitate and, after the warmth of friendship back in Canada, she realised her own English reserve was once again foremost.

'Is this all your house, Grand Mamma?' Bobbie gave Amy a coy smile as though to say, he had everything under control, before slipping his hand into his grandmother's. Quite taken aback by Bobbie's sudden boldness, she was grateful his words had broken the awkward silence.

'Yes, it is.' Mrs Attwood smiled at her grandson. 'Now come and sit with me.'

With the arrival of tea, Will and Sam escaped into the garden and Amy sat near the window so she could keep an eye on them. Her heart sank. After the freedom and equality they had left behind, this felt so antiquated and unforgiving. In spite of Freddie's insistence all those years ago, that after the war, things would have to change, it seemed to her right then, nothing had altered - nothing at all.

'And when can we expect George?' Her mother's disapproving tone jerked her into facing reality. She had dreaded the moment when she would have to explain his absence. It was obvious he would never be accepted as an equal in this household but she wasn't ready to admit their marriage had failed, even though right then it felt as if it had. George would be true to his word and would telephone Freddie soon.

'Oh, within a day or so,' she said, assuming an air of cheeriness but feeling very uncertain as to how long George would stay in London. 'He wanted to see his family and there really isn't room there for us all. Freddie's sorting out some kind of interview and he'll be here for that.'

'I see. So how long do you think that will take?'

Amy's reply was drowned out by the sound of breaking glass.

'Good heavens! What are those children up to?'

'I'll go and see,' Amy placed her teacup in its saucer and went to investigate. She discovered Sam on his hands and knees examining a broken crystal vase. Will was inspecting the shattered window.

'You were supposed to be outside. How did this happen?' she demanded.

'The ball bounced through the window …' Sam pointed to the smashed window.

'But the vase …? How did that get broken?'

'It - er - was on the window ledge,' Sam said.

She recognized the shards of glass as particles from a pair of elegant cut glass vases given to her parents on their wedding day. She looked at it and despaired. It was beyond repair.

'What were you doing? And the vase - it fell off the window ledge on its own?'

Both boys were silent.

'The garden's big enough. I really don't understand how you managed to break the window as well as a vase. I think you'd better come and apologise to Grand Mamma, don't you?'

She took Sam by the hand and hoped George's interview would be soon as it looked as if it was going to be a difficult few days.

\* \* \* \* \*

Violet told her mother the news of her pregnancy over afternoon tea several weeks after Phoebe had announced her engagement. She wanted the moment to be unique and not overshadowed by the excitement of her sister's engagement. At times she thought she would burst if she didn't tell someone. How she endured all the talk of weddings, when she wanted so much to share her own news, she would never know. Harold had caught her eye and she knew he wouldn't say a word until the moment was right. Their baby was special and deserved to be announced at a time when he would be the centre of everyone's attention. There had been too many disappointments. Now the weeks of waiting were over. After all the miscarriages and years of dashed hopes, it looked as if this was really going to happen. Today she felt the baby strongly for the first time – not these odd flutters which she wasn't sure about. Please, please let this one be all right.

'Oh, Ma, it seems such a long time to wait,' she said, looking at Harold who smiled and winked at her. He was the best husband ever and she knew this baby meant as much to him as it did to her. Now their world would be complete.

'Time'll go quickly enough, you'll see. Another grandchild. I can't keep up with you all. First Phoebe engaged to a Bank Manager and getting married almost at once and now you pregnant. My goodness ...' Ma shook her head. 'I'll have to get my knitting needles out again.' She poured tea into the three cups. 'You must ask Lizzie if you can borrow her cot and her pram. No point in buying – save the money.'

She had wanted to say this baby deserved the best and she was not going to have second-hand anything. Harold had said they could afford to buy a pram and cot and in any case, she wanted more children. She was prevented from saying anything by a noise in the scullery.

'What's that?' Ma asked.

'Anyone at home,' a voice called.

'I didn't hear the back door, did you?' Ma said and put the teapot down.

Vi got up – they weren't expecting any callers. She opened the scullery door.

'George! How - when - whatever are you doing here? Goodness gracious, you gave me such a fright. Ma, you'll never guess!'

'Well, I'm blowed,' Ma said, looking up in amazement as George stepped into the room. 'It's one thing after the other,' she said and still recovering from the surprise, struggled to her feet. 'Why ever didn't you write? Give us a bit of warning. Such a shock for Vi, the way she is.'

George looked at Vi and she smiled back and immediately noticed his tired, careworn face. She wondered if things had been more difficult than Amy had revealed in her last letter. 'I'm four months pregnant and, oh, George, I'm so happy. Oh, come here.' She hugged him then pulled away, suddenly shy. 'This is Harold.'

Harold shook George's offered hand.

'Nice to meet you after all these years of reading about you and the family.'

George gave his mother a hug, steadying her as she sat back onto her seat, where she continued to stare at him in amazement.

'I'll get another cup. You must tell us everything,' Vi called from the scullery. 'Where's Amy? And what about the boys? I can't wait to meet Bobbie. He sounds adorable,' she fired questions without waiting for any answers.

'Whoa, whoa! One thing at a time.' George sat down.

'Well? What are you doing here? Are you back for good?' Vi demanded and stopped, wondering if she had sounded rude. She hadn't meant to but she wanted to know so many things – such as where the money came from for the tickets. Could it have been Amy's mother? Surely George would never accept a penny from her? 'What about Amy and the boys – did you come on your own?' It was so long since she and Amy had had a good gossip. She might be her sister-in-law but Amy felt more like a real sister and understood her better than any of her own sisters ever did. She couldn't wait for Harold to meet her and it would be wonderful to tell her all about her pregnancy.

'George?' she said when he didn't answer straight away.

'So many questions,' Ma interrupted, pouring a fourth cup of tea and handing it to George. 'Give him a chance, Vi, he's hardly got in the door.'

Vi went to sit by Harold. She was shocked by George's shabby appearance. Her appraisal took in the withered, thin features, the greying lacklustre hair and his worn out clothing. The George she knew would never have gone about in a patched pair of trousers. Now she was anxious.

'Everything is all right, isn't it, George?'

He shrugged, glancing first at Harold and then at Ma before settling on a reply. 'Yes. Er - I - er - I mean no. Not really. Amy's gone to her mother's and sure as hell I don't know if she'll have me back.' He put his head in his hands, the weariness of it all overwhelming.

'What? That can't be so.' Vi leant forward to squeeze his hands.

George didn't answer.

'You haven't left her, have you?' Ma asked.

He took a moment to compose himself. 'Not exactly.'

'Not exactly? What does that mean?' Ma asked in a disapproving tone.

George looked up at her. 'Amy's at her mother's,' he said, adding in a quieter voice, 'and the truth is I couldn't face going there - not after all that's happened. I took the coward's way out and now I don't suppose she'll want me back.'

'She loves you.' Vi went across and put her arms round his shoulders and, as she hugged him, she felt the looseness of his jacket. She thought back to the day he arrived home after the war, after an absence of eight years. She had thought him slender then but he had been full of optimism. Now he looked defeated. Then she remembered the strength Amy had shown on her wedding day when, against her mother's wishes she had walked down the aisle and married him. She squeezed his arm. 'Amy really loves you, George. I know she does.'

'Vi, after what I've put her through I can't imagine her wanting me back. Not now she's under her mother's roof.'

She didn't know how to answer and she could see George was struggling to control his emotions. She searched for the right words.

Ma knew what to say. 'Hmm. That woman. Amy saw through her before - remember?' She placed her cup back in its saucer. 'And I'm certain we'll find nothing has changed. You'll see, son, but tell us how you managed to get back to England.'

Vi listened as George, little by little, began to explain the gravity of their situation. The appalling farm sale, the agony of losing everything they had worked so hard for. He gave answers to all the questions they fired at him but often they were evasive and sometimes he changed the subject. The more she listened the more horrified she was.

'Why don't you come to us for supper tonight?' she suggested. She could make dinner stretch and she knew Harold would understand. 'We only live in the next road. It isn't far.' She caught Harold's eye and saw his approval. 'It would give you and Harold a chance to get to know one another.'

'He's only just arrived,' Ma objected. 'You can't whisk him away before everyone else has had a chance to say hello.'

'Ma, it's only for an hour or so,' she said.

'That'd be good. I'd like that,' George said. 'And in any case I'd sure like to see the newly-weds home.'

'Not so newly-weds,' Vi corrected, noting the Canadian accent. 'In any case, Phoebe's getting married - then she and Richard will be the newly-weds. It's all happening so quickly, too. Oh, how lovely. You and Amy will be able to come.'

Later, after supper, as George settled into a more comfortable chair, she decided what he needed was a good night's sleep. The fatigue was etched into the lines of his gaunt, weathered face and she wondered if Amy, too, was as thin. Had she aged as much too? When they left England they had such great hopes and it was no fault of theirs they had been left starving - only God could know why.

She was certain George loved Amy as much as the day they met and somehow she was certain Amy still loved him. They belonged together but at that moment she was unsure how she would persuade George to face that bully of a mother-in-law once again. Maybe after a good night's sleep, things would seem better but of one thing she was certain - she had no intention of letting him return to their mother's house that night. The intensity and volume of their younger brother and sister's arguments, not to mention more and more questions from the rest of the family would be too much in one day. Ted and Lizzy and Albert were bound to be there - Ma would have made sure of that. It would be noisy and intrusive and right then, she could see he needed some peace and quiet. She hoped, with a good night's sleep, he would see things weren't so bad.

# Chapter Four

Freddie knew it had been rude to abandon his sister but he couldn't face any further scenes - three boys squabbling all the way home, not to mention George and Amy's argument were more than enough for one day. He wasn't quite sure what kind of reception his mother would give Amy but, right then, he didn't want to find out. No, he had enough of his own problems and, leaving Amy to face their mother on her own, he drove straight on into the village. He needed a drink. The pub might be closed but he knew Beth would be pleased to see him. He intended only to stop for one drink - something to give him the courage to face Enid and he found himself telling Beth about his sister over a large whisky. She was a good listener, sympathetically refilling his glass when it was in danger of being empty. He lost count of the number of whiskeys he downed so when she enticed him up the stairs … it was fatal. It always was.

'I have to go,' he repeated, making an attempt to leave her arms.

'Why? What's the hurry? Stay the night …'

He weakened and she pulled him to her. 'It's my night off. I'll slip down later and let Maisy in and she'll take care of things.'

'Won't it be busy?'

'Nothing she can't handle. Don't worry so …'

He could never resist her and, in spite of his intention, the time drifted into the whole evening, then the night. He often wondered what would have happened if he had been free to marry but it wasn't something to be contemplated. His mother would *never* forgive him and he needed her money to keep the garage going.

They enjoyed a lazy breakfast together, like newlyweds, he thought, and knew they would never be able to be that. He left after lunch, crossed the road and called into the garage where he was pleased to discover Donnie had completed the service on the two cars parked on the forecourt. Had he noticed the Vauxhall parked over at the pub? If he had, Donnie refrained from making any comment. When he looked in the diary, he was also pleased to see several more jobs booked for the following week.

'Things are looking up, Donnie.' He closed the diary. 'Thanks for doing it all so efficiently.'

'Do my best, Mr Attwood. I was about to do the bills.'

'I'll see to those. You get off home.'

It didn't take long to write out the chits and slot them into envelopes. After sticking a note of apology for early closure on the door, he was soon locking up, leaving the garage several hours early. Stopping to post his letters at the post box, he thought the day was too good to spend indoors and decided a ride in the countryside might cheer Enid up and compensate a little for his absence but, if he was honest, it was more to alleviate his guilt. He parked the car outside rather than in the garage. It was already mid-afternoon and the sun was beginning to get low in the sky. He might even be persuaded to visit Enid's mother but, as soon as he placed the key in the front door, he knew she would be in a difficult mood. He could hear her raised voice followed by a shriek. What had Jon done now? He felt sorry for his son and ashamed he wasn't at home more but Beth's arms were more welcoming than Enid, especially since her pregnancy. As he walked up the hall, the howls became louder as did Enid's voice

'Don't you dare bring that in here.'

He opened the kitchen door and was alarmed to find Enid balancing on a chair. He puzzled for a moment until he spotted Jonathan, standing in the doorway to the garden, holding a large brownish toad in his hands and looking pleased with his find. No wonder Enid was on the chair.

'Come on, Jon. You know your mother hates those things. Leave it outside, there's a good boy.'

His son gave him a sullen look but, without arguing, stepped out into the garden. He turned to help Enid step off the chair, wishing that the child she was bearing had arrived a few years earlier. It would have been far better for Jonathan - he would have had a playmate. Instead it was becoming increasingly apparent he resented the expected baby. Maybe it would have been better if Enid hadn't got pregnant in the first place since she had this morbid fear of childbirth. He could sympathise to an extent - she did have a very bad time with Jonathan and ever since his birth, she had been reluctant to share the marital bed. This pregnancy had been the product of one of the few times she had allowed him to touch her and she hadn't forgiven him for the result. The only person pleased was his mother but then she didn't bear the brunt of Enid's bad temper and hostility and neither had she got to cope with the depression – something which had lasted for months after Jonathan's birth.

'I was going to suggest we all went for a drive ...' he said as he steadied her. 'It would do you good to get out and it would take Jonathan away from his current pet.'

She shook her head. 'No. Jonathan's been impossible. Absolutely impossible. I've had a terrible day, I've got a headache and there are toys all over the place. I'm going to bed. You can sort things out. I need a rest.'

She disentangled herself from his arms and disappeared along the hallway, leaving him staring after her. He heard her climb the stairs and the bedroom door click shut. Their marriage could have been so different, he told himself, turning his attention to Jonathan who was sitting under a tree in the garden, talking to the toad. The sooner he went off to boarding school, the better but for now he would have to do the understanding father bit. Later he would go back to the pub.

\* \* \* \* \*

Amy stopped in the hall and in the dull light, stared at the telephone Funny, she hadn't noticed that when they arrived but, then, she hadn't expected to find one. Very little had changed in the house since she had left all those years ago and her mother was set in her ways, so she suspected Freddie had been involved with its installation. It would be just like him to have one connected for his own convenience, at her mother's expense, of course. But if only she had known, George could have called her here. Right then, she'd give anything to hear his voice but it was an impossible hope. She would have to wait until he telephoned Freddie. Maybe he would write or maybe she should but receiving letters here would be like history repeating. She shut her mind to the thought.

It had been a difficult few hours. Her mother's comments on her marriage were few but pointed and left little doubt as to her disapproval of their Canadian venture.

'Well, my girl,' she said when the children were out of earshot. 'You've spent your inheritance.'

That, apparently, was the price for being rescued.

Upstairs, the children had been slow to settle down and, even though she was exhausted and wanted nothing more than to slip into bed herself, she doubted she would sleep. She decided to satisfy her curiosity and, taking a candle, she went to investigate if there were any of the clothes remaining from her younger days. Maybe they had been thrown out? It would be like her mother to do such a thing in a fit of pique. Everything would be unfashionable – not that she cared. The years of eking out a living had changed her values. All evening, as she supervised the children and unpacked their few belongings, she kept wondering what would be in that wardrobe. And if her clothes were still there, they had to be in a better condition than the skirt she was wearing. The waistband was threadbare, she had stitched the hem up more times than she could remember and she had been living in it for weeks. In fact, she was surprised her mother hadn't commented on her dress or the boys' for that matter. They were all shabby and patched, several times in the case of Bobbie's trousers.

She opened the door to her bedroom and stepped inside, waiting for the candle to burn steadily. In the poor light, she could make out the pale pink and white window drapes, the solid oak dressing table, the huge wardrobe, the equally large chest of drawers and the thick oval rug which she had adored as a child. She kicked off her shoes and stepped onto it, enjoying the sensation of its silky thick pile. It was all here, just as she'd left it and it was a strange feeling - as though in another era - a time of luxury and indulgence. Here was her bedroom exactly as it was the day she left to marry George. With one big exception, of course. She crossed to the dressing table. Where were the letters she had addressed to her mother and to Charles? Had her mother returned Charles' engagement ring? And if she hadn't ..? What did it matter now anyway?

She placed the candle on the dressing table and sat on the bed, enjoying the sensation of the satin quilt. Next she pulled the covers back, felt the crisp white linen and was tempted to lay down to sleep her exhaustion away but knew she wouldn't relax until she had looked inside the wardrobe. She was certain her old clothes would fit. After years of hard manual work on the farm and the months with little food, she might even be thinner than when she first married.

She drew in a deep breath, then threw open the doors, gasping in delight. In the flickering candlelight she could make out an array of skirts and dresses. A neat row of shoes lined the floor of the cupboard and on the shelf were her handbags and hat boxes, gloves and scarves. How spoilt she had been and how she had taken it all for granted. She couldn't help but compare all this extravagance with the years of scratching a living in the Prairies. But the years of her marriage had been rich in so many other ways, she reminded herself as she closed the doors, deciding to make her choice in the morning.

Next she went to rummage in the chest of drawers, pulling out a white cotton embroidery anglaise nightdress, holding it up to admire and finger the delicate needlework. A clean nightie was a bonus. She sat on the edge of the bed, reached for the silver-framed photograph from the bedside table and then lay back onto the pillows, squinting at the picture. In the flickering light, she could make out her favourite dog. He had died so long ago, maybe it was time for a new photo …

She was awoken by very loud voices. It was hardly light and she peered at her watch. Seven o'clock. She rubbed her eyes, remembered where she was and then realised she had fallen asleep still dressed in the clothes in which she arrived. Goodness knows what her mother would think but she hadn't time to change. The boys were bickering already and it was Sam's raised voice she could hear above the others. Why did it always have to be Sam?

She opened the door and the voices became louder.

'Give it back,'

'No. It's mine,' Will shouted, holding a wooden truck aloft with one hand and his shorter brother at arm's length with the other.

'Give it or I'll … I'll kick you,' Sam yelled, red in the face.

'Stop it!' Amy shushed the boys and pulled them apart. She removed the truck from Will. 'Stop it, the pair of you. You'll wake the whole household. Whatever will your grandmother think?'

Sam was still in his pyjamas and Bobbie was sitting on the floor surrounded by a pile of books most of which had come from the nearby bookshelf.

'Sam, get dressed.' She opened the curtains and was disappointed to see a dull, rainy dawn. 'Will, please help Bobbie and all of you put those back on the shelf.' She pointed to the books and, stepping over them, headed for the door. 'I need a wash and when I get back I shall expect you all to be ready for breakfast.'

She hoped peace would reign and wondered if she and Freddie had quarrelled as children. She didn't remember but then he was quite a bit older and she had always looked up to him.

Returning to her bedroom, she discovered the maid had brought a jug of warm water which she poured into the matching china bowl. At last she was able to wash the grime of travel away. Next she spent some time pushing hangers backwards and forwards in the wardrobe. It was years since she'd had such a choice. Eventually she found an old favourite, a maroon skirt which had a matching jacket but not wanting anything so formal, she grabbed a black cardigan from the chest of drawers and slipped it on over a frilly white blouse. Ready to face the day she opened the bedroom door to discover Will astride the bannisters, about to slide down.

'Get down,' she hissed at him but it was too late. With a defiant look he let go, sliding with a whoosh. When he reached the elegant newel post at the bottom of the stairs he fell off, holding himself with a pained expression before falling into a heap at the feet of his grandmother.

'Perhaps, you would be good enough to explain exactly what you are doing, young man,' Mrs Attwood said in a stern voice, tapping him with her walking stick. 'I will be in the dining room.'

Will poked his tongue out and pulled a rude face at her back.

'Will, behave.' Amy hissed. If only George was here. He would never dare to behave like this.

Over breakfast there was so much petty squabbling with her mother glaring her disapproval so many times, she felt herself go hot with embarrassment.

'Haven't you taught them any manners?' Mrs Attwood said in irritation as Bobbie rammed a large piece of toast into his mouth and Will poked his elbow into Sam's ribs, causing him to drop the sugar bowl he had snatched from under her nose. Fortunately only a little sugar was spilled.

Amy was mortified but somehow she couldn't blame the boys for their behaviour. They hadn't seen so much food in their entire lives. Even though there was sufficient food on board the ship, it was much inferior to this spread, so how could she criticize the way they scoffed it down?

'The sooner you organise school for them, the better,' Mrs Attwood said again. 'And I'll speak to Freddie about this job.'

Amy didn't bother to answer. Her mother had said the same thing so many times already.

'I'll take them for a walk.' She knew the sooner she got them out of the house the better it would be for all of them. 'They need to run off some of their energy. We'll go and visit Freddie.'

'Freddie will be at the garage.'

'Then we'll visit Enid. It's about time we met and the boys will be able to meet their cousin.'

She called into the kitchen to scrounge a snack and they left through the orchard, the boys running ahead, revelling in the sight of green grass and kicking dead leaves into the air. The sky was fresh and clear - no dust or dirt and now the drizzle had ceased, it was turning into a pleasant morning. As she watched them play tag, throwing the windfalls which lay in the long grass and racing around the trees, she recalled the first moments spent alone with George in this very orchard and longed for them to be together now.

She couldn't believe it was a mistake for them to come back to England, yet she felt so homesick. The feeling was inexplicable and if she felt like this, how much more so would George? The loss of the farm and everything it meant, including his pride had taken a huge toll. His depression made her anxious. If only she knew where he was and what he was doing.

The moisture of early October made her shoes damp and, with a nip in the air, she was grateful for her warm coat. She snuggled into the fur neck. She had insisted the boys took coats with them but they didn't seem to feel the cold and she was left with a bundle over her arm.

The leaves on the trees were the reds, golds and browns of autumn, something she hadn't experienced in years. Back in Manitoba, winter followed summer, almost without pausing long enough for the leaves to turn yellow before they fell to the ground. In Winnipeg, there would be snow by Halloween. She had forgotten the smell of mud or what autumn was with its dampness and mellowness, yet, oddly, she longed for the crisp white mornings and big blue skies of the winters on the homestead - that was before they made the dreadful mistake of moving further south. She consoled herself. At least the air they were breathing now was free of the choking dust.

She paused at the gate and remembered her first kiss. It was this exact spot. She banished the memory of Charles - all she longed for was George.

'Come along you three. We've got a few miles to walk,' she called to the boys. She lifted the latch and led them all out onto the lane. 'And I want to show you The Grange.'

The boys ran ahead but the honking of a motor car made her call them back. She heard several more cars. The lane used to be very quiet. Perhaps there was some function on at The Grange. Keeping the boys close, she watched with amazement as even more cars turned into the drive and then, as they got nearer, a very large sign caught her eye. The words 'Holy Cross Convent School' were emblazoned in large letters. She stopped to stare and wonder. Had Lady Margaret sold the place? And if so, why? Surely, Charles should be there? More questions crowded her mind but she had forfeited her interest in any of this when she had broken off her engagement to him.

'Mom,' Will tugged at her arm. 'Why are we waiting here?'

'Oh, er, nothing, Will. Just remembering old times. You see The Grange was once a house and I used to go there every day for lessons. I shared a Governess with Charles and your Uncle Freddie. But that's a long time ago.'

'What's a ... a governess and who's Charles?' Will wanted to know.

'Just a boy,' she said not wanting to admit how she once nearly married him. 'He used to live here but he grew up like Uncle Freddie and me. And a governess is a sort of teacher.' She changed the subject. 'We've a mile or so to walk before we get to Uncle Freddie's.' She hurried them along, determined not to answer any more questions and to keep her mind on the present though it had a will of its own and returned to the past too often for her comfort.

It was approaching ten o'clock when they reached Freddie's road. Amy soon spotted the large, attractive Tudor replica, just as Freddie had described in his letters. She was astonished at how many new roads with new houses had sprung up in her absence. Then she remembered the reason they had emigrated was because the farm on which George was employed, had been sold for housing, following the extension of the Metropolitan railway. These were some of those houses and they looked very attractive.

Freddie's house was on a generous plot with a garage at the side. It would easily have coped with some extra visitors, she decided and wondered why Enid, who she had yet to meet, had chosen to be so unwelcoming. If only … then George wouldn't have gone to London and she wouldn't be enduring such a difficult time trying to control three boisterous boys under her mother's critical gaze.

She opened the gate and shepherded the boys in before shutting it behind them.

'Go on, Will,' she said and watched him lift the knocker.

'I don't think anybody's there.' Will said when there was no answer.

'That's a shame. It would have been nice to meet Enid and Jonathan. We'll have to come back another day.'

'Can we go see Uncle Freddie's garage?' Sam asked.

She thought about it for a second. It would mean another long walk. Then there was the mile or so home after but it might have the desired effect on the children, even if she would be exhausted by the time they got back.

'I suppose we can. We can stop and have our snack and then we'll pass the school on the way. We won't call in today,' she said and thought she really ought to do as her mother suggested but, in her heart, she knew they needed time to adjust to being in England. 'At least you'll all know where it is and, Bobbie, you'll be going, too. '

'But I started school when I was seven,' Will said.

'Yes, I know but children here start school much earlier. Come on, we've got to get a move on if we're going to catch Freddie before the garage shuts for lunch.'

'Shuts?' They all chorused.

'Yes and if we're really lucky he might drive us back to Grand Mamma's.'

They stopped only briefly to eat the apples Amy had brought but, when they arrived at the garage, she could see it was already shut. She read the noticed affixed to the door while the boys ran over to peep inside the two cars which were lined up with "For Sale" signs in their windows.

'Ah well, you'll have to look inside another day,' she said and thought of the walk home. Her feet ached and she would have to help Bobbie, who was already lagging behind.

* * * * *

The following morning, as Freddie had not called into see them since the day of their arrival, Amy decided they should walk straight to the garage. She was anxious to hear about George. Surely he would have telephoned by now?

'It's Saturday and Grand Mamma said it was a half day, so we'd better step it out,' she told the boys as they donned their coats.

Rain threatened but there were only a few spots and they arrived quite dry. Freddie was switching the swinging metal sign to read "closed".

'Hello. Didn't expect to see you here.'

'The boys needed to run off some of their excess energy before we're given our marching orders.'

'That bad.'

'Mmm,' she said with pursed lips. 'I wish I'd gone with George. I'm beginning to think squeezing into his mother's house might have been preferable.'

Freddie pulled a face. 'Look, I've got a couple of things to do but when I've finished, I'll drive you back. Why don't you go into the office? I won't be a jiffy.'

A loud clanging doorbell announced their entrance to the office which smelt of old engine oil. Amy glanced at the work schedule attached to a clip board which hung on a hook and thought the following week looked slack. Then she sat at the seat behind the desk. She lifted Bobbie onto her knee and peered at what, to her untrained eye, looked like bills - lots of them. Two dog-eared car manuals and two dirty cups which she viewed with disgust had been abandoned amongst the untidy heaps of correspondence. Balanced on a nearby shelf was a telephone. A cheeky calendar hung at an angle on the wall above and nearby was a red bucket marked "fire". One wall had shelves which were piled high with odds and ends including a dust-covered wireless. Nearby a battered wooden three drawer filing cabinet with curved metal handles and handwritten labels stuffed into the metal holders, supported a pile of new tyres and inner tubes. Next to it was a door on which was a collection of postcards which she hoped the boys wouldn't spot, since many of them were of briefly clad ladies.

So this was Freddie's office - not exactly what she had expected. From his letters she thought he had a showroom and somehow she had anticipated a leather-topped desk, much like her mother's and certainly one not as cluttered as this. At first glance, it didn't appear Freddie was doing as well as he had led her to believe.

Will and Sam were equally curious and pulled open the bottom filing drawer.

'Shut that this minute and go and sit down over there.' She ordered, pointing to two leather chairs, one with its horse hair stuffing protruding through tears in the leather. When he thought she wasn't looking, Sam picked at it.

A few minutes later, Freddie appeared from the workshop. Through the door she could see a bench, smothered in a mass of engine bits, above it a neat rack of tools.

'I ought to show you round. I have plans for this place – big plans. I want to expand. I'll tell you all about it while I drive you home.'

'Wow, Uncle Freddie. Are you going to sell new cars?' Will wanted to know. 'We had a Maxwell but Dad … he …' he glanced at Amy, who shook her head. She didn't want him telling Freddie about George's trip to Winnipeg. Destroying an engine might not put him in a good light, especially when it came to any job interviews.

'That's the plan but I'll show you another day, Will. We have to go now as I've got to collect Jonathan. He's at a friend's and I promised to collect him before lunch.'

'We walked over to see Enid yesterday but no one was at home,' Amy said. 'Then we walked here but you closed early.'

'Oh, er - yes. That's right I did.' He paused long enough for Amy to look up and see his sheepish look.

'You're the boss,' she said, wondering why he should feel guilty.

'Yes, yes. That's right. Just that I daren't let mother know I took a half day. She expects me to slave away and now Enid's more or less taken to her bed, I often have to go to the shops. That's why she wouldn't answer the door.' He shrugged. 'Sorry.'

'It'd be really wonderful to meet her. You do realise we've never met, don't you? And it would be nice for the boys to meet their cousin.'

'I know. I know, but there's not much I can do about that right now. If you remember when Jonathan was born Enid had a very bad time. I did write to you about that, didn't I? Anyway, she's been in a bit of a state about this pregnancy and I can do no right.' He pulled a face and then turned to the boys. 'Well, what d'you think of Uncle Freddie's garage then?'

'Sure is different from home. Your signs are funny and the gas pumps are … strange. I've never heard of National Benzole. At home we have Shell and what's Castrol? And what's that big sign on the roof?' Will asked.

'Sign on the roof? Oh, you mean the AA sign and it's not really on the roof, just at the top of the apex. AA stands for Automobile Association and they rescue people when their cars break down and Castrol is the oil we use. Now then, I think we'd better get you back to your Grand Mamma's.'

'Has George telephoned?' she asked as Freddie locked the garage door.

'Not yet. Give the chap a chance.'

'But it's been two days. He has got your telephone number, hasn't he?'

'Yes, yes. I'm sure he has.'

'It's not clever at mother's. It really isn't. I don't want to moan but the children … she complains or picks holes all the time. They're boys, Freddie, and they have so much energy. That's one of the reasons we're out now – to wear them out.'

'School. Best place for them. Get them into school. That'll soon sort them out.' He held the car door for her. 'In the back, boys and no misbehaving.'

'This job,' Amy said as soon as he was seated beside her. 'They will keep it open for George, won't they?'

'No worries, sis.' He put the car into gear. 'It'll all work out, you'll see.'

Amy looked at him doubtfully. She had glimpsed her mother's newspaper at breakfast and was shocked to read about the millions out of work. She hadn't realised it would be as bad as back in Canada. The paper was full of the marchers heading towards London and she didn't want George mixed up in that. Knowing her mother-in-law's political views, it was very likely she would be in the thick of it and she remembered only too well the letter they had received out in Canada telling them Ted had been injured in some rally or other.

'I wish you'd told George he needed to get on with things and not delay. I'd forgotten how difficult mother can be,' she said, beginning to wonder if Freddie really appreciated how trying living under the same roof as their mother was. She sighed. 'I suppose nothing will happen now till next week.'

'I'm not at the garage tomorrow if that's what you mean? It is Sunday.'

She ignored his sarcasm. 'I do hope George telephones soon. Please let me know, won't you, Freddie? I can't bear all this waiting. Mother is an absolute pain and I swear she's losing her memory. She keeps repeating herself.'

Freddie glanced down at his sister. 'You've been away how long? Seven years. You can't expect her not to have aged, you know.'

'I do realise that but she's so … I think she's forgotten what children are like.'

Freddie didn't answer and a few minutes later they were pulling up outside 'Hazeldene'.

\* \* \* \* \*

As soon as everyone was out of the car, Freddie sped off up the road. He didn't want to get involved in the domestic life of his sister and if he was honest, these days he avoided visiting his mother. The garage was not making the progress she would expect and he was certain there would be an interrogation as to why. She had no idea about running a business and even less about cars but Amy was right in one respect. Their mother was getting very forgetful. He had enough worries of his own and he didn't want to linger mainly because he was reluctant to admit to Amy he had a sneaky suspicion the job he had in mind for George might already have been filled. It wasn't his fault his brother-in-law had gone off to London, he told himself and pushed the matter to the back of his mind. First he needed to collect Jonathan and he dreaded going home. Enid had been so difficult that morning.

'I'm exhausted. You'll have to see to Jonathan. I can't cope,' she had told him when he had brought her an early morning cup of tea.

'But I've got to go to the garage.'

'It's Saturday. And anyway, what about Donnie? I seem to remember he was in charge when you went off to Southampton.'

He recognized the tone of her voice - the one she used when she felt she had been put upon. But he was the one being put upon, he told himself. He was the one whose wife was never there for him. Up until then, she was either visiting her parents or too tired but now, since she had become pregnant, things were even worse and far from being a reason to be happy, this pregnancy had put a greater strain on their relationship.

'It's because he looked after the place when I met Amy that I've let him have the morning off. He's a good worker and I don't want to lose him.'

'But there are plenty of others who would gladly fill his job. I can't see why you're so worried.'

'I need a reliable person who knows about cars. Donnie's got the morning off and that's that. I'll give Jonathan his breakfast, then he'll amuse himself. You'll have to get up at the very least.'

'Close the garage. It's only a half day. I can't manage Jonathan.'

He studied her. It was true, she did look washed out and he was alarmed by the black patches under her eyes.

'I feel dreadful,' she added and, for once, he believed her and had dropped his son off at his friend's house. That way, at least the boy would enjoy his morning.

When he got back to the house with Jonathan, Freddie knew something was wrong but if someone had asked him why that was, he wouldn't have been able to say.

'We're home,' he called but there was no answer. 'See if your mother's in the kitchen,' he said to Jonathan and opened the lounge door but the room was empty.

'Enid!'

He rushed the stairs two at a time, half fearing she had packed her things and left for her mother's. It was a threat frequently made and one which he had often wished she had fulfilled. He flung open the bedroom door, seeing her straightaway, slumped on the bed still in her nightie, partly buried in the covers, quite motionless.

'Enid,' he said in a half whisper and walked round the bed. He touched her naked shoulder but she seemed cold to his hand. 'Enid?' He shook her very gently and her eyes fluttered.

'Oh, my Lord.'

He looked about for pills, a bottle - terrified she had tried to take her own life. Finding nothing, he tried again to rouse her.

'Dad,' Jonathan called from the bottom of the stairs. 'Mummy isn't in the kitchen.'

'It's all right, Jon.' He went to the door and called down the stairs. 'Your mother's here but she's sick. I have to get her to the hospital. I need you to be a big boy because I need your help.' Thankful he hadn't put the car in the garage, he tossed the keys down to Jonathan. 'Can you open the car for me? I need the back door open as wide as it'll go. Oh, and leave the house door wide open, too. Can you do that?'

'Yes, Dad.'

He went back to the bed and pulled the quilt around Enid before lifting her into his arms, struggling to rebalance her weight. He managed the descent and was soon outside, somehow heaving her into the car, arranging the quilt around her before closing the rear passenger door.

'Quickly,' he yelled at Jonathan. 'Jump in. There's no time to waste.'

He drove at high speed to the Cottage Hospital where he sent Jonathan ahead to get help from the porter and between them they got Enid onto a trolley. He watched her being wheeled away.

After all the frantic activity, he and Jonathan were left staring at a closed door. His mind zipped back to the front in the last war. Images of blood and gore – men fatally wounded – flashed into his mind. He had survived that so why was this so much worse? He felt excluded and inadequate. Enid looked terrible and what about the baby? He should have listened to her that morning and now he was weighed down with guilt.

After several minutes wondering what to do, he decided to take Jonathan to his mother's. Amy would have to look after him while Enid was in hospital and, if she expected him to find that husband of hers a job, then it would be the least she could do.

## Chapter Five

Vi was quite awake and it wasn't because the baby was moving, though she was very conscious of its movements. They were so delicate, no more than a quivering of life but she was very aware of them. She supposed it had no idea of light or dark but maybe it sensed its mother had a lot on her mind and it was true her mind was whirring. Beside her, Harold, who was on the early shift in the morning, had been asleep since the moment his head touched the pillow, while she was bursting to discuss their conversation with George.

She had so enjoyed the evening even if her brother was reluctant to talk about his life in Canada but she was anxious because she suspected George was depressed. She supposed it wasn't surprising after everything he'd been through but, in spite of this, it had delighted her to see him getting on so well with her husband. While she rustled up a tasty cottage pie in the kitchen, she could hear them discussing the world and, more controversially, politics. George's views seemed to differ substantially from Harold's but she could forgive him for that. He'd been absent from England for so many years. He couldn't possibly understand what was going on in Europe from across the other side of the Atlantic. And it wasn't easily explained in a letter which, when written, took weeks to get there anyway.

Harold had lit the fire for the first time since the evenings had grown darker and cooler and, after supper, as they sat in the firelight, she had dragged more of the story from George. She listened to him as he explained the difficulties out in the Prairies. She was amazed at how bad things had been – very little had been in the newspaper she read. She was impressed, too, by how Amy had eked out the food since she had never made do in her life before she married George. Coming from a well-to-do family, she hadn't had to. Now, Vi realised, Amy had a very practical side even though she had been brought up with servants as well as all the advantages money could buy. She thought back to George and Amy's wedding when she had been the only bridesmaid and had caught the bridal bouquet. It proved to be a good omen because not long after she met Harold.

How could she forget their first meeting? She had been running to catch the bus outside Selfridges and had tripped, spilling the entire contents of her shopping bag. She had been so embarrassed but the conductor stopped the bus and helped her to her feet which had humiliated her even more. It was Harold and some weeks later, by chance, she happened to catch the same bus and this time he was a passenger. They had tea at a Lyons Corner House in the Strand and from then on they would meet there whenever his shifts as a bus conductor allowed. Next he had taken her to her first trip to the cinema to see Greta Garbo and it wasn't long before he proposed. At first she'd resisted. He was more than ten years her senior but they agreed on most things and she liked the way he looked after her and his charms won her over.

Her thoughts returned to George. He wouldn't talk about the final calamity - the tornado but he didn't have to spell out the ultimate humiliation - returning to England and having to accept the fare from his dreadful mother-in-law. No wonder he'd come to London instead of Buckinghamshire. How could she blame him? But she would be eternally grateful he and Amy and the boys were rescued from starvation because she knew their own mother would never have been able to find the fare. The thought reminded her she was in for a good dressing down for not sending George back for the night but she could hear George snoring in the next room and knew she'd made the right decision.

Harold's job meant he worked a shift pattern and he left very early but, for once, she slept through, allowing the cup of tea he brought her to get cold. She awoke with a start. The grandfather clock in the hall was chiming and she counted nine. Goodness, was it that late? She grabbed her dressing gown and went downstairs. It wasn't until she reached the bottom step that she realised, for the first time in weeks, she didn't feel nauseated.

She filled the kettle and put it on the stove. It was novel to feel hungry instead of sick. She found a saucepan from the cupboard and poured a couple of cups of oats into it, adding some milk. She was stirring the porridge when she heard George behind her.

'Morning. Sorry, I slept in,' she said. 'Tea?'

'That'd be good. Harold's gone to work, I suppose?'

'Yes, left hours ago.' She could see he was dressed. 'I couldn't sleep, then when I did ... well, I've only just got up. You'll have to excuse me.' She indicated the dressing gown.

'Don't worry on my account, Vi. I'm very grateful for a bed and you were right. There's no way I could have coped with the rest of the family last night.'

'I hope you can today. I have a feeling Ma's going to be a little put out.'

'Sure won't be the first time,' he said, pulling a face.

'She does like to be in control.'

'No change there then.'

Vi turned the flame down under the porridge and made the tea.

'You've got a nice house,' George said, looking round the scullery. His eyes rested on the butler sink and the blue enamel gas stove. 'Amy would love a place like this.'

'Harold's mother left it to him. She lived with us for several years or rather we lived with her. It wasn't always a picnic - we didn't exactly see eye to eye. You see, I think she thought I'd stolen her son.'

'And had you?'

'I didn't set out to. Oh, you know how it is with mothers and sons. Anyway, she'd got used to him being there for her, so when I came along she was a bit put out. More than a bit, I suspect but I suppose we can count ourselves lucky the way things turned out.'

'Harold's father was well off?'

'No, careful, I think. Harold hasn't any brothers or sisters.'

'I'm pleased for you both. Just hope Amy and I can get on our feet again.'

'You will. Of course you will but you shouldn't lose any time telephoning Freddie.' She was anxious he didn't lose the offer of employment which he had mentioned the previous evening. 'I don't think you realise how hard jobs are to come by these days. Didn't I hear Harold tell you about the hunger marchers? Things aren't any easier here in England, George, so don't let things slide.'

'Okay. Okay.' He was irritated by her words and she felt guilty for bossing him about. 'I only got back yesterday.'

She wasn't certain George really did understand how difficult things were and that jobs were rare, let alone a job which provided a house. Maybe she'd said enough. She knew Ma would push the point home soon enough, so she changed the subject.

'I'll come with you to Ma's after breakfast - that is if you want me to?'

'My younger sister come to hold my hand.' He laughed and gave her a hug. 'Yes, please. Sure need somebody to share the blame for not going back last night.'

She was anxious again. He sounded too cheerful as though he was putting on a front. 'Everything is all right between you and Amy, isn't it?'

'Sure. I know ... maybe I was feeling ... truth is ... '

She placed the cups on the worktop and turned to look at him.

'Just couldn't face everyone yesterday,' he said. 'That's all it was. Didn't want to fall out with anyone on my first day home.'

'Can't say I blame you but you still worry me.'

'There's nothing to worry about. Amy didn't think we'd all fit in at Ma's and she's probably right. And I'll give Freddie a ring this morning.'

'Good. Now let's have breakfast.'

\* \* \* \* \*

'Ma, it would have taken years to turn the whole thing round ... There just wasn't anything we could do and that's all there is to it,' George said in his firmest tone.

It was early afternoon and they hadn't long finished lunch. He and Vi had arrived at Ma's a little after eleven and he'd been answering her questions ever since - some questions several times and he'd had enough of her interrogation. The decisions he'd taken months before were irrelevant to his present predicament and no amount of discussion would change that. All it did was make him more depressed. Staying the night at Vi's had proved a comforting interlude and he'd like to head back there right that minute and hide.

'I don't understand why that woman couldn't see it in her heart to help you stay and make a go of things.'

'We've been through all that, Ma,' he said in exasperation. If she said that once more he'd scream. Didn't she realise how humiliated the whole business made him feel? Didn't she realise he and Amy had been over and over the same ground hundreds of times? He was here now, he wanted to yell at her, and money was going to be a big problem. But he hated the idea of being in even greater debt. He sighed and knew he would have to somehow psych himself up to ask.

'And what are you going to do about a job and what about money?' Ma asked, rummaging in her handbag. It was as though she had read his mind but, he reminded himself, Ma was always practical.

He hesitated. It was too embarrassing but she was staring straight at him.

'I didn't come for a loan …'

'But?'

"Truth is, I'm broke. Sure need some coppers for the telephone. Vi pointed out the telephone box when we walked here. Freddie's got a job lined up for me and as soon as we can arrange things I'll be going for an interview.'

'Take this,' Ma pressed some coppers in his hand. 'For the telephone call.' She found a ten shilling note. 'And you'll need this to get there. And don't let the grass grow under your feet, George. There's precious little employment and men are marching to London to protest.'

'Harold and I have been telling him how bad things are,' Vi said catching the end of their conversation as she brought in a tray of tea which she placed on the table.

They were drinking the tea when Ted arrived home from work.

'The wanderer returns,' Ted said and shook George's hand before giving him a hug. 'Welcome home but where's Amy?'

'Amy went to her mother's,' Vi answered for George, who she could see was sick of answering questions. She glanced at the clock. 'If that's the time already, Harold will be home too. I'd better get off.' She turned to George and said in a low voice. 'Bed's there if you want it. Stay as long as you need.'

'What's that?' Ma wanted to know.

'Nothing, Ma. Must go.' She dropped a kiss on her mother's cheek. 'Harold will be home in half an hour.'

Ted and George sat opposite one another, each studying the other's face. It was years since they had been together and George thought his brother had aged as much as he himself had.

'Never expected to see you again.' Ted was the first to speak. He took a gulp of the tea Vi had passed him before she slipped out of the door. 'Bit stewed.' He pulled a face then stood up and put his cup and saucer on the tray. 'What about a proper drink to celebrate your homecoming?'

'You know where the sherry is,' Ma said.

'No, Ma. I mean a proper drink. George 'ere can't have tasted beer for a few years. What about it?'

'Sure is the best offer I've had today,' George said and got up, glad to stretch his legs. 'Ma, it's a very long time since I had a pint in a public house. In fact, when I think about it, the last time was probably when Amy and I got married.' He felt a bit guilty at taking her money and then leaving for the pub. 'Why don't you join us?'

'No, son. I'm not up to walking that far these days. You go and enjoy yourself.'

George was relieved to avoid the rest of the family. It would only be a matter of time before they all crowded into the small room and he would feel stifled. He missed the solitude of the Prairies where he could be his own master. But if he hoped for peace and quiet, the pub soon proved not to be the place. There was quite a throng and Ted had a struggle to get two pints of beer to where George was standing without spilling them.

'Football?' George asked, remembering the last time he had been in this particular pub when it was full of West Ham supporters.

'No match today,' Ted said as they squeezed onto the two round stools they had found under the circular copper-topped table. 'Cheers.'

'Cheers.'

'You've heard of the Hunger marchers, haven't you? I think this lot are planning to walk along with 'em - you know give 'em some support.'

George was beginning to feel very uncomfortable. The drinkers around him were a bit bawdy and some of them had had a skin full. He knew it would soon be closing time.

'Let's drink up and get out of here.'

'No,' Ted said. 'Relax. There's still time for another pint before closing and anyway, there won't be no trouble. I say we join 'em. It's about time this government got the message.'

'Sure didn't realise things were bad enough for hunger marches,' George said. He took a gulp of beer. My, it did taste good but as he relished the long forgotten taste of hops, he was uneasy. He took another swig, anxious to down the pint and get Ted out of the pub. He'd forgotten how good beer tasted but it was doing funny things to his head. 'Strong beer, Ted?'

'No. Just the usual.'

George didn't reply. He needed fresh air before he made a fool of himself. He stood up. 'Look, let's drink up.'

Ted eyed him in surprise. 'Lost your appetite for beer? I remember you quaffing as many beers as the next man.'

'Sure,' George said. 'That was twelve years ago and I'm out of practice. Couldn't afford beer and in any case, there weren't pubs in the Prairies. And if you think things are bad here, just remember we were starving.'

'So are some of the lads marching down from Wales – starving that is. You aren't alone in 'aving a tough time. I'm going to stand with 'em. You can come if you want or push off 'ome but I thought you was more for standing up for your rights as I remember?'

George didn't answer. The last thing he wanted was to get caught up in some protest or other, especially when several of the participants looked as if they were drunk. But if he declined and headed back to Vi's, Ted would think him not a man of principles or, worse, a coward. He certainly wasn't that.

'Come on, lads. Down your drinks. It's time us left.' A big man said in an equally big voice.

'Shop steward,' Ted said.

The crowd began to edge towards the door and Ted tipped the rest of his beer down his throat and stood up. 'Coming?'

They were soon caught up and driven along with the horde. George looked for a gap. Somehow he had to get away.

He had just worked his way to the edge when he came face to face with Harold who was with a dozen or so other men.

'Glad to see we're all united,' Harold said.

'Not sure about that,' George replied.

'Come on, man. We've got to show this government they can't let the workers starve.' Harold said and with that pushed his arm through George's and turned him round. 'All stand together, now.'

'Does Vi know?'

'Yes, she does and she supports us. So does your Ma.'

George didn't argue any further. It seemed it was expected of him so, with Harold on one side and Ted the other, he found himself following the mob. It wasn't only Canada which let some of its population starve then and what harm could it do to show his support for their campaign?

\* \* \* \* \*

Vi was worried. She glanced at the clock on the mantelshelf. It was about to strike ten o'clock and still there was no sign of Harold or George. She had thought that Ted and George might have a drink in a pub but Harold had left a note to say he had gone to a meeting. Anyway he was on an early shift in the morning and it wasn't like him to be this late. Harold's note simply said *"Union meeting - back for supper"* but supper had come and gone. She had made enough for George but she could understand he might want to catch up with the rest of the family.

She tried to read but it was hard to concentrate. She reached for her bag of knitting which she kept at the side of the armchair. The baby's matinee jacket which she had started a week ago had been unpicked and restarted. She was determined everything should be perfect for this baby and a dropped stitch in the middle of the back had left a hole. She began to knit but gave up at the end of a row of rib and pushed the needles through the ball of white 4-ply. She wasn't in the mood and besides the fire was dying back and she felt chilly.

She warmed some milk and carried it upstairs, undressed and got into bed. The banging on the front door roused her and she realised she had nodded off.

'Harold?' she called. Had he forgotten his key? The banging on the door became louder.

'All right, I'm coming,' she said as she reached the bottom step.

She opened the door a fraction.

'Gawd 'elp us, Vi. You took your time.' Ted pushed the door open to reveal Harold, blood streaming down his face, supported by George.

'Whatever's happened? Harold? Oh, my Lord,' She held out her arm to assist but Ted stopped her.

'Put a kettle on. We need some hot water.'

It was dark in the scullery and she reached for the box of matches she kept on the table and re-lit the gas lamp. The mantle spluttered and popped before settling to a steady burn. Then she filled the kettle, placed it on the stove and lit the gas beneath. She returned to the dining room where Ted and George had got Harold onto a chair. She handed the matches to Ted to light the gas lamp and in the spread of light she could see Harold had a big gash on his head.

'Whatever's happened?' She knelt at Harold's side and he gave her a faint smile.

'Got a bang on the 'ed,' Ted explained.

'I can see that,' she said in irritation. 'But how? What's been going on? You said you were going to a union meeting …'

Harold didn't answer.

'Ted? George?' She glared up at them. They seemed unscathed, so why hadn't they looked out for Harold?

'Has the kettle boiled? I think we should clean that gash,' George said.

Vi went to organise a bowl of hot water and some clean cloths but the severe look she gave her brothers meant she wanted answers to some questions. While she waited for the kettle to boil, she remembered the wooden first aid box which Harold had purchased from Boots a few weeks earlier. At least there would be plenty of bandages she thought, climbing on a chair to reach it down and half expecting Harold's voice to boom out in reprimand for doing so in her present state. She carried the steaming bowl of water into George, placed it on the lino and thought right then, it wasn't her but Harold who was the one in a state.

Ted removed Harold's blood-stained jacket and loosened his tie and she bent over to inspect his head.

'This is a nasty gash. Maybe he should go to the hospital,' she said.

'Don't think that'd be too sensible tonight,' Ted said.

'And why not?'

'There's been a spot of trouble. The 'ospital'll be full and there's coppers everywhere. We don't want to get arrested,' Ted said.

'Arrested? Whatever for?' She looked up at George. 'What's been happening? Tell me. I think I have the right to know.'

'It'll be in tomorrow's papers,' Harold said.

'We went to support the marchers going to Hyde Park,' George said in a quiet voice.

'You did what?' She could throttle Ted. It must have been his idea. He was the radical in the family. 'You might have known there'd be trouble, Ted, and you of all people, should have known better, especially after that last time. If Ma gets to hear of this, she won't be too impressed.'

'They needed support. The rest of the country's been funding them so why should London treat 'em any different. We've got more jobs 'ere but we shouldn't forget there's them who 'aven't.'

'That's as maybe but there isn't any need for violence.'

'They charged with Police horses,' George explained. 'There wasn't anywhere to go. Things sure were tricky. Several men were knocked to the ground. There was a fair amount of panic. We were trying to get away but Harold tripped and … he got trampled on. Everyone was petrified.'

She turned to Ted. 'And I suppose you encouraged Harold to go.'

'No, Vi, love.' Harold squeezed her hand. 'It was my idea. I thought we should go and cheer them along. Lots of the lads were going.'

She was silent. She hadn't thought of Harold as an activist before but she supposed she should have realised. He had, after all, gone to a shop steward's meeting.

'I hope you won't lose your job over this,' she said and dipped a cloth in the warm water. She pulled it out with the tips of her fingers, holding it for a moment, allowing it to cool before squeezing it. She began to dab gently round the wound.

'Oofff. That's hot.'

'Needs to be,' she said with little sympathy and carried on. She peered at Harold's wound. 'This really needs medical attention.'

'No. I'll be fine. It's only a bang on the head,' Harold said.

'It looks a good deal more than that to me. It's quite a gash.'

'People had worse in the war,' George said.

'This isn't a war,' she replied. 'I don't know what this country's coming to. The whole world's gone mad.'

George went to wash his hands. When he came back, he inspected the wound, thought it looked clean so delved into the First Aid Box and found a dressing which he passed to Vi.

'I'm not sure this is going to be big enough but at least the bleeding has stopped.'

'Always bleed more from a head wound,' George said as a matter of fact.

Vi refrained from asking how he knew. She'd heard enough of the war and seen enough of the men who returned with legs and arms missing - quite a number from their street - men who could no longer work and whose families were destitute.

'You can't go to work like this,' she told Harold as she tied the bandage into place.

'I'm not taking a sick day if that's what you think.'

'Then you'll look a pretty sight in your uniform. Scare all the children you will and that eye's going to be a real shiner.'

'Enough of that, Vi,' Harold said. 'And I think in your condition you should be in bed. Leave us men to things now.'

She gave him a fierce look which was meant to tell him not to speak to her that way, never mind didn't she deserve some thanks for patching him up? She stopped herself from saying as much. It could wait until the privacy of their bedroom and then she'd have things to say. Harold couldn't afford to jeopardize his job when they had a baby on the way.

'I'll say goodnight, then.'

She went to sleep listening to the drone of conversation downstairs, annoyed she wasn't privy to what they were discussing. Ma would never have allowed herself to be sidelined. She would have been in the thick of the conversation she told herself but soon fell asleep and didn't hear Harold come to bed.

## Chapter Six

All four boys were asleep. Relieved and exhausted, Amy sunk into an armchair. Her mother had retired to bed early, complaining of a headache and grumbling about the noise and the mess. She wasn't the only one who found the constant arguments wearing. To say Jonathan and Will were not getting on was an understatement. How often had she acted as referee? She could make excuses for Jonathan because of the circumstances, but wished he wouldn't goad Will with constant allusions to his strange Canadian accent. Things had been difficult enough before Jonathan arrived … If only George would telephone, but, she reasoned, with Freddie at the hospital, there wouldn't be a reply anyway. She sighed. If only they had their own home. Her life consisted of so many 'if onlys' but any hopes of pressurising Freddie had been squashed. He had enough problems of his own. Living under her mother's roof might be far from ideal but how could she complain when she thought of poor Enid and what she must be going through. She would write to George. He had to know how difficult things were. It was unreasonable of him to abandon her like this.

She glanced around the room with its sumptuous furnishings and thought about life back in Canada - where everything from furniture to food had been basic. Memories of snow and the excitement of Halloween gave her pangs of homesickness. How bizarre to miss the cold but the truth was she did. The cold usually came with sunshine and clear blue skies and in the dampness of Buckinghamshire, she hated the dull days when there wasn't a glimpse of the sun. What fun it would have been to hold a little party at 'Hazeldene' with ghosts and ghouls, 'bob-apples' and other games but it was most unlikely her mother would agree to such a thing. She sighed and tried to banish the thought by picking up the paper which had been left on the small table beside the chair. In the light of the oil lamp, the headlines were large and she was soon engrossed in an article on the violence in London in which thousands of police were involved and many people injured. Her reading was interrupted by the arrival of Freddie.

She looked up when she heard his voice in the hall. 'In here, Freddie.'

He came into the room and placed a kiss on her cheek.

'I didn't hear the door,' she said, pleased to see him. She refolded the newspaper, intent on discussing the behaviour of his son but the expression on his face made her stop. 'Enid? Is she … all right?'

Freddie paced about the room, taking a moment to compose himself.

'Freddie?'

'She lost the baby.'

'Oh, my God.' It took a second for the enormity of the news to sink in. 'Oh, Freddie I am so sorry.' She got up and hugged him. 'Is there anything I can do?'

'Not really. Look after Jonathan,' he gulped.

She noticed the tremor in his voice and when she looked up at him she could see the tears welling in his eyes.

'God, Amy.' He broke down and sobbed in her arms. For a second, she couldn't believe this was her older brother to whom she had looked up to for her whole life. A moment later he pulled himself upright, inhaled deeply and went to stand in the window. It was pitch black outside and she could make out his reflection. He blew his nose and wiped his eyes.

'It isn't wrong to show emotions,' she whispered. 'It's your loss, too. Both of you have lost a child.'

It was some seconds before he turned to face her.

'You'll look after Jon? I need someone I can trust.'

'Yes, of course, I'll look after him. It's the least I can do and mother would say the same.' Now was not an appropriate moment to mention Jonathan's difficult behaviour, she thought and changed the subject. 'Would you like some tea? The maid's off tonight, but I can soon do it.'

'Something stronger. Mother keeps some whisky. I'll fetch it. What about you?'

'No, thanks.'

He opened the elegant oak bow fronted corner cabinet and reached for the decanter as though it was something he often did. She watched him pour out a good inch of whisky into the crystal glass.

'Isn't that rather a lot?'

'Need it.' Freddie took a slurp.

He stood by the window again and she felt at a loss to say anything.

'Will you tell mother or shall I?' she said after a while, breaking the silence.

'Tomorrow.' He drained the glass, poured another and then collapsed into an armchair. He held the glass up to the light as though to admire the amber liquid. 'I'll tell her tomorrow.'

'Jonathan will need some more clothes. Oh, and his school bag. Can you get them tonight?'

'Amy, I'm exhausted. I'm sure his teacher will understand why he hasn't got all his things. I'll drop them into school tomorrow after I've opened the garage and sorted Donnie out.'

She was going to have her hands full in the morning, she thought. They would all go to school, she decided. It was time Will and Sam were enrolled anyway.

'You didn't say but how's Enid?'

'Physically weak. She lost a lot of blood. They said something about an internal haemorrhage. Not sure about her mental state. She's been off balance ever since she's known about this pregnancy. Damn it, Amy. I've seen death in the war but it doesn't prepare one for the loss of an infant.'

'No. I don't suppose it does.'

'It was a little girl. They let me see her …' Freddie's voice cracked and he stared into his glass. 'I don't think we'll have any more,' he added before draining the glass.

'Stay the night. I don't think you should be on your own.'

He nodded. 'Yeah. You're right and I've probably drunk too much already.'

'Good. I'll organise your bed and I'll put the kettle on. And you're right, you don't need more alcohol tonight.'

\* \* \* \* \*

After a restless night, it was very early when Freddie pulled on his trousers and crept downstairs. He'd missed out on food the previous evening and was hungry so he went to the kitchen but by the time he reached the larder, his misery had manifested itself and tears were streaming down his face. He hadn't lost a baby, he'd lost his way, he thought. He sat down at the kitchen table and sobbed uncontrollably.

'Couldn't you sleep either?' Amy's voice made him jump and he looked up to see her standing in her dressing gown.

He wiped his eyes with the back of his hand. 'No. At least not much.'

She sat beside him and squeezed his hand. 'It's not a sin to cry. You don't have to be all strong and masculine in front of me. George - well, he and I have been there. We shed tears - buckets of them, I can assure you.'

'You?' He stared at her. 'It isn't just the baby.' He hesitated then decided he might as well tell her everything. He could tell Beth - she would listen - sympathise even but she didn't understand the pressure he was under. 'I've made a mess of … everything. My marriage, life, everything.'

'Don't be so silly. It only looks that way right now. It'll work out, you'll see.'

He'd like to believe her. If only he had a magic wand and could be whisked back to before the war and be the optimistic, easy-going person he was then. He remembered saying the war had changed everything. It was true, it had but it had changed some things in a way he wasn't sure he liked.

'You don't understand. It isn't just Enid …' He paused. 'There's someone else.'

Amy scrutinized him. 'Don't tell me you're still seeing that woman? Not while your wife's pregnant?'

'You are still seeing her,' Amy said with disgust.

He wasn't sure how to answer. How did she find out? She'd only been here a matter of days. He hadn't realised members of his own family knew. And his mother? Did she know and if so, why hadn't she said anything?

'Freddie, you're a fool. If mother gets to know …'

'If you know ... I'm not sure she doesn't know already.'

'But why? Why can't you be happy with Enid?'

'Enid's – well ... Some people might describe her as very highly strung. I'd say she was mentally off-balance. And a man has his needs ... do I have to say more.'

'Freddie for goodness sake put a stop to it. If this ... the gossips will have a field day.'

'I know. I know. But right now I need Beth. Sometimes I think I'll go off my head. If it wasn't for mother's money tied up in the business, I'd walk away from it all.' He sighed. 'After the war, I thought everything would be simple. A business and a career but mother kept on and on at me to get married.'

'Oh, Freddie. You have to give this woman up. You've got a son to think of.'

'Stay with Enid? It'll be unbearable. And I know it looks dreadful – to feel this way when she's so ill but ... I can't help it.'

'You have to stop this affair becoming public, if indeed it hasn't already but whatever happens, you must stay with Enid. I've disgraced mother already. She'd never cope with another scandal.'

'Yes,' he agreed and thought the outcome of any public recognition of his relationship with Beth would most definitely lead to the same treatment as Amy got when she wanted to marry George.

'Come on, big brother.' Amy shook his shoulder gently. 'We've got a day ahead of us and we can't start on an empty stomach. Let me cook you something. Eggs, bacon?'

'You? Cook?'

'You forget. I've had to do most things for myself since George and I married. I had no choice. I had to learn how to do a lot of things, even cooking for half a dozen hungry men.' Amy reached for the frying pan which was hanging from a hook. She placed it on the range, then fetched the eggs and bacon from the larder. 'Each year when the threshing gang arrived, I had to feed them and you wouldn't believe how much those men could eat – sometimes there would be at least six of them.' It took a moment to locate the lard, which she scraped out and placed in the pan to melt. 'And I did all that on a range half this size.'

'I didn't realise - I never gave it much thought before, but you - you sound as though … didn't you find it hard?' He'd never given his sister's life in Canada a great deal of consideration. He supposed he'd been fully occupied by his own affairs and one affair in particular. Beth. How he wished he hadn't allowed his mother to brow beat him into marrying Enid. He'd tried to love her but it was impossible when his mind was always consumed with Beth.

'I'd be less than honest if I said it was easy.' Amy placed several rashers of bacon in the pan.

He tried to concentrate on what she was saying.

'It was hard to begin with but we had wonderful friends. They were all lovely people and we all looked after each other. And another thing. In Canada there was none of this snobbery or class business and George and I were accepted for who we were which is more than can be said for around here.'

'Sounds as though you've enjoyed your life more than I've enjoyed mine,' he said and then regretted saying as much. In comparison, Amy would wonder what hardship he had really endured.

'I always thought you and Enid were …' she stared at him. 'You have a beautiful house - at least from what I could see from the outside. It'd be nice to be invited over sometime.'

Now he did feel guilty. He had avoided his family since Amy had arrived. He hoped she would overlook this because right then, for the first time in his entire life, he needed her help.

'Sis, I'm sorry. I've neglected you.'

Amy turned her attention to the bacon which was sizzling in the pan.

'One or two eggs?'

'Two. I could eat a horse. I skipped dinner last night and the smell is making my stomach rumble.' He watched her crack the eggs. The bacon was already on a warmed plate and she cut some bread. It was only a matter of minutes and the breakfast was placed in front of him.

'Thanks, sis. I'm impressed.'

'Tea? The kettle's almost boiling.'

When she had poured the tea, she sat opposite him and they began to eat.

'I never thought I'd be the one lecturing you,' she said in a low voice. 'But you know its unforgivable carrying-on with another woman when your wife is expecting your child.'

Freddie put his knife and fork down and took a moment before responding.

'Was. Was expecting and I know you don't approve but it isn't black and white.'

'It is from where I'm sitting.'

'If only I was more like you. You had the guts to marry the man you loved. I'm a coward. I should have made an honest woman of Beth.'

'You fought in the war, Freddie. I can't ever describe you as a coward but I will say one thing. You're married to Enid. So end with … with this woman. End it now.'

He didn't reply and was relieved when their conversation was interrupted by the sound of footsteps. A few seconds later, Jonathan burst into the room.

* * * * *

Amy arrived at the school out of breath with Jonathan holding one hand and Bobbie the other. Sam and Will lingered behind. It had been one long battle to get four wayward boys off to school and, leaving less time for the walk than she would have liked, she had frogmarched them down the lanes.

'Stop dawdling, you two. You are going to school and that's that.'

Jonathan ran off to his friends the minute they were inside the gate, leaving Amy with her three boys whom she bundled into school. It had been a noisy few hours, trying to get them all dressed and breakfasted and she was relieved her mother decided to take breakfast in her room. She was equally thankful when she was greeted by a teacher and taken straight to the headmaster's room. Matters were concluded in a very professional way and she left Sam and Will to be taken to their respective classrooms in no doubt that Mr Golding knew how to handle boys and pleased that Bobbie would be joining them next term.

She set off with Bobbie for the garage, intending to ask Freddie if she could visit Enid but she wanted even more to ask about the job for George. Surely he would telephone today? And it would be even better if he telephoned that morning whist she was in Freddie's office.

The big garage doors were wide open and she could hear the telephone ringing but there was no sign of Freddie. She could see a man, who she presumed must be Donnie, peering into the engine of a large black car which roared loudly whenever he pulled some lever or other. She wanted to shout at him to go and answer the telephone. At that moment the ringing stopped, the man looked up.

'Can I 'elp you, Ma'am?'

He left what he was doing and strolled towards her, wiping his greasy hands on a piece of rag.

'I was looking for my brother. You must be ..?'

'Donnie, Ma'am. Pleased to meet you Mrs Mills. Mr Attwood ain't bin in this morning. I 'spect he's at the 'ospital.'

'Oh. Right.' She hadn't expected he would still be there. But, of course, that's where a husband ought to be.

'News travels fast round these parts,' he said by way of an explanation.

She didn't want to discuss private matters with an employee.

'There hasn't been a telephone call from my husband, has there Donnie?'

'Can't say as we've 'ad any calls this morning.'

She wanted to correct him, wondering how many calls were missed because he didn't hear them.

'Never mind. I'll call in later.' She bent to speak to Bobbie. 'We'll do the shopping first and come back when we've finished.'

She crossed the road to go to the butchers and then realised she was standing right outside the pub - not any pub - but the pub George had talked of all those years ago - the one whose landlady was Freddie's mistress. The place was closed and then she realised it was Freddie's distinctive red car parked in the yard at the top of the passageway at the back of the pub. She didn't need to have the scene spelt out - she could visualise it all and she was resentful. If Freddie was that blatant, then surely Donnie couldn't fail to know. She gave him full marks for being discreet. But if he knew, then half the villagers must know and so, too, must their mother. Yet, she allowed this to go on whilst the way she treated George all those years ago was appalling. It was one rule for Freddie and quite another for her.

* * * * *

Freddie sipped his cup of coffee and glanced at the clock. It was mid-morning. No wonder Beth had not lingered. She had gone to get ready for opening time and he had better get dressed and over to the garage. It didn't do to leave employees unattended for too long, even if you did trust them.

He hoped Jonathan had settled at school after all the tears that morning. He had reassured him that his Mummy would be home soon but when he visited the hospital, he wasn't sure whether that would be the case.

'Your wife is asleep,' said the nurse, who barred the way into the ward. 'Visiting times are six o'clock tonight until eight precisely,' she added in a voice which told him he was very unwelcome and no rules would be bent no matter how serious the matter or who he was. Angry with the nurse, he left intending to drive straight to the garage. It was a dark morning and, as he entered the High Street, he couldn't resist looking up at Beth's window. He was surprised to see the light on. He parked in the yard.

She was still in her nightdress and with her long blond hair and blue eyes she had been an open invitation and he hadn't been able to resist. Now Beth was downstairs, so he took his time dressing before wandering into the bar. He should have gone straight to the garage but stopped to consume a beer, his excuse being that it gave him fortification to face the rest of the day. In reality, he knew he was putting off the evil moment.

He told Donnie, when he enquired, that his wife was making progress and slipped into the office before he could ask another question. He worked through the paperwork, ordering parts and making out invoices and thought how good it would be to have an office girl and have the bills typed instead of handwritten by him. Maybe if he could talk his mother into financing an extension on his bank loan, he'd be able to do just that but, for now, he'd have to continue getting his hands greasy as well as do the office work. Doctor Fraser's Ford would be arriving for a service that afternoon and with Donnie fully occupied with a head gasket, he knew he would be the one to crawl under the thing and grease it. There was no way he'd skimp on this service. The doctor would be sure to check all the work on the invoice had been completed and he would be punctual about collecting it.

At lunch time, he walked to the newsagents and purchased a paper before crossing the road to the pub for a quiet sandwich. He took his beer and sat in a corner, leaving Beth to see to her regulars. The headlines shocked him. There had been more rioting in London but the Prime Minister, Ramsay MacDonald, had agreed to an urgent review of the Government's policies on unemployment. Then he remembered George. He had clean forgotten his promise to do something about that chauffeuring job. In fact, now he thought about it, it was surprising Amy hadn't been on at him. He'd better make a few telephone calls and see what he could organise. It would be a sensible idea to be in Amy's good books after this morning's confession.

He was rather glad he'd given it priority after lunch. The outcome was not going to please his sister as the vacancy had been filled. He picked up the telephone intending to make some further enquiries but Doctor Fraser arrived and he'd got involved with the service. Dressed in overalls and flat on his back under the car, he was pumping the grease gun when he heard the telephone ring.

'Damn,' he said out loud, very tempted to let it ring. Donnie had gone off for his lunch break and he couldn't afford to miss business so he began to manoeuvre himself out from under the car.

'Shall I answer it?'

'Amy?' He squeezed out and sat up in time to see her disappear into the office and by the time he reached the door, he knew she was talking to George. He wiped his hands on his overall and listened to Amy's half of the conversation.

'So that's why you haven't called. I've been so worried. There's so much going on here. Enid's in hospital and Will is ... I do wish you were here, George. He's being impossible ... What's that you say? Pips? Oh. I see. Yes, he's here and I know he's fixed that job for you.' She handed the receiver to him.

He hesitated for a second. How could he admit there wasn't any job at all?

'Hello, George? George? Hello? Damn the phone's gone dead.' He replaced the receiver. 'Must have run out of change. Maybe he'll call back in a while.' He rather hoped not or at least not until he'd had time to speak to one or two of his acquaintances. He had several numbers but he wasn't hopeful and he knew Amy would be furious when she realised there wasn't a job. 'Now, did you want something especially? Only I need to get that car finished. Doc Fraser wants to collect it at four.'

'No. I - er - You have fixed that job for George, haven't you?' Amy queried.

He thought a moment. He had to say something but what. Be honest, he told himself. Be honest.

'Truth is Amy, I spoke to Miles this morning and I'm sorry the job's taken. Said he couldn't wait any longer. He's told me of another possibility and I was going to make a call after I'd finished this service.'

'Is it the same sort of job? You know, with a house?'

'I expect so.'

'And if it doesn't work out ...'

'Look, if it doesn't, I could do with an extra pair of hands here. We'll tell George to get here asap. That suit you?'

'Please, Freddie. It's so difficult being at mother's. And you will give him a job if this doesn't work out?'

'I said I would and I'm a man of my word,' he said, recognizing he'd spoken yet another untruth. Hell. What did it matter now anyway?

## Chapter Seven

George stared at the scene before him. It hadn't changed much in twenty years. He couldn't see any sailing ships – he supposed it was the end of an era. He surveyed the long line of crane jibs and wondered if Ted was somewhere on the dockside. As a stevedore he would be unloading one of the ships but he hadn't thought to ask in which dock he might be found. The previous evening, patching up Harold had been the most important thing and staying in Vi's good books. He didn't fancy staying at Ma's with the rest of the tribe.

It felt odd being back here. It was as though he had completed a circle. The thought disheartened him. His life was a mess - he was a mess. He'd imagined hearing Amy's voice would cheer him up but the truth was he felt even more of a failure and even more miserable. He would love to be there with her but it would involve staying in his mother-in-law's house where he didn't belong. How could he forgive that woman for what she'd done? It was a stroke of luck, he'd met Freddie on the station that day … otherwise Amy would have been lost to him forever. But right then, how he wished he'd stayed in Canada. Yes, it was true in London, he had family around him but what a state the country was in - men fighting in the streets. It felt worse than when he'd left in 1925. He supposed it was. The stock market crash had made life as difficult in Europe as it had in America and Canada. At least in Canada, he had friends. What was more, they were all equal - they shared the same difficulties and helped each other. Here, there were those with money and those without and those with jobs and those without.

Amy. He remembered slamming down the receiver with a thump when the call was cut short by the pips. He felt cheated of his money and he didn't have any more change. This button 'A' and 'B' business had flummoxed him and he felt like giving the black box a good thump, too.

There had been a rattle on the kiosk door and an angry man stared in at him.

'You finished in there. There's a queue out 'ere.'

He had felt like letting the door go in his face, but, controlling the urge, he had held it open as the man muttered something about an urgent call.

The activity in the docks drew his attention. There was a ship bound for Canada. He had boarded such a ship years ago when he was a boy and then, after the war, on his return to England from the fighting in Europe, he had stood on this exact spot and made a life changing decision - to go back to Canada - only he hadn't – at least not right away. He'd married Amy. Now he was here where it all started but this time there was no hope of a life in the prairies – what hope of anything? So how was he to stomach life back in England? He thought of what he'd seen since he'd been in London - the appalling dirt and grime of a city choked by coal fumes, hungry children, some without shoes, playing in the streets, men without jobs, sitting on their doorsteps with the hopeless expression of destitution on their faces. That was what he'd seen with his own eyes and he'd been told it was far, far worse in the north of the country. The poverty and the filth horrified him. No wonder people were marching. So how could he ever think of England as his home?

* * * * *

Vi put her shopping away - two very heavy bags. She looked at the clock - mid-afternoon. Harold would be home soon and they would sit and enjoy a cup of tea together before she got on with the supper. But it wasn't the same these days - not since Harold's injury. He'd gone to work the day after the riots with a his head bandaged and a real shiner of a black eye. It was fading now but the memory of that evening was not. Whatever had happened, when he got home from work that day, he wouldn't talk of it and from then on, he was a changed man. She tried to understand, she really did but it was no use. Whenever she asked him what was wrong, he'd snap right back at her. His state of mind was a puzzle and she kept finding herself wondering if she'd done something to upset him. It she had, she couldn't think what it was. She wished she could talk to someone but none of her sisters would understand and Ma would simply tell her to toughen up and get on with life.

The house was quiet. George was out, too. For the past few weeks, he was the silent, moody visitor, often lying in bed until mid-morning. As she put the tins of peas and spam in the larder, she thought she would have to talk to him about his keep. It was true, they were not on the breadline but feeding an extra adult was taking its toll on her housekeeping and Harold, who had always been so generous before, was unapproachable. It was over a month since George had arrived and he really ought to go back to Amy but how could she say that without him thinking he wasn't welcome any more? Sometimes she thought she was the only 'normal' person in the household - that is, if pregnancy could be counted as normal. The thought amused her and, feeling the baby change its position, hoped its arrival would bring back the Harold she loved.

George hadn't returned by supper time. She had minced the remaining meat from Sunday's joint of lamb and supplemented it with chopped carrots and onions, piling on a good topping of mashed potato to make Harold's favourite dish, Shepherd's pie. Maybe with a tasty dinner inside him, his mood would be better, she thought as she scooped out three helpings. Whatever was on Harold's mind, he wasn't prepared to share with her and she found choosing a moment to raise the subject of money difficult.

'Mmm. That was good,' he said, mopping the last bit of gravy up with a slice of bread. He glanced at the empty place setting. 'He should've told us he was going to be late.'

'I'm worried ...'

'He should do something about a job. Hasn't that brother-in-law of his got something lined up?'

'I thought so. Can you speak to him?' She thought it would sound better coming from a man. 'I shall need some more money in my purse, soon,' she added hoping he would take the hint.

Harold didn't reply and they finished dinner in silence.

After clearing the table and washing up, she joined him, sitting by the fireside in the chair opposite. He was reading the paper and she rummaged in her knitting bag. An hour elapsed and, pleased with the evening's effort, she glanced up at the clock.

'Goodness, look at the time. It's nearly ten o'clock. Think I'll go on up.' She gathered her work together and shoved it all back in the bag. 'I'm worried. George missed supper. It's not like him.'

'I keep telling you - he can look after 'imself,' Harold said from behind his paper.

'I'm still worried. It's not like him.'

'You go to bed.' Harold dropped the paper into his lap. 'I'll have words with him when he comes in.'

'Now don't be hard on him. He is my brother.'

'That's as may be, but he ought to let us know if he's going to be out.'

'I've left his supper on the side,' she called as she went upstairs.

George's state of mind also worried her. It wasn't the only time in their lives George had gone missing. She remembered the uproar when he walked out as a boy. Her father had been furious but rage turned to worry when he was never found and her father had been dead many years before

George turned up at the end of the war. He had no responsibilities then but he was a family man now and she couldn't believe he would walk away from Amy and their boys.

The sheets felt icy and she hoped Harold wouldn't be too long so she could snuggle up and warm her feet. She was beginning to feel sleepy when she heard the front door. Thankful George was home, she allowed herself to drift off but she couldn't have been asleep long when she was awoken by raised voices. She got out of bed and went to the top of the stairs.

'There's no need to shout at me,' George said. 'You'll wake Vi up.'

'Somebody needs to get the message through to you. It's time you got off your backside and found work. You've been 'ere more 'an a month. In fact, it's getting on for six weeks. You can't sponge off us forever.'

'Vi invited me and I've never sponged from anyone in my life. In any case, we're family, aren't we? I'd do the same for you.'

'I don't care if you're related to the bloody Queen - it's time you was gone.'

'Believe me, I would if I could ...'

'For Gawd's sake man, I've only got so much patience.'

Vi was alarmed by the tone of Harold's voice. She'd never heard him talk to anyone like that before. She began to go downstairs.

'Well, you're certainly trying mine,' George snapped back.

'Now you listen, here,' Harold said and Vi entered the room in time to see him grab hold of George by the collar. 'This is my house and you're outstaying your welcome.'

'Harold! How dare you speak to my brother like that.'

Harold let go of George so suddenly he almost fell over.

'Don't worry, Vi,' George said, regaining his balance. 'I know when I'm not wanted.' He straightened his collar and pushed past her.

'George!' She followed him down the hall. 'Where are you going? George?'

He grabbed his coat from the hook on the wall and, ignoring his sister, opened the front door, banging it shut behind him.

'Now look what you've done,' she said to Harold when she returned to the parlour. 'You've got to stop him.'

'I'll do no nothing of the sort.'

'Where will he go?'

'Your mother's - where by rights he should be. Now go to bed, Vi.'

* * * * *

Amy was thankful her mother was later than usual for breakfast and even more thankful the children weren't arguing. It took the pressure off.

'If you've all finished, then get ready for school,' she said, glancing round the table. They looked as if they had been awake half the night. Maybe that was why they were so quiet. Jonathan, in particular, had dark patches under his eyes. Poor little boy. He must be missing his mother and father, although Freddie did call in between finishing at the garage and visiting at the hospital. The visits were brief, with most of his time spent upstairs with Jonathan but the previous evening, he had stayed a little later and there was an opportunity to talk and to find out if George had called.

'Are you sure you haven't missed his call?' she said, remembering how Donnie failed to answer the telephone. 'I don't think Donnie hears so well.'

'There's nothing wrong with Donnie's hearing,' Freddie said in a dismissive tone of voice. 'But it's been busy and with engines revving, I suppose it's true we might have missed the odd call. But the office is a problem. I can't be in two places at once and now I'm visiting Enid, my evenings are fully occupied. I don't get the chance to catch up with the paperwork.'

'You see, you do need some help. George would be able to do all that for you - he used to keep good accounts when we were farming. Everything but everything was accounted for but, then, it was a case of having to. There was nothing to spare so we needed to know where every cent went.'

Freddie didn't answer.

'I've an idea. Why don't I help? That way I can answer the telephone and maybe do some of your accounts. Being under mother's feet all day is driving me mad.'

'You? Work in an office?'

'Do say yes. I'm so bored.'

'But it wouldn't be right. In any case, what do you know about paperwork?'

'You keep forgetting. I'm not the empty-headed young girl who left for Canada all those years ago. I've had to do everything for myself. In any case, it can't be that difficult. Give me a trial - until George comes and if I make a mess of things, you can dismiss me and it won't cost you a penny.'

'It may well cost me a customer if you cock things up.' He grinned at her.

'I can write and add up. What more do you want?'

'Oh ... all right, but ...'

'But?'

'What about Bobbie?'

Amy thought a moment. 'He gets on well with mother. I could leave him here ... or ... I could bring him with me.'

'Not sure that's a good idea. Not that I mind but it isn't a place for children, is it? Never know what he'd get up to when you weren't looking.'

'I'd like an excuse to get out of the house ... please say yes.'

Freddie sighed and she knew she'd won her way. Now she couldn't wait to speak to her mother. She was tempted to knock on her bedroom door before she went off to school with the boys but it was certain to court disaster. Mother could be so moody first thing in the morning.

It was lunch before the opportunity occurred.

'I do wish Freddie would stay longer in the evenings,' Mrs Attwood said. 'We never get a chance to chat. Couldn't you persuade him to come back after hospital visiting?'

'I think he would but he's so busy at the garage and the evening is the only opportunity he has to catch up with his book work.'

'Oh, dear. Isn't it about time he had someone to do that for him?'

'We were only discussing that yesterday, mother. I could help Freddie.'

'You?'

'Why does everyone think I'm incapable? You forget I helped run a farm.'

'And look where that ended.'

'That's unfair, mother. Nobody could overcome what we faced or at least not without money …' she wondered if her mother would realise her last comment was intended to make her feel guilty. 'And, unfortunately, we didn't have any …'

Mrs Attwood's face was expressionless. If she felt any guilt, she didn't display it.

'Do you think you could take care of Bobbie for me for a couple of hours each day? Or just a day or two a week even?' Amy asked and hoped her mother was feeling just a little pang of guilt – enough to grant her request. 'When the others are at school, of course,' she rushed on. 'And Bobbie would like that, wouldn't you?' She glanced at him and could see he was uncertain. 'And I could help Freddie. I know he could do with some help.'

'Good heavens, Amy. I can't have any daughter of mine working in a garage.'

'But it wouldn't be the garage. It would be in the office and it's only for a few hours. Freddie does need the help.'

'No. Your place is here, looking after Bobbie. There's no way I could agree to you working in the garage. In any case, it's time that husband of yours was here.'

Amy wanted to shout that was the whole point but, instead, she tried another tactic.

'Freddie's under so much stress, mother. If you want to see more of him, then he needs some help. I don't mind helping temporarily.'

'No. That's my final word.'

Amy stared at her in disbelief. Everything must be seen to be correct and, even if it wasn't, then no one in the outside world must know. Of course, it wouldn't be acceptable, in her mother's eyes, for her to be seen working in a garage but it was perfectly acceptable for Freddie to have a mistress. The whole situation was beginning to feel like her worst nightmare. Maybe if she pinched herself, she would wake up back in her own little house where they belonged. How she loved it and how it had hurt so much to leave and return here - to her mother's house where it had all begun. She sighed. She was half inclined to go to London but how could she abandon the children and now there was Jonathan.

'Ma'am, could I have a word, please?'

Mrs Attwood looked over her spectacles at the maid.

'There's a problem?'

'I hate to mention it Ma'am but is there any chance of some extra help. With all the family - well, things are getting …'

'Yes?'

'The laundry's piling up and I've only got one pair of hands.'

'Yes, yes. I see. I'll give it some thought.'

'Amy,' Mrs Attwood said after the maid had left the room. 'You have to tell that husband of yours to find you all a home. I'm not employing more servants.'

'Yes. I see that, mother.' She had to do something but what?

# Chapter Eight

Freddie stared in disbelief at the Sister. Right then he could only see the top of her starched hat as she was bent over, recording something onto a sheet of paper. When she looked up at him, he shifted his eyes to the bow which held it in place, then to the equally stiff collar with its shiny stud before staring blankly at the pristine white apron on which was pinned an upside down watch. They were sitting in the little office to the right of the entrance to the ward, where he had been summoned on his arrival. It was dark outside and the room was illuminated by a dull light hanging from the ceiling. He couldn't quite take in her words and there was a long silence.

'You can't be serious?' he finally said.

'Yes, I am and this is serious – very serious. Your wife needs psychiatric help and I think the best place is St Johns.'

'A mental asylum?' Freddie was aghast. Whatever would his mother say about that? Maybe she might understand your need for Beth, a little voice said inside his head. But he couldn't imagine a worse stigma - a lunatic for a wife? Besides he couldn't, didn't believe Enid was mad. It was the pregnancy which made her unstable and she'd got over that before, hadn't she?

'Physically, your wife is doing well.'

'But she's still very sick isn't she…?'

'She's made slow progress these last few weeks but a few days more here should see her recovered enough to return home though, physically, she will be very tired to begin with. She lost a lot of blood but it's her mental health which is causing us concern. She needs psychiatric help. We can't help her here. St John's is best place for that,' the sister repeated.

'I'm sure you mean well but my wife …' Freddie had recovered from the initial shock. Now he fully understood what the sister was suggesting but he was still horrified at the thought of Enid being labelled a lunatic. 'My wife, when she had our son, had bad depression – very bad depression but she got over it. In time - she got over it. This is so much worse for her … I mean, losing a child. Of course, she's going to be depressed - more so than last time, but she'll recover. It may take longer, of course and, possibly, be more difficult. I agree she no longer needs to be here because you have done a miraculous job saving her life even if - ' He still found it difficult to believe they had lost a daughter. 'Even if you couldn't save our child's life.'

'Yes, but that's why she needs help.'

'She isn't mad?'

'No.'

'Then I don't think St John's is appropriate. My wife can be looked after at home by her family - where she belongs.'

'If that's what you wish but - '

'If my wife isn't mad, then she doesn't need to be in any asylum. She'll be leaving hospital immediately.' He would get in touch with Doctor Fraser. He would know what to do. And Enid would get over this. He wasn't certain he trusted the sister. 'I'll take her home now.'

'There's no need. I'm sure all this can wait 'til the morning.'

'I'd feel happier if she came with me right now and I refuse to allow my wife to stay in a hospital which thinks she's insane.'

'I didn't say that, Mr Attwood.'

'No, you didn't but you inferred it.'

'I really do think it would be better to arrange for her discharge in the morning.'

He hesitated. Was he being hasty? And if he left Enid here overnight - was it possible they would move her to this asylum without his knowledge? The thought was too horrendous to contemplate. Enid was enough to try the most saintly of men and he couldn't claim to be that, but he could never condemn her to a lunatic asylum. It would be cruel beyond words. No, he would take her home tonight and sort out the mess in the morning and it would be a big mess. God, what a mess. He wouldn't be able to leave her alone and then there was Jonathan to consider. And what about the garage?

He shoved all those unsettling thoughts to the back of his mind. Somehow he would cope.

'No, if there's nothing more which can be done, then I'd like Enid home now.'

The Sister sighed and stood up. The meeting was concluded.

He left the room, walked along the short corridor, then pushed open the door to the ward. He could see Enid leant back against the pillows, looking very pale and staring blankly ahead.

'Hello, Enid,' he said and pulled up the chair next to the bed. He took hold of her hand and squeezed it. 'You're coming home. How about that?'

There was no response so he set about gathering up her belongings and once he'd packed everything into the bag he'd retrieved from the bedside cupboard, he managed to persuade her on to the edge of the bed. Then he wrapped a dressing gown about her and pushed her feet into her slippers.

A nurse hovered at the end of the bed.

'Isn't it rather late to be doing this, Mr Attwood?'

'Are you telling me, nurse, that it's a crime to take my wife home?' Freddie carried on with what he was doing and, satisfied he had everything, put his arm around Enid and helped her to her feet.

'Come on, Enid. We're going to take you home,' he said and was relieved when she allowed him to guide her past the other two beds to the door. She leant on him and progress was slow so he was even more relieved when he got outside without being accosted by the ward sister.

It was dark but there was a full moon and he could see in its light the way to the car. He was thankful he'd parked close to the entrance. A nearby clock struck eight. Visiting time had come to an end and other visitors were leaving their sick ones for the walk home. It was then he was grateful for his mother's wealth. How would he have got Enid home without a car? He settled her into the front seat, retrieving the blanket from the back seat and wrapping it around her.

He couldn't believe the turn of events. Now he was wondering how he would manage. Or more particularly whether Enid would cope with being at home but this had to be better than admitting her to a St Johns - anything had to be better than that.

* * * * *

After settling the boys for the night, Amy was upstairs sorting dirty washing. As she picked through the garments, she wondered if it would be too extravagant to send George a telegram. How else could she contact him quickly? And they did need to talk but, if she sent a telegram, without any prospect of a job, what was there to talk about? She held up Bobbie's muddy trousers and considered the problem of laundry and employing more staff. She supposed her mother's life had been disrupted by the arrival of three - no four children and all boys - boisterous ones, who never sat still for a second. The house was noisy and untidy whereas she had been used to order and solitude. No wonder she was bad tempered. Now the maid had complained about the extra work. Of course, she could help - she'd had to do all the washing in Canada but she knew with complete certainty what her mother's reaction would be to this suggestion. The best thing, she thought, was to slip in unannounced and do some of the ironing and, whilst this might not be her favourite occupation, it would relieve her boredom.

There was a tap at the door and the maid entered. 'It's Mr Attwood for you on the telephone, Mrs Mills.'

She rushed downstairs wondering what on earth could be wrong. It was nearly ten o'clock and Freddie hadn't looked in on his way to the hospital. Had there been an accident?

'Freddie?'

'Amy, thank God. Is there any chance of you coming over in the morning?'

'Oh, is that all? I rushed to the telephone - thought you'd had an accident at the very least.'

'Sorry, I realise it's late and I do apologise. I hope I didn't get you out of bed?'

'No. Not quite.'

'I need your help. To be honest, I'm a bit desperate.'

'The garage?'

'No. No. It's Enid.' There was a pause. 'She's home.'

'Home?'

'That's what I said,' he sounded annoyed.

'What? Is she well enough? I thought ... For goodness sake what's going on?'

There was silence at the other end and the line crackled.

'Freddie? Freddie? Are you there?'

'I can't discuss it now. I need to speak to you in private. Can you come over to the house tomorrow? Please? Please, say you can. I don't know who else to ask.'

'What on earth's wrong -'

'Don't ask questions. Just come. Tomorrow.'

'It's all very well for you - '

'Amy, please. Just do this for me. I need your help.'

'All right. After the boys have gone to school. I can't trust Will. I have to take them and make sure they all go in. I'll be there as soon as I can. But whatever is it? Can't you say?'

'You know as well as I do that the old biddy on the exchange ... ' there was another crackle on the line. 'Just be here, tomorrow.'

It was mid-morning before Amy arrived with Bobbie and there was a fine drizzle in the air. She stopped to admire the newly cut lawn. It was late in the year to cut a lawn and possibly this would be its last before winter really set in, she thought as she pushed open the garden gate. She noticed a pink climbing rose which, in spite of it being November, was managing to flower and realised there would have been snow by now in the prairies. She and Bobbie would be dressed in thicker coats and would definitely have needed gloves and a warm hat. She was deciding whether she preferred the English dampness when the front door was flung open.

'Amy! Thank the Lord.' Freddie stood in the doorway and she didn't think she'd ever seen him so anxious. He looked exhausted. She gave him a hug.

'Whatever's going on? You look as though you haven't slept,' she said once inside the hall. 'I've never seen you so - well, agitated.'

Freddie held his finger up to his lips.

'Come through into the sitting room.' He guided her along the hall. 'I'll get Doris to make some coffee.'

He opened the door and for a second she took in the extravagant furnishings. The window drapes were generous to say the least with more material, she thought, in the pelmets than she'd had to make curtains for her entire house. The red velvet, trimmed with gold, was extravagant – not her taste – but spoke of wealth.

'Make yourself at home. I'll see about this coffee.'

Bobbie charged straight to the window and stared into the garden.

'Who's that, Mom?' He pointed at a garden ornament and Amy laughed.

'Why it's cupid,' she replied, still trying to take in the luxury. In comparison to the house they'd left, which had thrilled her when they moved in, this was lavish indeed. From the huge Indian rug covering the parquet flooring to the extravagant fire place over which hung an ornate, gold mirror, everything spoke of affluence. The room was square – bigger than the whole of her first house – and it had a beautiful view into the garden and across unspoilt countryside. She wandered round, admiring the paintings before picking up and studying the photograph on top of the piano. It was Freddie and Enid at their wedding.

'Who's cupid?' Bobbie asked.

She was replacing the photograph as Freddie entered the room.

'Doris'll be in with some coffee in a jiffy.'

If he noticed her examining his wedding photograph, he didn't comment and she went to sit on the settee, indicating for Bobbie to sit beside her.

'Enid came home last night,' Freddie said without preamble.

'Yes, that much I gathered from our telephone conversation but that's much too soon, isn't it?'

'Yes, probably - I think so. They said there wasn't anything physically wrong with her that wouldn't mend better at home but ...'

'But?'

'Mentally, she's a mess. I can't leave her. I rang Doc Fraser and he came out and gave her a sedative - not that I thought she needed one.'

She thought the doctor ought to have given a sedative to Freddie at the same time.

'He said he'd look in later today ...' he continued.

'And?'

'I can't be here and run a garage, can I?' he snapped.

She was annoyed by his tone of voice but before she could say so, their conversation was interrupted by the arrival of coffee. Once the door had shut behind Doris, Freddie began to explain what had happened the previous evening.

'So you see, don't you?'

She nodded, now understanding why he was in such a flap.

'There's no way I could let Enid go to St John's.'

'St John's?' Amy thought she remembered the name. 'Isn't that a - a mental - '

'Shshsh.' Freddie indicated Bobbie. 'Let's not refer to it - at least not directly by its name. I don't want the whole neighbourhood whispering about us.' He lowered his voice. 'In any case, she's far from insane. If you remember when she had Jonathan …'

'You've forgotten. I was in Canada but you did write and tell me about it but then, I had no idea it was so serious.' She tried to recall Freddie's letters. 'Mother wouldn't be too happy about an asylum either,' she added.

'Shshsh. Please don't mention the 'a' word or use anything resembling that meaning in front of anyone - especially the boys. Jonathan's pretty sharp and this is between you and me.'

'So what do you want me to do?'

'Can you come over each day?'

She thought a moment. The most obvious solution was for her to move in. It would be bliss to get away from mother but moving in could make Enid worse.

'You know, Freddie, maybe I should meet Enid before we decide.'

He looked at her in surprise.

'I'd forgotten … I thought …'

'For goodness sake, I haven't been back in England for long and most of that time Enid has been in hospital. Of course, we haven't met.'

'She's asleep. Can you stay this morning? Just so I can check what's happening at the garage. I spoke to Donnie on the telephone but there's other things I need to do - things I can't trust him with.'

'I suppose so,' she said with reluctance. 'But this can't be a permanent arrangement. It's exhausting walking the boys to school then coming over here - I don't want to do that every day.'

'I still don't understand why they can't take themselves.'

'Yes, you'd think I could trust them but …Will is twelve, almost thirteen. He could leave school within a year and without George around, he's a real handful. For the last day or so he's been saying he doesn't want to go to school and when I ask him why, he won't tell me. I get the impression from Sam it's something to do with his accent and I also get the impression that given half a chance he'd skip school.'

'I see but what's wrong with his accent?'

'It's Canadian, that's what's wrong. Do I have to spell it out? Children can be very unkind sometimes.'

'I see. I wouldn't have thought it was that big a problem,' Freddie said.

She almost yelled back he could have no idea how big such a thing might be since he had never experienced it. Poor Will. He'd been through so much. If only they'd been able to bring Spot with them. That dog had been Will's constant companion and he'd been devastated to leave him behind. And, coming to England, had meant such a huge adjustment for him. George had trained him to drive the wagon and hitch up the horses and even to step in whenever he was needed. That's what all the farm boys in Canada were expected to do. That expectation had gone - his dog had gone - his whole life experience gone. And now his accent was something the other children poked fun at. No wonder he was so difficult.

Freddie was thoughtful. 'What if I take them to school in the morning and collect you at the same time?' he eventually said. 'Then would you stay with Enid?'

'What about her own mother? Surely, she'd want to be involved?'

'Heavens above, Amy, that'd be – unworkable. She's – dare I say it – on the verge of … ' he stopped. 'Enid takes after her, don't you see. It quite probably would make matters even worse than they already are. That woman is difficult enough in normal times, there's no way I want her here.'

'All right, all right. But first I have to meet Enid. We might not get on.'

Freddie was silent for a minute.

'I know Enid didn't want you to stay but maybe we can all understand why that was now. She's not very strong so I'm sure she'll be as grateful as I am if you look after Jonathan. I know mother's been an absolute pain and, I suppose it would make sense …' He hesitated. 'But why don't you and the boys move in here?'

'That's a good idea,' Amy said, grateful he had finally suggested it and hoping she didn't sound too eager. 'It would give mother some peace and quiet,' she added and thought it had to be the most sensible solution. What a relief it would be to leave 'Hazeldene'.

'And it would make life a lot easier for me if I could get down to the garage first thing in the morning. I could drop the boys off at school and save you a lot of walking.'

'Mmm, that'd be good and I bet the boys will find it a novelty arriving at school by car. But I have to pack our things and I don't think we could carry our bags all the way here.

'That's the easiest thing of all to organise,' Freddie said. 'Doris will be here for a while. I'll get her to organise the beds while I drive you back. Then Donnie can collect you later and bring you all over here.'

\* \* \* \* \*

'Where's Will?' Amy asked when the boys came in from school. The short time she had spent at Enid's bedside was enough to convince her that her brother was right. She shouldn't be left alone. She had been home long enough to discuss the situation and to inform her mother she and the boys were going to stay at Freddie's. Now she was collecting items from around the house.

'Don't know,' Sam said and followed Jonathan, climbing the stairs two at a time.

'Come back here, young man. I want to know where Will is.'

Sam came down one stair at a time, pulling a face at Bobbie who was grinning at him.

'You, too, Jonathan.' She waited till Sam and Jonathan were standing in front of her. 'Now, I know Will went to school. So why didn't he come home with you?'

Sam shrugged.

'He wasn't in assembly,' Jonathan said.

'Where was he then?'

They didn't answer.

'You must know something. You must have seen something. The school isn't that big. Now think. Did you see him at break?'

They shook their heads.

'So if you don't know where he is, where do you think he might be?'

'He goes down to the river sometimes,' Jonathan said.

'What? Is that where he is now?'

Jonathan shook his head. She looked at Sam.

'He doesn't tell us anything.'

She thought a moment. If Will was playing truant regularly, he had always made sure he got home with the others. So where was he now? And why did he have to choose this exact moment to go missing? As if she hadn't enough to do with only a couple of hours in which to pack.

'Jonathan you should know your mother's home from hospital. She's very sick still and needs a lot of help so we're all coming to stay at your house.'

'We're going ...?' Sam began.

'Yes, we're all going,' she said and began to go upstairs. The boys followed. 'It'll give Grand Mamma some peace and it'll help your Uncle. I want you to pack up your belongings so we're ready for Donnie to collect us. Do you understand?' she said when they all stood on the landing. 'Seeing them nod, she continued. 'I'm going to look for Will and I want you to keep a strict eye on Bobbie, both of you. You're the eldest, Jonathan, so you're in charge.'

Sam pulled a face.

'No misbehaving now,' she said at her bedroom door. 'You're all to be on your best behaviour. I'll be back as soon as I've found Will. And don't upset Grand Mamma by being silly.'

She pulled on her shoes and lifted her coat off its hanger, slipping it on as she walked along the landing. There was a knock on the front door and she heard the maid open it. She could hear someone asking for her.

'Mrs Mills, Mrs Mills ...' the maid called. 'There's a policeman asking for you.'

Will! She ran down the stairs, arriving at the bottom as a policeman entered the hall.

'Mrs Mills?'

'Yes, yes,' she said. 'Is it my son?'

'There's been an accident, Ma'am. He's in the hospital.'

'Is he all right?'

'Can't rightly say, ma'am. Something to do with a go-cart? Can't say more than that.'

'A go-cart? What's he doing with a go-cart? Whatever that is. I don't understand. Is he badly hurt?'

'I think it best if you come down to the hospital.'

'Oh - er - I will. Right away.'

She opened the door to let the policeman out. It was raining and she watched him collect his bike from the side of the house, trying to decide what to do next. She needed to get to the hospital straight away but she might be there for hours. She told the maid to inform her mother where she was going and, in spite of the wet weather, left the house, running along the road with her coat still unbuttoned.

Wet through, she arrived at the hospital quite out of breath. She hadn't been there since she was a girl and it was so much smaller than she remembered. She stopped a nurse and panted out her enquiry.

'My son's been admitted. Can I see him?'

'Name?'

'Oh - er - Will. William Mills.'

The nurse consulted her notepad.

'I believe the doctor's with him right now.'

'Whatever happened? They said a go-cart. He hasn't got a go-cart.'

'I can only tell you that he got his foot trapped in a rusty wheel. I think it's quite bad.'

'Oh, my God.' She felt faint. 'Can I see him?'

'Not before the doctor's finished. I suggest you have a seat over there.' She pointed to two empty chairs.

'Can I see my son when the doctor's finished?'

'That depends on the doctor.'

## Chapter Nine

'I think … he, maybe … jealous,' Ma said. 'Can't think of any other reason for what you're telling me.' She shuffled across the room, holding the arms of the chair and steadying herself as she sank into the only upright chair in the room. 'This blessed arthritis. It's always worse in winter.'

Vi observed her mother. She was very slow these days and she could see a time when she would need more help. She hoped she wouldn't be the one responsible. She had done her bit with her mother-in-law.

'Harold? Jealous? What of?' Vi couldn't think of a single reason. Was it George? Why should he be envious of her brother? George had so little to be envious of. She dismissed the idea. Besides, George had been gone for two days and, if anything, Harold's behaviour had become worse. No, it couldn't be that.

'The baby, of course.' Her mother interrupted her thoughts.

'The baby? It isn't even born yet so how could that be possible?'

'I've known of men who don't cope too well with their wife's pregnancy.'

'Really? But why? I don't understand.' She racked her brains. She had tried her best to be a good wife, so how had she failed? She couldn't think of a single thing to justify Harold's irrational behaviour. He found fault with everything and everybody but most of all her. It was so unlike the man she married.

'Do you think it could be that bang on the head? It's healing nicely but it was quite a nasty injury. I'm so grateful he's stayed away from any more of those marches.'

'It's possible, I suppose,' Ma said. 'But it's much more likely he's worried about becoming a father. Up till now, the only people in his life were his mother and you and he didn't have to share you with anyone. It won't be like that once the baby arrives. It'll mean a huge adjustment for him.'

'Hmm. It's us women who have to do all the adjusting.' She thought of her waistline and the clothes which were beginning to get tight.

'You shouldn't forget Harold was over forty when he married you. People get set in their ways. Being a father is life changing.'

'I can't believe that's causing him to act like a - like a spoiled brat.'

'And another thing. You've done nothing but indulged him since you got married.'

'I've what?' She'd only done what any woman who was in love would do.

'You've let him get away with an awful lot, Vi, and you wait on him, hand and foot. He can see you won't have time to do that in future. It is possible, he's having doubts about this baby.'

She stared at her mother in disbelief. It was an extraordinary suggestion. Harold had wanted this baby as much as she did. He couldn't possibly resent it - or could he? What Ma was saying did sort of make sense. Though she still thought allowances, if there were any to be made, should be for her. After all it was she, who was sharing her body and it would be she who would be going through labour and what's more it would be she who would be getting up in the middle of night to feed the baby. Men, she thought in exasperation, have it made. She could put up with everything a pregnancy meant going through without complaint if only she could have the old Harold back.

'What can I do? Oh, Ma, he's such a wonderful man and we both wanted this child. I remember how thrilled he was when I told him.'

'I don't know the answer, Vi, love. Make us a cup of tea, there's a good girl. Things always seem better after you've had a cuppa.'

Vi stood up. If Ma was right, then there wasn't going to be an easy answer. Why, just when she thought she was the luckiest girl alive, did this have to happen?

'Don't suppose you've heard from George?' Ma called after her as she went into the scullery.

'Nothing. Not a word. Do you think I should write to Amy?'

She left the kettle to boil.

'I suppose so,' Ma said. 'It's more than likely that's where he's gone but just the same, it might be sensible.'

'I'm really worried about him. Even before the row with Harold, he wasn't his normal self. He was so depressed and, if you heard half the things they went through, it wasn't any wonder really.'

Ma didn't answer.

'So you think I should write?'

'Yes, but don't say anything to alarm her.'

'And how do I do that? He's been gone nearly a week. I don't think I could tell her George isn't here and we don't know where he's gone without worrying her. And where could he have gone? He had next to no money.'

'To Buckinghamshire and Amy, I hope. I gave him the money.'

Vi looked at her mother in surprise. Now she knew how he could afford to go to the pub.

'I gave it to him so he could make a phone call and some for the fare. Let's hope he's there already.'

Now she was worried. She didn't like to say George had been at the pub most days and on more than one occasion, he'd returned the worse for wear. But more than anything she hoped he hadn't done anything silly.

'I'll write to Amy. When I get home.'

*****

Freddie was exhausted - he hadn't felt like this since the war. The trenches. His mind conjured up the most appalling images - images he'd tried to shut out but, no matter how he tried to forget these memories, there was no doubt the hospital reminded him of it all - carrying the injured to safety, giving orders and being hungry - he'd forgotten what it was like. He'd got Enid home, carrying her upstairs and getting her into bed. Then he'd persuaded Amy to look after her, at least during the daytime when he was at the garage. Now he was doing his best to fix himself something to eat. Somehow in all of this activity, he'd missed out several meals. Funny, but he hadn't noticed. On his return home after his visit to Beth, he should have asked Doris to fix something for him, but he felt he'd burdened her enough for one day. He'd had to bribe her with an extra ten bob to get her to stay with Enid for longer as it was. He'd told her he needed to go to the garage but the truth was he needed Beth - needed her to get his head straight - needed to lose himself in sexual abandonment.

'I can't take responsibility for the sick,' Doris had protested.

'Enid's asleep and will be for at least another couple of hours. The Doctor gave her a sedative so she'll be no trouble.

Please, Doris. Tomorrow my sister will be here and it won't be necessary.'

When he'd pulled out a ten shilling note, her eyes had lit up.

'So long as I don't have to do it tomorrow. I've my own family to look after,' she grumbled but was quick to take the money.

He felt a little guilty then, considering he wasn't planning to go to the garage at all. He'd already telephoned Donnie and organised for him to collect Amy. He was going to see Beth. A stolen hour - an hour of bliss when he could forget his problems.

'Where've you been, stranger?' Beth greeted him and her coolness hit home.

'I've had the most God awful time,' he started to say and almost blurted out that he'd rescued Enid from a fate worse than death - a mental asylum.

'You're not the only one who's had a bad time,' Beth said and shut the door behind him. 'Maisy walked out. Heaven alone knows why I put up with that girl all these months. Now she's left me in the lurch and I've got to run this evening without much help. Oh, I know Henry will put in some extra hours, but he is getting on …'

He threw his arms around her.

'I came here to forget my troubles. Please don't burden me with more.'

Her blue eyes looked up at him with a frown and he realised he had been taking her for granted - expecting her to be there for him - not to have cares of her own.

'I didn't mean that,' he said, worried he'd offended her. 'It's just that - well - I feel like I'm sinking into a quagmire. I had to get away. Let's not talk about our problems. I need you.'

He kissed her and buried his face in her soft fair hair. It smelt of lavender and he wanted to drown in it. It wasn't long before she led the way upstairs. Soon their frantic love making blotted out their problems.

After, Freddie reached across to the chair at the side of the bed.

'Cigarette?' He opened the silver cigarette holder and put one in his mouth. Then he reached for his lighter. Lighting up, he lay back on the pillows. After two puffs, he took it out and offered it to her.

She shook her head. 'I thought you'd given up.'

He sighed. 'I smoked in the war. It calmed my nerves.' He inhaled again. 'Truth is, I feel as though I've been through some big battle.'

'I wish you wouldn't - smoke, that is.'

'It's like you. I need it right now.'

'Huh. I don't like being compared to a cigarette.'

'I didn't mean it like that and you know I didn't.'

She didn't reply.

'Enid's home from hospital …'

'And?'

'It's like last time, only far, far worse.'

'How do you mean? Far worse?'

He hesitated, then told himself he could trust Beth.

'She's mentally unstable. The hospital … they, er … they suggested she should go to St John's.'

'That's a mental asylum isn't it?'

Freddie puffed on the cigarette. He didn't want to tell her any more. He'd said enough.

'It is isn't it?'

He exhaled again and then reached for an ashtray and pushed the stub into it.

'I wouldn't let her go - the stigma …'

'I see. So she's mad and she's at home?'

'You make it sound awful. Oh, I suppose it is awful but the thing is, I don't trust those institutions. Once they get their claws into you … Need I say more?'

'I suppose not. But … you've left her alone? She oughtn't to be left on her own - not if she's like you say. You never know what she might do.'

'Doris is with her and Amy and the boys are moving in tonight, thank God. I don't know how I'd cope otherwise. Doc Fraser gave her a sedative and since she's been home, she's been sleeping mostly.'

'I'm so sorry, Freddie. I had no idea. Makes my little spat with Maisy seem tame really.' She kissed his cheek. 'How long can you stay?'

'I need to go soon. I bribed Doris - not sure how she'll cope if Enid does get out of bed but I don't think that'll happen. She's very weak.' He pulled her to him. 'I do so wish you were my wife.'

'Tut, tut. Your mother would never approve - you married to the Landlady of a public house. I can't see that going down too well.' She laughed.

'Sometimes I wish I could re-invent myself - you know - have a simple life.'

'Freddie, you of all people should know that money and privilege comes with responsibilities. Let's face it, you're upper class and I most definitely am not.'

He thought of those words as he broke some eggs into a saucepan. Class. It was all about class. He had thought the war would be the end of it but people like his mother still lived their lives according to this elitist system. If she hadn't been so class conscious, there wouldn't have been all that trouble over Amy marrying George. He had to admire Amy - she married the person she loved. She had given up everything for George while he had married Enid, his mother's choice, knowing he didn't love her. And in so doing, he'd condemned them both.

In his anger he crushed the shells in his hand.

'Damn!' He peered into the saucepan. Now how could he get the fragments of shell out?

He'd finished the last mouthful of scrambled eggs when Donnie arrived.

'Where's Amy?' He held the door open and counted three boys. 'And where's Will?' His stomach sank. Had the boy done what Amy feared and played truant?

'She's at the hospital, Mr Attwood,' Donnie said.

'The hospital?' Now what had the boy been up to?

'Seems young Will has had some kind of accident.'

'Yes, yes but do you know what's happened?' He directed his question at everyone.

'No, Uncle Freddie,' Sam answered for them all. 'Mum telephoned and said to make sure we were ready when Mr Donnie arrived. She said we were to come here and that she would telephone you later.'

'I see.'

'I'm hungry, Dad. What's to eat?' Jonathan asked.

He sighed. He'd done his entire repertoire when he'd made scrambled eggs.

'I think we'll have to do something on toast tonight. I'm no cook, so we'll all have to muck in.'

He thought he couldn't keep Donnie any longer, yet Amy would need collecting from the hospital. How he was going to achieve that, he hadn't worked out.

'I see it's still raining,' he said as he opened the door. 'I hope to see you in the morning. Not sure what's going on so you open up as usual, Donnie.'

He closed the door and realised then, not only would he not be going to the garage in the morning but the boys would be missing school if Amy didn't make it back that night. Leaving Enid alone was too risky.

'Now come on, boys,' he said on his return to the kitchen. 'I need some help. Let's see what's in the larder.' He inspected the contents of the cupboard and realised he needed to go shopping. 'I think it'll have to be …' There were six eggs left which by his calculation, might feed three hungry boys with toast to top up. He reached for a large tin marked Huntley & Palmer and shook it gently. It didn't sound like biscuits. He prized the lid off and inside was the remains of homemade fruit cake. 'Haha. Cake for afters.'

In the following hours, his admiration for Amy increased several fold. Refereeing arguments and preparing food not to mention the numerous times he'd climbed the stairs to see if Enid needed anything, left him exhausted. It was late by the time the boys were in bed and peace had descended on the household. As he came downstairs, having checked once again on Enid, his eyes rested on the telephone.

He would call the hospital and find out exactly what was going on.

*****

Vi re-read her letter and then folded it and slipped it into an envelope. She would post it when she went to the shops. She glanced up at the clock and realised it was later than she thought. Harold would be home soon and she'd better get on with preparing the dinner. She couldn't bear the thought of another row. Yesterday it had been because dinner wasn't exactly on the dead of five.

'You know I get bad stomach cramps if I eat late,' he'd moaned.

'It's hardly late, Harold.'

'I expect to eat at five and it's almost six,' he'd snapped at her. 'Now my mother would have had everything ready -'

'I'm not you're mother,' she snapped back.

'No, you're my wife and should know better. And another thing, where were my shirts, this morning? It's all right you sleeping in but I was nearly late by the time I found them down here. They should've been in the wardrobe.'

The rest of the meal had been conducted in silence and, instead of helping with the dishes as he usually did, he slunk into his armchair and buried his head in the newspaper.

She was determined not to be late that evening and dinner was simple enough - sausages and mash so it wasn't far from ready when Harold arrived home. She ran to greet him, relieved she'd caught up some time.

'Have a good day?' she asked.

'Usual.' He didn't kiss her, but kicked off his shoes and went upstairs to change.

She went to count out the cutlery and set the table. Their wedding photo, framed in silver stood on the top of the sideboard. She picked it up. She looked beautiful that day and Harold looked very dapper in his dark grey suit.

'What the hell are you doing to the dinner?' Harold demanded from upstairs.

She looked up. The air was blue. How had that happened? She ran to the kitchen in time to see the frying pan burst into flames. She hesitated in the doorway. What on earth should she do?

'What in gawd's name have you done?' Harold peered over her shoulder. 'You've set the house on fire, you silly bitch.'

'Harold!' The insult hurt. If he hadn't put her under so much pressure and been so critical, she wouldn't have been trying to set the table instead of supervising the frying pan.

'Come out of the way, will you?'

He shoved past her and grabbed the tea towel, thrusting it into the water which was in the sink.

'But it's dirty ...' She wanted to say it was full of potato peelings.

He wrung out the cloth and covered the pan, then shut the gas tap before opening the backdoor. Coughing, he ran outside. Vi, held her handkerchief over her nose and followed.

'I thought you knew better than to leave a frying pan unattended.'

'I ...' What was the use. He wouldn't see it her way.

'We're very lucky the whole house didn't catch fire.'

So much for her hopes of a pleasant evening. Now look what she'd done. She didn't think she could stand much more of Harold's criticisms. Couldn't he see how unfair he was being? She felt jumpy and on edge in his company so not waiting for the air to clear, she returned to see if she could rescue some of the sausages.

'Don't touch it,' he yelled from the safety of the garden. 'For gawd's sake, don't touch it. For all you know it might still be alight.'

There was a tremendous thud, followed by the splintering of wood. She ran into the hall to be confronted by a fireman pushing his way in through the front door. Everything after that was a blur. Someone was asking her if she was all right. Yes, of course she was. Wasn't she? She tried to sit up but felt the room spinning.

'I shouldn't do that.' It was a strange voice. 'Just relax. The doctor will be here any minute.'

'No, please. I'm fine. Just fine,' she said. Harold would hate all this fuss and who was this man anyway? Everything was blurred, so she closed her eyes.

'Mrs Smith. Mrs Smith.'

She roused and tried to focus.

'It's all right Vi. It's the doctor.' Harold's voice sounded muffled.

'What's going on?' She recognized another voice - it was Ted. 'I was on my way home and saw the fire engine. What's happened.'

The room was full of people - the doctor who was attempting to take her pulse, two huge firemen and Ted. Harold was thanking their neighbour for calling the fire brigade. All this for four measly burnt sausages. Was it really worth it?

\* \* \* \* \*

Amy replaced the receiver. It was still raining and so the nurse had taken pity on her and allowed her to use the phone on the desk.

'Make it snappy or I'll be in trouble,' she had instructed, so her conversation with Freddie was justifiably short and it was just like him to expect her to go there that evening. But how could she?

In the midst of their conversation, there had been a loud commotion with trolleys and nurses rushing about and it had been hard to focus on what he was saying to her. She hoped she'd made it clear, she wasn't leaving until she knew how Will was. Anyway, she could hear the rain thrashing against the windows and it was pitch black outside. It would not be sensible to venture out and, if she did, it would be unpleasant enough walking to 'Hazeldene' which was a good deal closer than Freddie's house. She might need to stay at the hospital all night even if it meant sitting bolt upright in a less than comfortable chair. No she was not going to walk to Freddie's house at this late hour and in this weather. It was unreasonable of him to suggest it and he would have to send his driver over in the morning. She wandered back to the row of seats and sat down.

Will was in the operating theatre and they were fighting to save his foot. Such an idiotic thing to do - race down that hill with no way of stopping. She couldn't imagine where Will had acquired this thing they called a "go-cart" or how he'd managed to crash it in such a way it had resulted in his foot being wedged in a rusty wheel. It was a wonder he was alive. And she didn't believe for one moment he was alone. There had to be another boy involved, maybe two but Will was not letting on. If only George was here. Will would never dare to lie to him. She could feel tears creeping into her eyes and dashed them away with the back of her hand. It was all too much. Now she blamed herself for not going to London with him in the first place. She should have agreed even if there was going to be a shortage of space of and, if she had, none of this would have happened.

'Amy? Why it is Amy?'

A male voice penetrated her thoughts. It was a second or so before she reacted. Charles? The voice was unmistakable - unforgettable. She looked up and caught the look in his eyes and in his gaze was all that had passed between them. His face was plumper, creased with lines of worry and he looked so much older than she remembered but, she reminded herself, she hadn't seen him since - she thought back - since 1919. The year she broke their engagement and ran away to marry George - thirteen, nearly fourteen years ago. Had he forgiven her? Had he married? And did he think she looked old? Probably. The trials of the last few years and the harsh climate had taken its toll. But what brought him to the hospital at this time of night? Was he … a father in waiting?

She stood up, hoping she would be speaking on equal terms but he still towered over her.

He made as if to give her a hug – then changed his mind, stepping back and increasing the space between them.

'I can't believe it. It is you. They said you were in Canada.'

'Yes. I - er - we were.' She didn't want to tell him of their failure. 'Farming - we were farming.'

'When - how long are you here for?'

'We're not going back to Canada.' She didn't want to answer more of his questions. 'And You? Are you well? Did you marry?'

'Yes.'

'Children? Do you have any children?'

'Yes. A boy and a girl. You?'

'Three - all boys.'

'There's a lot to catch up with.' He indicated the chairs. 'Shall we sit down.'

She waited until he was sitting beside her.

'Your wife ... is that why you're here?'

'No. Actually it's mother.'

'Lady Margaret?' she said with surprise. Then she remembered the painting adorning her mother's drawing room wall and realised that it would have been painted years ago and the lady in the picture was now the same age as her own mother, if not older. 'Is she going to be all right?'

'It's her heart. She hasn't been well for ... well, several years. The doctor thought it best if we got her here but ...'

'I'm sorry,' she said. The arrival of Charles and his mother must have been the mayhem which had been going on when she had been talking to Freddie on the telephone but she had been too absorbed in their conversation to notice.

'And you? You're here …' he said.

'My son. He's had an accident.'

'You're on your own?'

'George is in London, if that's what you mean.' She didn't want to tell him why he was in London.

'Is it serious? Your boy?'

'Yes,' she said, looking down at her own feet. How were they going to cope if Will lost his foot? George would, of course, blame her. He wouldn't understand how impossible it was to keep track of Will once he was at school even though she had walked him there every single day. 'Yes,' she finally said. 'He might lose a foot.'

'Oh. That is serious. I'm really sorry to hear that.'

She looked up and found him staring at her. Disconcerted, she looked away. She could see in his eyes what she had seen when she accepted his marriage proposal and she didn't want him to see any hint of regret in hers. All those years ago, she had made the right decision and nothing could change that now.

'I never stopped loving you,' he whispered.

'Charles, please …'

'Are you happy?'

She nodded and for some inexplicable reason felt tears welling into her eyes. She blinked them back. It was all too much but she didn't want Charles' sympathy - she would be unable to stop the tears if that happened. She stood up.

'I'm glad. I couldn't have born it if we were both unhappy,' he said, catching the tips of her fingers.

She allowed him to grasp them for a few seconds before pulling her hand away. He was telling her his own marriage had not been as blissful as she had imagined it might be but before she could think of how to reply the door opened and a nurse appeared.

'Mrs Mills? Would you come this way?'

'The car's outside,' he said. 'It's pouring with rain … I could take you home, Amy.'

She nodded her thanks and turned to follow the nurse.

## Chapter Ten

'Thanks, mate,' George said as he got down from the cart. He supposed he'd been lucky to get a lift out of London. He knew lorries, having delivered their loads, would leave from the Markets, so it had been a question of finding one, going in the right direction, with an obliging driver.

He didn't know quite when he reached the decision to go to Buckinghamshire. He knew he'd been a coward. He should have faced up to things much earlier – in fact weeks ago. Now he felt an enormous burden of guilt. He should never have left Amy to cope with the boys when he knew Will was resentful and difficult. He sympathised. Just as his son felt so did he. He had lost a way of life which he loved and Will was only doing what he, who should have known better, had done. He had been bitter and angry. Poor Amy. How could he ever make it up to her?

He had mooched around the docks before heading back, disgracefully late, to Vi's. He'd been feeling sorry for himself and resenting the hand he'd been dealt in life and he knew he'd been taking Vi and Harold's hospitality for granted. He supposed it was only a matter of time before they - or Harold, at least - asked him to leave. He still found it difficult to realise he'd stayed with them for six weeks. Six whole weeks and during that time all he'd done was to drink his sorrows away. No wonder his brother-in-law was angry –

he had every right to be. Once he got settled, he must write and try to smooth matters over. It was possible Harold's actions had been the spur needed to make him face up to reality. If Freddie had managed to hang on to that job for him, then maybe he could start to claw his way back to a more normal life and he wanted nothing better than to settle into his own home with his own family. He hoped, in his stupidity, he hadn't left things too late and he hoped, more than anything, Amy would forgive his selfish behaviour.

When he left Vi's, he walked to his mother's in the hope she would take pity on him but, the place was in darkness. He hadn't the heart to wake them up and confess to falling out with Harold. Instead he headed towards Smithfield but most of the wagons were going back the way he'd come. Exhausted by now, he'd slept on a park bench. It wasn't the most pleasant of nights. He was awoken more than once, first by a vagrant who wanted his bench. He didn't fancy sharing, so he'd moved. Then a policeman shone a torch in his eyes and asked him a few questions. In between times, he snoozed, awaking cold, stiff and very hungry. At least the overnight temperature had been above freezing. He would never have survived sleeping rough in November in the Prairies.

He left the park and wandered aimlessly along the streets when the smell of sizzling bacon in a nearby café made his stomach rumble. He felt in his pockets but all he had was sufficient to purchase a large tin mug of milky tea. He regretted spending Ma's money on the demon drink. He had always regarded men who did that as fools, yet that was exactly what he'd done. He now understood how the hopelessness of life impacted on the mind - understood why men drunk themselves senseless. He mentally thanked his brother-in-law for attempting to knock some sense into him for he realised it was only Vi's intervention which had prevented that from actually happening. But it was enough to shake him out of his despondency. He was alive. He had a wonderful wife. He had three sons. He had a life and he was going to reclaim it not give it away to the fiendish drink.

He was in the café when he struck lucky. They told him to go to Spitalfields where numerous carts came in everyday with fresh vegetables from the nurseries on the edge of London – many of them on the north west outskirts of the city which was the direction in which he needed to travel.

'There's bound to be a cart going out 'Hillingdon way.' The man who spoke was a meat porter and his overalls were smeared with blood. He was tucking into a large plate of bacon and eggs while George tried not to drool.

Hillingdon, at least, from his memory was roughly in the direction he needed to go but getting from there to Chalfont was probably going to mean a very long walk.

'Thanks, mate,' he said and sat in a corner well away from the door, warming his hands on the mug, intending not to move until he had thawed out. Right then, he felt colder than he often did in the Prairies when it was minus 20° but there, it was a dry cold whereas here, the overnight November dampness had penetrated his clothes and made his bones ache. No wonder he was so stiff.

''Ere, mate.' The man serving the teas said in a low voice and pressed a slice of toast into his hand. 'Don't let the gaffer see.'

George mumbled his grateful thanks and shoved the bread into his jacket pocket and, having finished his tea, got up to leave.

'Good luck,' the man said in a louder voice.

By the time he got to Spitalfields most of the carts had already left. He wandered round the market, eyeing the produce, longing to stave off his hunger. He had been thankful for the bread but it had only filled a tiny corner of his stomach. He spied some sacks of carrots and wondered if there might be some left-overs he could filch.

'If it's work you're after, there's nothing 'ere.' A man was shifting sacks of potatoes onto a barrow.

'Just looking for a ride out west,' he replied.

'Out west, you say?'

'Need to get towards Uxbridge.'

The man thought a moment.

'Jack goes to Ruislip but he's gawn already.'

'Any chance you go that way?'

'Surrey, mate, I'm from Surrey. You wanna see Jack. Gets 'ere early hours. His cart's yellow. St Leonards Farm. That's 'im.'

He thanked the man and spent the rest of the day meandering in meaningless circles. It was dark by four and beginning to get foggy. The gas lamps gave an eerie light. He'd forgotten about fogs and he hadn't got a scarf. He sheltered in a doorway, coughing. Dam his chest. This was as unpleasant as the dust storms back in Canada. They had set his chest on fire, though he'd never admitted to Amy, how bad he felt at times.

He returned to the market a little after three o'clock in the morning. It was a hive of activity. Horse-drawn carts contended for space amongst smart new wagons. He admired the liveries on some of the Foden steam lorries as he squeezed between barrows and men, while trying to spot a cart painted up in yellow. Finally he found it, wedged between two others, the horse with its head in a nosebag, resting a hind leg and half asleep but no sign of the owner.

He asked about and soon learnt that Jack was in "The Golden Heart". A pub was the last place he wanted to go, besides he had no money. He hung around the market for what seemed like hours and was about to give up when he thought he spotted Jack. The man walked with a limp which George suspected might have been exaggerated by the amount of alcohol he'd consumed. He got up from the doorway where he had been sitting and followed him back to his cart.

'A chap told me you go out to Ruislip,' George began.

'Who said?' Jack's voice was aggressive.

'Don't know his name - said he came from Surrey. Told me you'd be here tonight and that I might get a ride that way.'

'Depends. Who's asking?'

'George. George Mills.' He held his hand out. 'I need to get back to my missus. Any chance?' he said, trying to sound like a local but wondering if the Canadian influence might put the guy off.

Jack hesitated, looking him up and down.

'Ruislip, you say?' He shook his hand.

'That's right. Be really obliged.'

'Don't go as far as Ruislip. Nursery's afore you git there but there's room enuf.' He indicated the cart with a nod of his head.

'Thanks.' He didn't wait for a proper invitation but climbed onto the cart and made himself as comfortable as he could amongst empty sacks and boxes. The cart jolted and juddered into movement and he tried to console himself with being grateful he'd got a ride for part of the way. He knew, if he wasn't going to get as far as Ruislip, then the walk was going to be several miles longer than originally planned. In spite of the rough bumpy ride, he slept for a couple of hours and had no idea where he was when he awoke coughing. When his cough subsided he realised the steady clop of the horses hooves no longer echoed as it did in the London streets, so he guessed they must be in a more rural area. The fog was thicker still and he snuggled down inside his coat trying to cover his nose but it was difficult to breath.

When the cart jarred to a sudden halt, Jack announced it was as far as he went.

'If you want 'illingdon, you keep straight on.'

George eased himself down from the cart. His legs felt odd as though they didn't belong to him until the pain of the blood flowing through his limbs again made him realise how numb he'd become. He was getting too old for this lark, he thought and longed for a large plate of eggs and bacon and the chance to get clean, dry and warm.

'Thanks,' he said, adding almost as an afterthought. 'You wouldn't happen to know if there were any jobs round these parts. Only I'm out of cash.'

Jack stared down at him.

'Short of cash, you say?'

'Yeah. Kinda hungry, too.' That was an understatement. He was starving, so hungry in fact, he thought the front and back of his stomach were stuck together – much like in Canada. He shut the thought out of his mind.

Jack rubbed his chin with the back of his gloved hand.

'Can't say as I do, not regular, like. But I could do with some 'elp. A couple days to sort out me green 'ouses. Got to get the whitewash off. Bugger of a job but your's if you want it.'

He climbed back on the cart for the last half mile to the nursery. Cleaning whitewash off greenhouses didn't sound too arduous, just depended how many there were but at least it meant he'd have a few bob in his pocket.

*****

'You stay right where you are,' Ma said and shuffled towards the scullery door.

'I'm not incapable, you know,' Vi said. She had never been idle so it wasn't easy to have everyone fussing over her. Since the fire, everyone had insisted she stay at Ma's. Harold had argued the kitchen and dining room both needed redecorating and it would be much better for her not to breath in the fumes. He'd been less critical and more caring recently but the previous evening he hadn't called in to see how she was and the evening before that he smelt of drink. She wondered how much painting he was really doing.

'The doctor said rest. Complete rest, Ted told me and so did Harold. So you stay where you are and I will make the tea.'

'I'm so bored …'

'Have a nap.'

'I've done nothing but nap for days now.'

'I'll get Lizzie to get you some more wool and I'll ask Ted to go to the library for you. Now let me get that tea.'

Vi listened to the sound of the kettle being filled and the gas being lit. It was so frustrating being trapped here on a borrowed chaise longue which had been squeezed into the parlour in order that she didn't have to stay upstairs all day when all she really wanted was to be at home in her own familiar surroundings. The baby didn't seem to move so much these days and the doctor was concerned about her blood pressure. She knew his advice was right but oh, how she wished she could be whizzing about the shops choosing the pram and the layette much as she knew most of the other pregnant mums would be. True, Lizzie had lent her a pram and there were so many boxes of baby cloths she didn't really need to buy much at all. But all the same it would be fun looking. She smiled to herself. This baby was going to have a far more extensive wardrobe than she herself currently had.

'Have you heard anything from George?' she asked when her mother returned with a tray of tea. The cups rattled on their saucers and she was alarmed at the angle of the wooden tray. She remembered that tray – it was the one Thomas made when he was at school. At the time, everyone had been impressed and agreed he should become a chippy and he was lucky enough to get an apprenticeship. 'Ma, do be careful. You're tipping it. If you're not careful it'll all slide to the floor.'

'No, I'm not.' Ma placed it on the table and collapsed into the nearby chair.

'Are you all right?' Vi was concerned as Ma didn't seem as fit these days.

"Course I am.' She took a deep breath before picking up the milk jug and pouring it into two cups.

'I wondered if you had heard anything from George? Has he written?'

'Not a word. Not a word.'

'I don't remember posting my letter to Amy. With all that commotion over the fire I can't recall what I did with it. I'll have to ask Harold when he comes.'

'I should do that.'

'I wish I could go home. I feel so guilty about putting Thomas out of his room.'

'Don't be. He's not here most of the time and when he is, it doesn't hurt him to sleep in Ted's room.'

'All the same …' She had been going to say it was hardly fair on Ted but the sound of Lizzie made her stop.

'Cooeee!"

Much as she loved her sister, between her and Ma, she was being smothered.

'How's the patient today, then?' Lizzie said as she pushed open the door.

'Fine. There's absolutely nothing wrong with me.'

'Not what the doctor thought. In any case, you should by rights be in bed.'

Vi inwardly groaned. Since Lizzie had become a Mum herself she did nothing but fuss.

'Tea, Lizzie?' Ma asked.

'Ta, Ma.' She pulled a chair out from under the table, sat down and rummaged around in her shopping bag. 'Now look what I got for our patient.'

'I do wish you'd stop calling me a patient when I am most definitely not,' Vi said unable to contain her irritation any longer.

Lizzie frowned at her. 'Remember, you're supposed to keep calm and not get worked up to a frenzy.'

Frenzy? She'd get worked up into a lot more if Lizzie kept on in that vein. She inhaled slowly and counted to ten. She learnt a long time ago, it was best to let Lizzie have the last word.

'Look what I've got in 'ere. Ta da!' She held up a small brown paper bag which had been carefully twisted at either end. 'I know you've got a craving for liquorice allsorts and I got the man in the shop to pick out lots of your favourites. Those round pink ones - you know - the ones with the little tiny balls all over them.'

She dropped them into Vi's lap.

'I don't think liquorice is sensible in your condition, Vi,' Ma said before she had a chance to thank Lizzie.

'Why?' Lizzie wanted to know.

'I heard somewhere liquorice is used to alleviate constipation. I don't think Vi needs to eat something like that.'

'Ma, please stop fussing,' Vi said. 'Thank you, Lizzie. It was a nice thought and I shall enjoy them and,' she turned to Ma, 'I promise I won't eat enough to turn me out.'

Lizzie giggled. 'I'd better take some home for Albert. He's always complaining about constipation.'

Grateful though she was for all this attention, Vi was really glad when her sister left to get Albert's tea ready. It wasn't long before Ted was home and he helped Ma cook the dinner. They were half way through when Harold arrived and she knew, at once, something was wrong. He gave her a peck on the cheek before sitting at the table.

'I'll get another plate,' Ma said and shuffled into the kitchen.

'Everything all right at home?' She hadn't meant to enquire in front of the others, but she could see Harold was angry about something.

'No,' Harold said. 'And I'm not beating around the bush so I'll come straight out with it. When I went to put some more money in the gas meter, I found the tin empty. Now I know there was at least five bob in there because I put it there. But it's all gone - every last shilling and the only person who would know where I keep that tin is your brother ...'

'George? Don't be silly. George wouldn't do that.'

'How else do you explain it then? '

'George didn't need to steal. He only had to ask.' Ma placed a plate of stew and dumplings in front of Harold.

'Thanks, Ma,' Harold said. 'Well, have we heard from him? Do we know where he is even? I've a good mind to report it to the Police.'

'Listen here, Harold,' Ma said in a stern voice. 'I won't have anyone sitting at my table and accusing other members of my family when they're not here to defend themselves. I brought all my children up to be honest. So I'd be pleased if you would keep your assertions to yourself.'

'Sorry, Ma but I can't help thinking …' Harold picked up his knife and fork but Vi knew by his face, he hadn't changed his mind about George.

'What about when you had the fire?' Ted said. 'There were so many people in your house that day, could have been any one of them. Someone turned the gas off, didn't they? They'd have seen the tin wouldn't they?'

'That's right,' Vi said. She turned to Harold. 'It could have been anyone.'

Harold didn't reply and for the rest of the meal the subject was avoided. Vi hoped to be able to speak to Harold in private but there wasn't any chance as Harold left soon after dinner saying he had decorating to do.

\* \* \* \* \*

It was still raining when the car stopped on the gravel outside 'Hazeldene'. Amy reached for the door handle but was prevented by Charles' hand. Since the moment she had got in the car, she had avoided her arm touching his. The look she had seen in his eyes spelt danger and, with George away, she was so tempted to fall into his arms. She was tired of being strong, being both father and mother to three energetic boys. She was exhausted, too, by the worry of Will's injury as well as the potential responsibility of looking after Enid. Freddie would only think of himself and as for her mother … well, there was unlikely to be any sympathy in that direction. She longed for an arm to lean on and Charles was offering one …

'Stay where you are and I'll get the brolly,' he said but his hand remained where it was, resting on her own. She tried to remove it.

'Stay a minute, Amy. I only ask for a little of your time - a chance to explain myself. You never gave me that. Remember?'

Yes, that much was true. She had shied away from facing him with the truth. She had written that letter and taken the coward's way out.

'It won't change anything. I love George. We've been through a lot together and I still love him. So please … I have to go.'

He squeezed her hand before removing his. He was silent for a few moments and she wondered if he had forgotten her. She glanced up at him and saw he was staring without seeing, as though he was in another world.

'After the war,' he said in a low voice. 'Men acted like maniacs. They did all sorts of things they later regretted. I was one of those men. I just need your forgiveness. That's all I'm asking for. Can your forgive me?'

'Charles - I - er - there's nothing to forgive. It's history. We can't change a thing by going over it and, in any case, it doesn't matter now.'

'It does to me. It matters a lot. All these years ... all I wanted was the chance to say sorry. I'm glad you married the man you love. I wish I could say I'd married for love but the truth is - Sylvia ...'

She waited for him to say more but he was silent. 'I don't think I could have made you happy either ...' she began to say.

'You didn't give me that chance.'

'It's late ...'

He turned to face her.

'It's never too late.'

For one awful minute she thought he was going to kiss her and when he changed his mind, she felt guilty. She had wanted him - she had actually wanted him to kiss her. How could that be? When who she really wanted was George.

He opened his door, retrieved an umbrella from the back and walked round the car.

'I'll walk you to the door,' he said, holding up the umbrella.

She didn't argue. The rain was lashing down and she was grateful for the shelter but uncomfortable at his proximity and even more thankful there were lights still on in the house.

'The Grange,' she said out loud. For some inexplicable reason she was reminded of the shock of seeing The Grange in its new role as a school. 'You don't … live there?'

'No.'

They had almost reached the door and she should have gone but she was curious. They stopped on the steps.

'Why?'

He sighed. 'It's a long story. You're getting wet and so am I. Meet me for lunch and I'll tell you all about it.'

'Lunch? I'm not sure.'

'Not sure about what?' There was a note of irritation in his voice. 'Don't you think I know all about gossip? When you ran out on me there was plenty of that.'

'I didn't …' she wanted to say she hadn't run out on him. Rather, it was he who was at fault. Now she realised she hadn't given a thought for how it might have appeared for him. Neither had she given any thought as to how he might feel. She had cared only for herself and her desire to marry the man she loved.

'A married man meeting a married lady for lunch?' he continued. 'We're both adults. Village gossip? Let them gossip.'

She chose not to answer. It was better to leave things the way they were.

'Good night, Charles and thank you for seeing me home.'

He watched her go into the house. Once she'd shut the door she listened for his footsteps on the gravel. He didn't go immediately.

'Is that you, Amy?'

She was surprised her mother had waited up.

'Yes, yes, it is. Just taking my wet things off.'

## Chapter Eleven

It was midnight and Freddie had long given up on Amy. Once the boys were in bed and after he'd looked in on Enid, he took solace in several glasses of whisky. His life was becoming impossibly complicated and he supposed he would have to behave himself whilst his sister was living under his roof. If only Enid would return to some sort of rational being - someone he could reason with. He would accept her absence from the marital bed if that made her see sense but only if she would accept that he needed Beth. If they could come to some kind of arrangement, though he doubted if she would agree to any arrangement, it might allow them to live a more normal life - whatever normal was.

And he would have to do something about George even if it meant him working at the garage. True, there was plenty of office work to do but he couldn't afford to pay him a penny unless he could persuade his mother to extend her credit a little longer. Another problem.

Then there was Jonathan. He wanted him to go to boarding school but that was going to be expensive - too expensive without his mother's indulgence. It was true she had hinted at Harrow with the suggestion she might pay but she was getting so forgetful these days. Yes, he was going to have to see if he could wheedle his way into her good books and that would mean staying married to Enid. There wasn't a hope of him doing what Amy had done. He would never be able to marry the love of his life, not without bankrupting himself and, in any case, he knew Beth enjoyed the expensive gifts he often gave her. Did she like him for his money and not for himself, he wondered but immediately shut his mind to the thought - he needed her. For the past few years, she had kept him sane.

He stared at the amber liquid in his glass, before emptying it in one gulp. He placed it on the table and dozed in the chair.

He awoke with a jump and with a crick in the neck. Something had made him wake, but he wasn't sure if it was the uncomfortable position he had slept in. He glanced at the clock. Three in the morning. God, he felt awful. He rubbed his neck and twisted his head from side to side. He listened but couldn't hear any other noises so he staggered to the kitchen, found a glass and filled it with water.

'Dad?'

'Jon? You made me jump out of my skin. What are you doing down here?'

'Couldn't sleep,' he said in a small voice.

'Here. Come and sit beside me. Do you want a glass of milk or something?'

Jonathan nodded and he went to the larder. Poor Jonathan. His mother was half crazy, his father was seeing another woman and he had been sent to his grandmother's and then sent back home again. No wonder he couldn't settle. He felt guilty when he thought how he wanted to send him away to boarding school. Was he being selfish? Maybe the boy needed more of a loving and caring home and so far, he'd failed to provide that.

'Here you are.' He placed a glass of milk in front of him.

'Thanks, Dad.' He took a sip. 'Is Mummy going to be all right?'

'Of course, she is.'

'She didn't seem all right when I said good night to her.'

'She's very tired that's all.'

'Auntie Amy said the baby had died. Is that right, Dad?'

Oh, my God. He'd left his sister to tell him. Poor boy. The child would have been his sister. Tears welled in his eyes. She would have been his daughter and now he knew there wouldn't be another child.

'Jonathan, I'm sorry. I should have told you myself but I was …' the truth was he had sought his comfort with Beth but he couldn't tell him that. 'I was too upset to tell you. It was a little girl and your Mummy is very upset, too.'

Jonathan didn't reply and he hoped that would be the end of the questions.

'Dad.'

'Yes, Jon?'

'There's something I ... '

'You need to ask me something else?' He prompted, dreading what might come next.

'Dad, I ... Will ... I don't know how to tell ...'

'Jon, if you have something to say, please say whatever it is. I'm sure we can sort it out.'

'You see ...'

'No, I don't see,' he began and realised he sounded impatient. 'Just tell me what's worrying you,' he said in a kinder tone, wondering what problem was.

'The go-cart ...'

'Yes?'

'I sort of told Will where it was.'

'Do you mean you told Will where to find this go-cart?'

Jonathan nodded.

'And?'

'It was Micky's. He wanted me to go but I knew I'd get into trouble if I sneaked out of school.'

'You were out of school?'

'No. Sam and me - the teacher made us do a job for her.'

'So you might have sneaked out but you didn't?'

Jonathan looked uncomfortable.

'It seems to me both you and Sam had a lucky escape. Tell me about this go-cart. And anyway what exactly is a go-cart?'

'That's what Micky calls it. It's only some old wheels he found in a ditch and an old notice board.'

'Some old wheels and a notice board? How does that work?'

'I think they were from a pram thing - you know, like the one Mummy …' Jonathan couldn't stop the tears.

Freddie pulled his son into his arms.

'Better?' he said after a couple of minutes had passed. How many times had he sobbed in his boyhood and been told to grow up and act like a man. He had wanted a hug of reassurance and he hoped that was what he'd given Jon. 'Now tell me what else you know about this go-cart?'

'He kept it in the hedge near school,' Jonathan sniffed.

'I see. And how does this - go-cart - work?'

'You have to push it and jump on.'

'Is that why they took it up the hill on the common?'

'Yes, but Dad. It wasn't Micky's fault.'

'And why do you say that?'

'He didn't go. He told Will not to ...'

'I see.' Freddie said and thought he understood now what Amy meant. Will was out of control and it was definitely time for George to take him in hand.

* * * * *

'Phoebe's wedding seems to have been forgotten in all this pandemonium,' Ma declared as they sat together in Vi's newly painted parlour. 'First George going off like that - without so much as a word, then the fire and then you having high blood pressure. That's three things, so now maybe things will begin to be normal again.'

Vi knew she was right. The wedding had been almost forgotten but at that moment she didn't much care. In fact, she resented her sister and her wedding. Phoebe had landed well and truly on her feet. There was never going to be any shortage of money in her life and that was going to be permanent, she reflected. Her mind went back to their childhood. Even then, Phoebe always had ideas well above her station. The niggling resentment she felt right then was mainly caused because Phoebe always considered herself superior and never failed to make it clear that cleaning, which is what Lizzie still did and she herself did until she married Harold, was below her. She had set her sights right away on becoming a store girl. From an early age, Phoebe always implied she was better than the rest of them and at an even earlier age, had announced she didn't want her name to be shortened to "Phi". Phoebe had turned into a snob and now all the men in the family would have to go to the expense of hiring suits because, as she put it, "she didn't want to be let down".

'I'm beginning to think it would be better if I didn't come,' Vi said. 'The doctor said not to do anything upsetting and Phoebe …' she took in a deep breath. 'Phoebe has this way of making my blood boil.'

'Yes, yes, I know,' Ma soothed, squeezing her arm. 'But she is your sister and she's my daughter and I think she must take after her father. He most certainly could be difficult at times.'

Vi thought back over the years but her father's memory had faded with her adulthood and she only remembered happy times.

'I don't want to spend a fortune on getting a dress I'm hardly going to wear,' Vi said. 'It's not economic and then there's this business of Harold having to hire a suit. It's all right for her, she's marrying money.'

'Harold isn't the only one who has to hire a suit. It's going to cost us all a lot of money. Isn't there something in your wardrobe we could dress up for the day? I'm sure we could make one of your outfits more glamorous. You can borrow some of my beads.'

'I suppose my navy dress might do. But I haven't got a smart coat and it's bound to be cold.'

'I'm sure Lizzy still has some of her maternity clothes. We must ask her but, judging by the size of your bump, I don't think you'll go full term anyway.'

'I hope not. I can't remember when I saw my feet last.'

Life had settled into a very boring routine now she was back home and whilst she was allowed to move around a little, the doctor had insisted she continued to rest. As though she was ill. The thought exasperated her. It was almost the end of November and Phoebe's wedding was only days away and then there would be Christmas.

\* \* \* \* \*

'Are you going to the hospital today?' Mrs Attwood asked over breakfast.

'Yes. I'm very worried. There's a strong possibility Will might lose the use of his left foot. The doctor told me it was a pioneering technique he used and he has no idea if it will be successful.'

Mrs Attwood was silent.

'I'm going to stay with Freddie tonight, mother. I can't just abandon Sam and Bobbie and in any case, I'm supposed to be looking after Enid not to mention Jonathan. This accident couldn't have happened at a worse time.'

'No, it couldn't. And where's George when you need him? I don't understand what he's playing at. He should be here right now. It's high time he took responsibility for his family.'

Yes, Amy thought, she was right. Where was he, indeed? They all needed him. She needed him but, more than anything, she longed for a place they could call home. The thought that, if the operation was unsuccessful, Will might lose his foot was still uppermost in her mind. How would they cope? She thought back to her meeting with Charles the previous evening, then realised she hadn't told her mother about Lady Margaret.

'Last night …' She hesitated not sure how to break the news. Lady Margaret was her mother's lifelong friend. 'Last night,' she began again. 'Mother, Lady Margaret … she was brought into hospital. She's had some kind of heart attack, I think.'

Her mother paled.

'How do you know that?'

'Charles – I saw Charles. He was with her.'

'He was? Is she all right?'

'I - er - I'm not sure. Charles said something about the doctor wanting her there - some kind of precaution, I think.'

Mrs Attwood placed her napkin on the table and stood up.

'I must telephone the hospital and find out.'

Amy watched her leave the room. It was the first time her mother had actually mentioned the telephone in her presence and she was left pondering if she would have to endure her mother's company at hospital visiting time. She also wondered if Charles would be there and was horrified to discover part of her hoped he would be. Then told herself, she only wanted him there to take her mind off the possibility of Will losing his foot.

Amy was relieved to hear visiting time for children was earlier than for adults. Not only would she not have to endure her mother's company, it was unlikely she would meet Charles so she was very surprised, as she entered the hospital, to find him sitting in the corridor. Had Lady Margaret taken a turn for the worse?

'Charles?'

He looked up, his face grey and, over night, older by years.

'Mother ...' he began.

'Is it bad?' She touched him on the arm.

'Yes. She might not make it. Look, I need some air.'

'Of course.' She watched him walk towards the door and wished there was something she could do or say. He looked so alone; she thought and turned towards the children's ward. There were only two beds and, to her relief, Will was lying on top of his, laughing and joking with one of the nurses. His left foot was thickly bandaged.

'And how's my big son, today?' she said trying to sound chirpy, though right then she didn't feel in the least bit cheerful. In spite of everything, she had been fond of Lady Margaret and it was a shock to hear she was so ill. She gave Will a hug.

'Look. Look. I can move my toes, Mom,' he said in an excited voice.

'Really?' She looked at the nurse for reassurance. 'The doctor said …'

'Yes, I know what he said but he just wanted you to know what the odds were - not to raise false hopes. He's an incredibly gifted man and this hospital is blessed to have him. But I think you should know, there's a long road to recovery for this young man. Now, come on, Will, show your mother.'

She watched him move his toes and felt an enormous waive of relief.

'Will, that is amazing.' She hugged him again, blinking back tears of relief.

'It's very important for Will to stay off that foot for some time to come - maybe even a few months. And he's likely going to stay with us for several more weeks, I should think.'

Soon the hour's visiting time was over.

'I'll be back tomorrow, I promise. Is there anything you'd like me to bring? Something to read?'

'Yes, but I'll be home soon.'

'I don't think so. You heard what the nurse said. Maybe now we know you're going to get better, you can think about explaining to me why you were out of school?'

Will didn't answer.

'I want to know, Will, and so will your father but it can wait until tomorrow. Now you must do what the doctors and nurses tell you because you mustn't undo their good work.' She bent over and gave him a kiss on the forehead. 'It's dark outside and it'll be time for sleep soon. So settle down now.'

When she left the hospital, even in the poor light, she recognized Charles' car and assumed he must be inside.

'Amy, I hoped I'd see you.'

He had followed her out of the hospital.

'You're still here?'

'I went home for a while. Can I walk you home?'

'But your car ..?'

'I know it's here but I don't feel up to driving. It's a fresh evening and I need some exercise. In any case, you shouldn't be walking alone.'

She looked up. The night sky was full of stars and reminded her of the nights in the Prairies. There was likely more danger lurking back there than here. She smiled to herself. Charles would never understand.

'Tell me why you no longer live at The Grange?' Since he had insisted on walking beside her, the least he could do was to satisfy her curiosity.

'Sylvia hated it and mother wasn't capable of managing it alone after my father died. Letting it seemed the obvious thing to do.'

'Yes, I seem to remember Freddie writing your father had died. But a convent school?'

He shrugged. 'Does it matter?'

'I suppose not. So where do you live now?'

'Home Farm was vacant - the house was big enough for us all.'

'Not sure I can remember where Home Farm is.'

'On the east side of the estate. Remember where the woods are? After the war, we amalgamated three farms into two and that meant the house wasn't needed.'

She did remember the woods and she couldn't help wondering how his family together with his mother fitted into the house. The Grange was huge. It must have taken some adjustment.

'It needed a bit of renovation but it's quite a big house,' Charles said as though he had read her thoughts. 'And it works quite well. Mother has a ground floor bedroom and bathroom. The children settled in very quickly. Margaret has her pony and Alex likes going fishing. Only Sylvia is dissatisfied with the arrangement.'

'Why's that?'

'I think she wanted something less remote. We're about two miles further from the village. But nothing ever seems to please her.'

'Oh, dear. Things are not so good then?'

Charles didn't answer and she realised she was prying. What Charles' wife did or did not like was none of her business. But she and Charles went back a long way. They had shared their schooldays - once she had been engaged to him and, even though George had won her heart, she was still very fond of him.

'Will you be at the hospital again tomorrow?' she asked.

'I'm going back as soon as I've walked you home.'

'It's really serious then?'

'They're not sure she'll live through the night though I'm sure mother is tougher than they think.'

'My mother planned on visiting tonight. Shall I stop her?'

'No. They were such good friends. I should have brought the car then I could have driven her.'

'I think she's arranged for a man from the village to take her. She doesn't walk far these days. In fact, she hardly leaves the house.' She sighed. 'It's so depressing. We're all getting old.'

'If I learnt anything in the war, it was to live for today because there isn't any certainty about a tomorrow. Maybe you can understand what I said yesterday. You know, about how stupid men could be ...'

She didn't answer.

'If I could change one thing in my life, it would be my hurting you. I was a fool and I've lived every day regretting it.'

She was flattered by the thought that Charles still wanted her and shocked to discover part of her still wanted him.

'It's all in the past. We have to move on.'

They turned into the lane and it was only a matter of yards before they reached 'Hazeldene'.

'Will you come in and break the news to mother?'

'Yes. It'd be better if I tell her - better than the shock of finding out when she gets to the hospital.'

\* \* \* \* \*

'We still haven't heard a thing from George.' Phoebe pranced around in Ma's back room, dressed in her wedding dress, straining over her shoulder to see the effect of the train, which was held in place by a delicate lace headband.

Vi tried not to be jealous but the dress was gorgeous and must have been very expensive. It came from Selfridges – apparently Richard had taken her to see the roof gardens and she hadn't been able to resist going back to look at the wedding gowns. Then, she had taken Ma along to choose one and Ma had been talking of nothing else since. And what was more, Phoebe had bought the most stunning going away outfit Vi had ever seen. She had examined it in its special box. The soft material – a wonderful shade of deep blue – was to die for. She sighed. How nice to have that amount of money. Though, right then, all she really longed for was to be slim enough to wear such a dress, not huge and the size of a bus as Harold had joked last night.

Phoebe turned right round. 'What do you think?'

Ma came in from the scullery, wiping her hands on a towel. She nodded her approval. 'You look beautiful.'

'I suppose I'd better get out of this,' Phoebe said, capturing the train, laying it over her arm and lifting her skirt so as not to trip and, in so doing, revealing her white lacy shoes. Vi felt a pang of envy at the dainty ankles displayed to effect by the shoe's pearl straps. Phoebe held the skirt up higher, preparing to go upstairs but stopped in the doorway. 'You know, I can't understand George. He had an invitation. I put it in his hand. You'd think after all these years in Canada, he'd want to be with us for the wedding but I haven't heard a thing. I think it's extremely rude of him.'

Ma sighed. 'I suppose we'll have to count him out. I shouldn't think Amy will come either.'

Trust Phoebe to think of her own arrangements, Vi thought, wriggling on the chair and pushing a cushion behind her in an effort to make herself more comfortable. Her back had ached for days and her feet had swollen again. But she was more concerned about George, who could be lying dead somewhere for all they knew. Phoebe only ever thought about how things would affect her.

'A letter arrived for him yesterday,' Ma said.

'Not another one?' Phoebe pulled a face and shook her head.

'Those on the sideboard?' Vi had spotted the envelopes on the way to the garden to visit the toilet, the umpteenth time in the last hour. She was tired of making so many journeys but her bladder always wanted emptying. 'I thought it looked like Amy's writing. She probably doesn't know where he is any more than we do. We ought to do something. Maybe we should to go to the Police.'

'The Police? I don't want them sniffing around just when I'm about to get married. Richard would be horrified especially if the press got hold of it. In any case, it isn't the first time George's gone missing, is it?'

'What do you think, Ma?' Vi asked.

'Phoebe's right. George has done this before. In any case, I think he can look after himself. We should leave things until after the wedding. It's only a few days away now.'

'I'll change into my going away outfit then,' Phoebe said. 'I want to check they've done those alterations properly and I want to see how it goes with the hat.'

Once Phoebe had left the room, Vi shut her eyes. She was so tired but how she wished her mother and sister would be more concerned about George. Maybe they were right and they'd hear from him soon. Such a pity it was unlikely he or Amy would make the wedding. She had been looking forward so much to seeing Amy after all these years. It was the main reason she was going to the wedding. Now, she was wondering if she could make an excuse.

\* \* \* \* \*

The wedding day dawned as a crisp winter morning. There was frost on the inside of the window but when Vi scratched away enough to look outside, the sun was shining and she couldn't help but make comparisons with George and Amy's wedding day when it had poured with rain. She had shared Amy's bedroom the night before and had helped Amy into her wedding dress before getting into her own bridesmaid's outfit. Then, she thought, she really did have a waist. She sighed as she pulled on the maternity dress she had borrowed from Lizzie. It wasn't exactly her choice of colour and when she looked in the mirror, it made her seem larger than ever but it was better than spending the little money she had on something she would hardly wear.

She spent a few minutes, re-arranging her hair for the umpteenth time. Then she put on some lipstick before rummaging in the bottom of the wardrobe for her shoes. Since her feet were swollen again, they were going to be a problem but she would squeeze into them at the last possible moment. She adjusted her hat and took her coat of its hanger. It was never going to cover her tummy. She would have to wear it unbuttoned but it was better than nothing, especially when it was so cold outside.

'Taxi's here, Vi. Hurry up. Every second on that meter is costing me money.' Harold called from the bottom of the stairs.

'All right, all right. I'm coming.' Vi pushed her feet into her shoes, using a shoe horn to get them in the final bit. She picked up her handbag and started down the stairs. She could see Harold frowning up at her but she was not going to risk losing her footing by hurrying.

The taxi took them from the East End of London into the Square Mile of the City. Ma had insisted to Harold that Vi should not travel by public transport in her current condition and so he had been forced to organise a taxi.

'This had better be worth it.' Harold banged the taxi door shut behind him and sat beside her.

'You look very handsome in that suit,' Vi said trying to distract him. Harold's moods were becoming the norm but today he was more ill-tempered than usual and she knew it was because her family were not in his good books. He resented the whole cost of Phoebe's wedding – the cost of hiring his suite, never mind the taxi, while he still blamed George for the missing money from the gas tin. This was going to be a difficult day, she thought and, as the taxi bumped along the cobbles, gripped Harold's arm. She was relieved when they came to a halt outside the church. She looked out of the window with surprise. It didn't look like a church at all, squeezed between other buildings. She would probably have walked by without realising what it was but for the words "St Mary's Church" over its impressive portico.

'Bloody Roman Catholic,' Harold muttered in her ear as he helped her out. Now that was news to her. Did Ma know? She waited while he paid the cabbie and then took his arm to walk into the church. Inside were the ushers who enquired whether they were 'Bride or Groom' and indicated on which side they should sit. She could see her mother and the rest of the members of the family towards the front of the church. The organ was playing a familiar tune, though she couldn't place it but concentrated instead on persuading Harold to stay at the back of the church.

'Don't want to go too far down. I might need the lav,' she whispered in Harold's ear. At that moment she had no idea where the nearest one was and prayed she would last.

A nearby woman turned and frowned at her. This, she thought, was going to be a "them and us" sort of wedding and she hoped her part of the family would not let Phoebe down.

It was another ten minutes before the organist began to play the "Wedding March". She turned to watch Phoebe walk down the aisle on Ted's arm. The choice of the only bridesmaid had upset two members of her family – Lizzie who thought her four year old daughter should have been one and May who felt that, as the bride's sister, she had as much right as Richard's sister. As she watched the bridal procession progress, Vi knew Phoebe had made the right choice. May would never have carried it off and Phoebe wouldn't have had any patience with a child.

Later, as she stood outside waiting for the photographer to finish the family picture, she thought her sister looked radiant and the dress stunning. The service was so much longer than she expected and she was feeling a bit light headed, so she leant against Harold for support. And she really did need the loo. The day was chilly and with the photographs completed in record time, the bride and groom climbed into the wedding car, an expensive looking Bentley, and everyone else departed on foot for the nearby Great Eastern Hotel.

It was only a five minute walk and she didn't think she would be the only one impressed by the size of the hotel or of the opulent room in which the wedding breakfast was located. She had never seen such a large room or amazing ceilings which reminded her of pictures she'd seen in some magazine years ago. It was all very imposing.

'Congratulations!' She kissed her sister and Richard on the cheek then moved on to meet the bridegroom's parents. They shook hands – it was very formal. A glass of sherry was placed in her hand though the location of the "Ladies" seemed much more important at that moment. She looked about for somewhere to leave her glass. What happened next, she wasn't sure but she could hear Ma.

'Where's Harold?' Ma's voice sounded so far away and the room was beginning to dim. Then Ma was shaking her gently and she could hear her shouting to get a doctor.

*****

Freddie was angry. He had wasted the whole day when there was so much to do at the garage. Where was Amy? She said she would come that afternoon and now it was dark, she probably wouldn't come at all.

It had been a challenge from the moment he got out of bed, more so with Enid now mobile and needing his attention. It was difficult to know what to say to cheer her up and even more difficult to discuss the loss of their baby. Whenever he approached her, she shrank away. He wanted to comfort her but she was more distant than ever. When she said she wanted a bath, he insisted she didn't lock the door and, terrified she would slip away under the water, he kept looking in on her. Each time he couldn't help thinking she looked so thin and fragile, porcelain white and delicate that he worried she would never be well again. The doctor called in the afternoon and declared she was making progress but Freddie could only see how much further there was to go and how tortuous a journey it was going to be.

Somehow that morning, he had managed to get Jonathan and Sam to school, taking Bobbie along for the ride, while Doris was doing her three hours of cleaning, though, since he had asked her to prepare a meal for them, he knew not much housework would be completed. They arrived at school late but it was better than not going at all and he had gone into the headmaster to explain the situation and apologise. Then he called in to the garage to organise Donnie to collect them after school and bring them home.

But it was all far from satisfactory. Work at the garage was beginning to fall behind. If he wasn't there, repairs and servicing were down to Donnie alone and if customers didn't get a quick enough service, there were other garages nearby. He despaired at the sight of the paperwork on his desk but chose to ignore it, picking up the unopened mail to take home with him. As he got into the car, he glanced across at the pub, half tempted to cross the road and call in but it was more than he dared do right then, especially as his young nephew was with him. He wondered if Beth was missing him as much as he was missing her.

Later, in the evening, when he slit open the envelopes, he discovered most were bills, some were reminders. He needed to get back to work. If they weren't careful they would lose clients and, worse, if he couldn't send out invoices, there wouldn't be any money to pay the bills. Maybe he should speak to his mother about employing a nurse - at least until Will came out of hospital.

With the boys in bed and Enid asleep, he took consolation in a glass of whisky. It was beginning to be a habit and he knew he was drinking too much but it helped and sometimes it was the only way he stayed sane. He had just poured out a second glass when there was a knock at the front door.

'Amy!' he said when he opened the door. 'Am I glad to see you.' Thank the Lord. Maybe he could get into the garage in the morning after all.

'Sorry I'm so late.' Amy took her coat off.

'How's Will?'

'It's a miracle. He can feel his toes. What a relief. It's going to be a long time healing, I think, but I can't tell you how grateful I am. Sad news, though. Lady Margaret's in the hospital. She's very ill - not expected to last the night.'

'Sorry to hear that.'

'Mother went to visit her – some local chap drove her so I persuaded him to drive me here.'

'You didn't walk?'

'No, of course not. It was dark really early.'

'Yes. You were quite right not to walk in the dark and to be honest, I didn't expect you to come. But thank the Lord you're here now. You have no idea how the work is piling up at the garage and if I'm not careful, I'll be losing customers.'

'Any chance of something to eat and I could do with a cup of tea.'

'You haven't eaten? There's not much in the larder.' Freddie pulled a face. 'I'm no good at this domestic lark.' He led the way into the kitchen and she followed him, watching him fill the kettle. 'There's some cheese left. Will a sandwich do?'

Amy nodded. 'How's Enid?

'She's been up a bit today but –.' He hesitated then added in a low voice. 'I really wonder if she'll ever be the same again. You know, mentally.' He opened a cupboard and took out some cups and saucers. 'I am so pleased you're here. I really need to get into work tomorrow.'

Amy had slumped into one of the kitchen chairs.

'Amy - whatever's the matter?'

'Everything. Oh, it's all too much,' Amy sobbed and burst into tears.

He stopped what he was doing and put his arms round her. He hoped his sister was not about to crack up. Right then it seemed as if his entire family was falling apart. It was the first time he'd seen Amy give in to her feelings. She was always in control, always so resolute and, from what he'd heard, it was her determination which brought them safely back to England. Her tears made him feel inadequate. He was lost for words. Damn it! Where the hell was George? He knew more than one letter had been sent. So why didn't he get in touch? There was the telephone these days. Had he misjudged the man when he'd walked down the aisle and given his sister away? He had thought him honourable but now he was wondering if George had abandoned his wife and sons.

Amy reached into her bag and retrieved a handkerchief.

'Sorry about that.' She wiped her eyes. 'I suppose, it's relief. I've been so worried about Will. And I need George …'

Freddie patted her on the shoulder.

'You need some food inside you.' He opened the bread bin and began to cut the loaf of bread.

Tomorrow had to be better. After a good night's sleep, things would be all right.

\* \* \* \* \*

George was pleased to have some money in his pocket. It was unpleasant work, outside in the damp and cold and scrubbing greenhouses had left his hands split and chapped. It had been dangerous work, too. He had stood on walls, balancing between the glasshouses. They were uneven and wet and one slip would have sent him crashing through the glass. But Jack had been satisfied with his efforts and had given him twelve shillings for his two day's work and he'd been allowed to sleep in the hay loft in the stable. Better still, Jack's wife had been kindness itself and had brought him out a large bowl of stew. It was the best meal in days.

He left early on the third morning, having had a strip wash in freezing water. He hadn't braved Canadian winters for nothing, he told himself as he dunked his arms into the rain barrel. He set off in the direction of Ruislip. It might mean a change of trains, but knew that the Metropolitan Railway would take him out towards Amersham and he had enough money in his pocket for the fare. He whistled a tune as he set off, convinced he would be with Amy by afternoon.

# Chapter Twelve

'You've got a little girl,' the midwife said in a cheerful voice. She remembered now – she was in hospital but how did she get there? It was all so vague. Had she dreamt it all? No, she didn't think so, but she'd slept so long. The noises in the ward had woken her. How long had she been there and did she really have a baby?

'I see you're awake now, Mrs Smith.' A nurse stood at the foot of the bed. 'Nice to have you back with us. I expect you're still feeling woozy?'

Did she dare voice her worst fears? 'My baby?' she asked surprised at the sound of her voice. It came as a whisper.

'She's fine. We've been looking after her. We've been very worried about you.'

So she did exist, Vi thought and drifted off again. When she awoke next time, Harold was sitting beside the bed and it was dark outside.

'Hello.' He held her hand. 'Are you feeling better?'

She smiled at him and nodded.

'They tell me you've slept most of the day. Not surprising. You've been very ill.'

She drifted away again and it was light when she awoke next and the ward was bustling with activity. She could see visitors arriving and then Harold was beside her.

'Harold … What happened? The nurse said I had a baby. Is it true?' She began to panic now. Had it been a figment of her imagination or had she lost yet another child?

'She's fine. Just fine. Got a good pair of lungs, the nurses tell me.'

She stared at him, not sure whether to believe what he'd told her.

'She?'

Harold nodded.

'Can I see her?' She tried to shift into a sitting position but her body ached and there was no strength in her arms. Harold plumped up the pillows.

'I'll ask the nurse if we can get her.'

A few minutes later, he returned with a nurse, who placed a tiny bundle into her arms. She stared into the baby's face.

'Hello. I'm your Mum.'

'You've no idea how relieved I am.' Harold smiled at her. 'Thought we'd lost you.'

'Oh?'

'The doc saved your life. Some relative of Richard's. Got you in here.'

She looked down into the little face, trying to digest this bit of information, trying to take in the fact she was now a mother. How? It didn't make sense.

'I don't remember ... I was at - the wedding? Oh, my God. Phoebe's wedding.' She might not have wanted to go to the wedding, but – oh, how awful. She could only imagine the scene.

'You were lucky one of the guests was a doctor.'

'Really? But, oh, Harold. The last thing I wanted was to mess up Phoebe's big day. She might be the most irritating person in the world, but I would never have wanted that.'

Harold squeezed her hand. 'That's the least of your worries. And you didn't anyway.' Harold sounded reassuring. 'I don't think she noticed to be honest and Ma said not to say anything.'

'I don't understand – how couldn't she notice?' She had visions of all the guests rushing to her aid.

'Slumped – that's what you did and luckily it was straight onto a chair. Phoebe was too busy meeting all her guests and then they went into the sit down bit. Got you in an ambulance and brought you here into Barts – Lizzie and I did. Never been in one of those before – a Police Ambulance.'

The baby murmured and she stared into her tiny face. She pulled the shawl down and examined the minute fingers.

It was quite incredible and it all felt very strange. This little person had been inside her and now she was here. And she had very little memory of any of it.

'How long have I been here?'

'Seems like forever. She's two weeks old tomorrow.'

She took a second or so to absorb what she'd just been told. It was hard to believe she had lost two weeks of her life but, she told herself, she was going to make up for it.

'I still can't believe I don't remember ...'

Harold laughed.

The nurse appeared at the foot of the bed.

'Visiting hour's over. I'll take baby.' She held out her arms. 'You need to get stronger so you can look after her.

The nurse lifted the baby from Vi's arms and took her to the nursery.

'Night love, so pleased you're back with me,' Harold said and kissed her.

She allowed herself to drift off again. She had a little girl - it was a miracle.

* * * * *

Amy found herself immersed in all the household chores with which Freddie hadn't coped and Doris didn't do. The first thing she discovered was that the larder was empty.

She was used to empty larders but even the basics such as flour and butter were missing. Although she discovered a large amount of washing, she decided food was the priority and, over breakfast, she talked Freddie into waiting until Doris arrived before he took the boys to school, so that she could come with him and do some shopping.

'I haven't got any money, Freddie,' she said in a hopeful voice.

He pulled out his wallet and she almost gasped at the wad of notes he pulled out.

'Sold a car yesterday – haven't got to the bank with the money,' he said as though reading her thoughts. He handed her two £1 notes – a fortune, it seemed right then. She trapped the notes under her saucer, wondering if Freddie was paying Doris suitable wages. She was doing much more than cleaning the house these days and she would be keeping an eye on Bobbie as well as Enid while she was out.

She was quite excited at the thought of a trip to the shops. Before leaving England, she'd shopped in a village close to where they lived but that was years ago and things were bound to be different.

The morning was sunny and the clouds were high and cheered her as she walked along the High Street. She could see little evidence of unemployment and there were a number of large houses with wealthy occupants, so it seemed to her that things weren't as bad as the newspapers would have her believe or, at least, not here.

The first shop she stopped at was a greengrocer which had crates of fruit and vegetables stacked up in wooden boxes outside on the pavement. She'd forgotten displays such as this. In fact, she hadn't bought vegetables in years. They had grown most or went without.

Then it was off to the butchers. She stood under the striped canvas awning which kept the sun off the window, staring at the display of beef and pork joints and thinking the chickens hanging on hooks outside looked decidedly fatter than the last one she'd eaten. Inside, standing on sawdust, she watched the lady ahead of her in the queue selecting some pork which was cut into large joints, the size of which she'd never seen before. Such luxury, she thought as she appreciated the cuts of meat displayed on the marble counter and admired the glazed tile pictures on the walls. She decided to buy some sausages – something she hadn't tried for so long, she wasn't sure if she would like them. Then she bought some sheep's kidneys and a pound of minced beef.

Outside the delivery van was a surprise – a sign of modernity, she thought, remembering her mother's meat had always been delivered by a boy on a bicycle. But she was even more surprised to see the Memorial Hall had been converted into a cinema. What a treat that would be and if only she had the money.

She spent sometime in the grocer's shop as she needed advice on what brands to buy and kept the lady behind the counter running to and fro with different items but once she'd ticked off everything on her list she debated whether to leave the shopping with Freddie for him to bring back later.

Deciding it would be nicer to take it all back in order to plan and prepare the meals for the next few days, she struggled along the road with four heavy bags. Some of the items were, in her opinion, extravagances such as biscuits and the pot of Marmite which Jonathan adored and for which Bobbie was developing a taste, since at breakfast there had been a squabble over who had the scrapings.

As she walked along the High Street, she compared today's experience with the times when she had visited the General Store in Canada. In England, it was easy to pop to the shops to purchase a forgotten item but out in the Prairies, it was very different. The trip into town was only made when they had eggs or milk to sell but since, in the bitter cold of winter, there was little milk and no eggs laid by the chickens, it was often a month or more before they made the journey. The mail was also collected at the General Store, so it might be many weeks before she received news from home. They would buy large sacks of flour and bigger quantities of other items to see them through and that would be the only chance to exchange gossip with friends.

Yes, the experience had been quite strange with brands she'd forgotten and new ones she hadn't heard of but, that evening, she was looking forward to enjoying a cup of Ovaltine – something she and Freddie, as children, used to love before bedtime. Surely, that had to be healthier for Freddie than the whisky he'd been drinking lately? And also she'd been very naughty and spent some of the housekeeping on herself. Freddie had asked her to visit the tobacconists and purchase some Senior Service cigarettes and when she saw the price of his indulgence, she felt justified in spending 2d on the Woman's Own magazine which had been on the counter. The thought of the two coppers it had cost reminded her of the struggle with the currency. Pounds, shillings and pence were very different to dollars and she'd quite forgotten about three penny pieces and half crowns.

Overall, she thought, it might be easier to get into the shops in England, but there were also a greater number of temptations. She would have to be careful when she came to budgeting for herself as every shopping trip would have something attractive which would entice her to spend more money than she should. Maybe there were advantages to being stuck out on a farm in the middle of nowhere she mused and, with a sigh, thought how she missed the life. She now understood why George, in his letters all those years ago, had described the big skies and she couldn't help yearning to be there. She blinked back tears at the impossibility of it all. Why did she keep getting so emotional?

The weight of the bags became too much and she stopped, putting them on the pavement to rest her arms, and reconsidering her decision not to take them to the garage for Freddie to bring back later.

'You shouldn't be doing that,' Charles' voice broke into her thoughts, making her jump. 'Sorry, didn't mean to startle you. What or who were you thinking about? Hope it was me.'

She didn't answer but allowed him to lift the bags for her, trying to think of a sensible answer.

'I had to call into the bank. My car's up there.' He indicated with a nod of the head. 'Let me drive you home.' He didn't wait for an answer but led the way.

'No chauffeur, Charles?' she said, spotting the car.

'Not these days. Not since mother left The Grange. Once old Petersen retired, we didn't replace him. In any case I prefer to drive myself.'

She stood admiring the car, something she hadn't done since the time the Maxwell arrived at the farm and how she had adored that. Since then, cars had never interested her much but this one had a cream canvas roof and was a very sleek, shining deep red. It was quite the prettiest car (if you could call a car pretty) she had ever seen. It was also much smaller than anything she thought Charles would drive.

'Nice isn't she?' Charles said catching her admiring look, having stowed the shopping.

'Yes, it is but it's very small, isn't it? Why, it's only got two seats.'

'But that's why I bought it. I didn't want to be seen driving round in father's old Rolls or the Bentley. I haven't had a Morris before but I must say I'm rather pleased with it.' He opened the passenger door for her to get in. 'Roof comes down and it's ideal for short trips to the shops.'

As she settled into her seat, she noticed two ladies outside the shoe shop staring in their direction and a ghastly thought struck her. She could hear them: *"that husband of her's has left her and now she's picked up where she left off ..."* She glanced up at Charles and knew he wouldn't care but surely there could be no harm in him helping her with her shopping?

'How's your mother? Shouldn't you be at the hospital?'

'I called in on my way here. Mother never ceases to amaze me - or the doctor.' Charles put the car into gear and sped off. 'She's much improved. Says she'll be home before the week's out, though I have my doubts. She's very frail but she has such determination.'

'How incredible. I thought ...' She had understood Lady Margaret was unlikely to get through the night. What a turnabout. 'Well, I am pleased.'

'Now. Your mother's, I presume.' He looked straight ahead.

'Oh, er, no. Actually, we're at Freddie's. Mother always has her shopping delivered. I wasn't sure what Enid did and in any case I didn't know what was in the shops – we've been in Canada for seven years. I thought it better if I did it myself.'

They were heading out of the village and Amy relaxed, beginning to enjoy the ride.

'Don't suppose it's that different,' Charles said.

She thought of the small packs of flour and sugar packed in her shopping bag and giggled.

'If only you could see the huge size sacks of flour I used to buy - . ' She stopped. There hadn't been much in the way of food in the last year or so of their time in Canada.

'You must do that more often.' He glanced at her.

'What? Shop?'

'No. Giggle. I like it when you laugh.' He grinned. 'You used to do it a lot.'

'There's not much to laugh about these days. Did you know Enid's been very ill?'

'No, I didn't. Freddie and I …' he shrugged and she knew they were no longer the friends they used to be and it was because of her. 'Sorry to hear Enid's ill.'

'She miscarried and it's led to all sorts of mental problems. She's getting better but it's slow progress.'

They were silent. Then it occurred to her that he might not know where Freddie lived.

'Don't worry, I know the way but I was thinking of visiting that little tea room we used to go to all those years ago. You promised me lunch, remember?'

'I did no such thing and in any case I can't. You forget, I'm a mother of three boys and one of them is waiting for me. Besides, Enid mustn't be left alone at the moment and Freddie's "lady who does" finishes soon. So please take me straight home.' She glanced at her watch. 'Doris has to leave in half an hour.'

She could see he was disappointed.

'Why don't you stop for a cup of coffee at Freddie's?' The words slipped out before she'd thought it through. Was it appropriate? What was suitable in Canada where everyone was equal might not be seen as such in England. At that moment she was not sure what was correct in 1930's England but there couldn't be any harm in inviting an old family friend to stop for refreshments? It was only polite, since he was taking the trouble to drive her home and, in any case, she wanted to hear all his news. There were years of news and gossip to catch up on and it would be so nice to relax and chat.

'That'd be nice but I'd better not be caught by Freddie. He and I – well – let's say I wasn't exactly polite when I saw him last. Truth was, I got hold of him by the scruff of the neck.'

Amy was aghast. 'You did what?'

'That was a long time ago.'

'I knew you two fell out but I didn't know you'd had a fight.' She felt guilty. 'I'm sorry.'

He glanced at her and his hand strayed to her arm to give it a gentle squeeze. 'It's not your problem and, in any case, we're grown men with our own families now. I guess we should be able to be polite to each other.'

He replaced his hand on the steering wheel and nothing more was said until she had to identify Freddie's house and they pulled up on the driveway. He gathered the bags of shopping and followed her into the house and into the kitchen.

'Everything all right?' she asked Doris, who, with sleeves rolled up was scrubbing the sink.

'I think so,' she said into the sink. 'Young Bobbie's playing upstairs and Mrs Attwood was asleep when I looked in ten minutes ago.'

'Thanks, Doris. We'd like some coffee … Can I …?' She could see the kettle steaming on the hob.

Doris looked over her shoulder and saw Charles in the door. 'Not to worry, Mrs Mills. I'll make it.'

'That is kind of you, Doris. I'll put the shopping away later.' She turned to Charles. 'Doris has been an absolute angel,' she said and led the way out of the kitchen.

'Nice,' Charles said as Amy shut the lounge door behind them. 'It's the first time I've been in one of these new places.'

'And to think this was the reason we went to Canada … funny old world.'

Charles was puzzled. 'I'm not sure I understand.'

'Sorry. I'm talking in riddles.' Of course, he wouldn't realise George was made redundant because the farm he was working on was sold for development. Nor would he realise that George lost not only his job but they had lost their home and this had led them to leave for Canada. 'You did know George was working for the Burtons?'

He looked surprised. 'No. No, I hadn't realised.'

'Of course not. Why would you?' She indicated for him to sit down. 'The place was sold if you remember …'

'It was sold for …' He sat on the settee. 'These houses were built on their farm? I'm sorry, I hadn't realised the connection before … but how ironic Freddie should buy one.'

'It is a bit but you're right. It is a lovely house and I must confess to being a little envious.'

'You? Envious? That's not like you. I've never known you to be envious of anyone.'

She sighed. 'Maybe not but experience does change one. It was tough out in Canada. We had a very hard time of it and I learnt a lot – had to learn a lot and now I suppose I am a little – well – now we're back … The truth is I'm resentful.' How could she explain her feelings? And if she did would Charles understand she was angry because Freddie was bankrolled to do what he liked – to carry on with that woman while it was a very different story for George and her. Maybe she had said too much.

'Resentful? Resentful of what exactly?'

'It doesn't matter.' She didn't want to explain more. 'I didn't mean it to sound so … Just that life is unfair sometimes.'

'Mmm. You can say that again.'

There was a moment's pause as she tried to put such irritating thoughts out of her mind. She tried to think of something else and wondered if she had really treated him shamefully all those years ago? Looking back, if she was truly honest, she knew she'd acted disgracefully in some respects. When they first met in the hospital, he had been keen to apologise but maybe it was she who should do some apologising also.

'I guess you aren't the only one who should ask for forgiveness. Maybe I should be asking that of you, too. After all, it was very cowardly of me to run out on you like that. Only leaving a letter - I should have had the courage to tell you to your face.'

Before he could reply, the door opened and Doris brought in a tray which she placed on a nearby table.

'Thanks, Doris. We'll look after ourselves.'

She poured two cups of coffee and noticed as she handed Charles a cup, it was the best bone china. Freddie had told her, when she had got some plates out the previous evening, it was a wedding present and not for everyday use. She had put them back and used some plain white ones instead.

'It's time I was off, Mrs Mills,' Doris said on her way out.

'Thanks, Doris. See you tomorrow.'

The door closed and Amy glanced up at Charles and caught his eye.

'Now we're quite alone …' he began to say. 'Come and sit beside me.' He patted the seat beside him. 'You need some support and I'm offering.'

The shake of her head denied what they both knew was true. She needed and wanted the strong arms of a man. She avoided his eyes. His presence was dangerous - so very dangerous.

'I didn't take George for a fool but he is, for leaving you here alone.'

'You don't understand,' she said in a firm voice and went to sit in a chair opposite him. He would never appreciate what they had been through together - never in a million years would he comprehend why she could never be untrue to the man she had married. 'George has had a lot to cope with.'

'So have you and that doesn't excuse him for abandoning his wife.'

'He hasn't abandoned me as you put it.'

'So why is he in London? He should be here, especially now with Will in hospital.'

'He doesn't know.'

'What? Haven't you telephoned?'

'Not everyone has a telephone.'

'Heavens above, Amy, send a telegram. That's the least you could do. He has a right to know, especially as it's so serious.'

She didn't like to tell him she hadn't the money and in any case, she had been so busy coping on her own, she hadn't even thought about a telegram.

'The whole thing's a nightmare. Coping with three boys – no four – and with Enid. Will's accident …' She brushed away some tears. She was not going to get all emotional. 'Will's accident happened at the exact moment Enid was discharged from hospital and couldn't be left alone. There simply hasn't been a minute.'

But he was quite right. George should have been told and she would write – again. Now she was beginning to doubt George. Was Charles right? Had he abandoned her? There had been no word since his phone call and that was – when? She'd lost count of the time.

'What about Sylvia?' she changed tack. 'Does she come to the hospital with you?'

'That's different.'

'Is it?'

When he didn't answer she sipped her coffee. She wanted to tell him about their life in Canada but right then, it was impossible. There was something else in the room - it crackled, sizzled and made her ache but to give into temptation would be a mistake - a big mistake.

He gulped down the rest of his coffee and got up.

'I think I'd better go.'

She didn't know what to say. She wanted him to stay longer but he was bound to misunderstand if she were to say so. She stood up.

'Thanks for bringing me back.'

In three strides, he had covered the distance between them and had folded her into his arms. She melted so desperate was she for someone to share her troubles. She relaxed, wanting to stay but it was wrong – oh, so wrong.

'God, Amy. We've made such a mess of our lives.' He said into her hair.

'Mom,' Bobbie's voice cut across anything which might have said and, she thought later, regretted. She broke away.

'What is it, Bobbie?' She walked unsteadily towards the door.

'Daddy's here.'

'What the bloody hell do you think you're doing?' Freddie had followed Bobbie into the room.

'Freddie, please.' She didn't want Bobbie to hear such language and she glanced at Charles with embarrassment.

'I was just leaving.' He grinned as though he understood.

'Charles was kind enough to bring me and the shopping home.' She turned to Charles. 'I'm sorry about Freddie.'

'Amy, it doesn't matter. I'd do that for you any time.' At the lounge door he confronted George.

'And what exactly would you do for my wife?'

## Chapter Thirteen

'George! George! Oh, thank the Lord.'

Amy ran into his arms and he had a vague recollection of the front door closing behind Charles. He put his arms round her but he knew he was stiff and unwelcoming. He felt an intruder and what had he witnessed? He struggled to make sense of it. His mother's words "while the mice are away…" echoed in his head but, despite feeling guilty for his absence, right then it didn't feel right with Amy in his arms – nothing felt right. He hadn't cheated but had she?

She looked up into his eyes and he wanted to kiss her but she burst into tears and her arms tightened about him while she sobbed into his chest.

'What's all the noise?' Enid's voice broke across whatever he might have said. Still in nightclothes and, in George's opinion, half naked, she stood at the bottom of the stairs and, with her white garments and pallid looks, if it were night, he was sure she would have been mistaken for a ghost.

'George's home, that's all,' Freddie said coming into the hall. He took her hand. 'And this is George,' he added as he guided her into the lounge. He took her to the settee and sat beside her. 'Bobbie, do you think you could get Aunt Enid's dressing gown? Its cream and I think it's still on the bed.'

George disentangled himself from Amy's arms and decided that, even though it was a sight better to be living with Freddie and Enid, there was going to be little privacy in which to sort things out.

'Shall I make some fresh coffee? Or tea?' Amy said. She blew her nose and tried to compose herself.

'Good idea,' Freddie said.

George went to sit in an armchair near the window and stared into the garden. His homecoming was a disappointment – a big disappointment. What did he expect, he asked himself. It was a surprise finding Charles here – in Freddie's home – a bit brazen since he and Freddie had fallen out and not spoken in years. He was astonished at Amy inviting him into the house in the first place. Why? Why would she do such and thing? What had been going on? Right then, nothing made sense and he tried to console himself with the fact that he wasn't going to be sleeping under his mother-in-law's roof that night and for that, he was extremely relieved.

He undid his shoes. The sole of the left shoe was beginning to develop a hole and he wondered if he could find some more cardboard to insert to make it last a bit longer. His feet were weary from the long walk, though he'd been lucky enough to get a lift right to the garage. As soon as Freddie had finished work on the car in the workshop, he offered to drive him home and during the journey, he learnt about Enid and the loss of their baby. Then Freddie had informed him about the job – or rather, the lack of it. He'd been such a fool rushing off to London – so determined was he not to have anything to do with Amy's mother, he had thrown away the only chance he had of providing for his family. True, Freddie had offered him work at the garage. The irony that it should all turn out the way Amy planned all those years ago was not lost on him. But did he really want to work with Freddie? Could he work with Freddie? With no other job in view, there was no choice and the thought depressed him. Living and working with his brother-in-law was far from perfect.

Bobbie appeared trailing the dressing gown along the floor.

'Be careful you don't trip up, old chap,' Freddie said with a smile. As soon as Bobbie had given the gown to Freddie, he went across to George.

'Daddy, are you going to see Will and can I come?'

George was deep in thought. The prospect of providing a home for Amy and the boys was never going to be easy but now it seemed impossible.

'Daddy?' Bobbie pushed at his knee.

'Tea. I made some tea,' Amy said appearing with a large tray on which was a teapot, a jug of milk and cups and saucers.

'What is it, Bobbie?' George asked when he realised Bobbie was tapping his knee.

'Can I go to the hospital with you to see Will?'

'What? Hospital? What's this about Will?'

There was a moment's silence.

'Would someone kindly tell me what the hell's going on.'

Amy placed the tray on the low table in front of the settee and looked at Freddie.

'I thought ... Didn't Freddie tell you?'

'I'd hardly be asking if he had.' He couldn't keep the irritation out of his voice. Ever since he'd stepped foot in this house, he had had this sneaky suspicion nothing was as it seemed. They were all hiding something. 'Well?' he prompted.

'Will had a bad accident and hurt his ankle,' Amy said.

'Damn nearly cut his foot off,' Freddie intervened.

'Freddie!' Amy gave him a stern look.

'Don't beat around the bush, for goodness sake, Amy. George needs to know.' Freddie said.

'Well?' George repeated.

'He played truant from school –.' Amy began to explain.

'He did what?'

'He's been very difficult. Apparently he got hold of a go-cart thing – whatever and, er – crashed it.'

'Where did he get that from?'

'I don't know. Anyway, the wheel cut into his ankle just below the joint. But George, he's been so lucky because the doctor at the hospital has been clever enough to stitch it up and he can feel his toes.' She began to pour milk into the cups.

'Bloody hell. When did all this happen? Is he going to be able to walk?'

'The doctor seems to think so,' Amy said.

'It happened the day Enid came out of hospital,' Freddie answered. He was helping Enid into her dressing gown. 'Now you know what I mean, when I said things were a bit difficult here.'

George took time to digest the news. He blamed himself. If he'd been here, maybe, just maybe Will would have stayed in school. He'd never have dared do otherwise. Amy always was a soft touch. Amy and Charles – he had his suspicions. And now Will.

'And what else has been going on?'

'I should think that's enough.' Freddie laughed. 'I don't think Amy and I could cope with much more. Thank God, mother hasn't been playing up for once.'

## Chapter Fourteen

## Christmas 1932

They arrived at church in Freddie's car. Amy got the impression that Freddie was glad not to be going as he seemed very willing to stay with Enid and Jonathan but she supposed she, George and the boys did impose on his privacy a little – a lot, she corrected herself – and it would give them some time together. Still in his dressing gown, he had handed George the car keys with the request to collect their mother and to take her to church after they had visited Will in hospital. That, of course, was the downside to being given the privilege of the car.

It would have been an even grander arrival at church if she had felt as fashionable and glamorous as Charles' wife, who wore a jaunty hat and a coat with a generous fur collar and who she could see sitting beside him towards the front of the church. Instead she felt dowdy and crumpled, following a journey in which she had been squashed between Sam and Bobbie in order to enforce a Christmas Day truce.

She helped her mother into a pew at the rear of the church and concluded the boy and girl sitting on each side of Charles and his wife must be his children. Of Lady Margaret, there was no sign – possibly she wasn't well enough to attend.

She tried so hard to concentrate but her eyes kept finding people she recognized and hoped they didn't spot her – she felt so scruffy and she was certain they would be whispering about how she and George had failed in their Canadian venture. Then she found herself drawing parallels to the services in the schoolroom in Canada. How she missed John and Ellie. Would she ever get used to being back in England with its snobbery and class system? George was forever telling her she was a snob – was she? And, if so, why didn't she feel as though she belonged here?

Charles and his wife were amongst the last to leave the church and it was obvious, not only to her mother but to George, that he had made a point of lingering behind the rest of his family in order to speak to them. He wished them a happy Christmas but as he said the words, he was looking at her and she had been foolish enough to catch his eye.

'And a Happy Christmas to you and your wife and, of course, Lady Margaret,' her mother said not disguising the sharp edge in her voice. Amy thought she noticed an emphasis on the word "wife" but she dismissed this as her being oversensitive to anything to do with Charles, especially when it was said in front of George.

There was an awkward silence, broken by Mrs Attwood asking after Lady Margaret.

'I hope your mother is better?'

'Er, yes. Thank you. She's much better,' Charles said.

'Amy, where's my stick?' Mrs Attwood said before anyone had a chance to say anything else.

Amy handed over the stick and, once her mother was in the aisle, she felt George's firm grip on her arm. He guided her out into the sunlight before she had a chance to wish anyone a "Happy Christmas". She was certain she could feel Charles' eyes on her but she didn't look back. The words he had said when he had wrapped his arms around her echoed in her mind.

*"We've made such a mess of our lives."*

It was a relief when they reached the car. She didn't want Charles to compare her with his stunning blonde wife.

'He doesn't waste an opportunity does he?' George almost growled at her as he opened the car door, leaving her to get in while he helped his mother-in-law.

She didn't want to understand what George meant and thought it safer to ignore the comment. Anyway she could see Charles had followed them out of church and she didn't want them to make an exhibition of themselves or spoil the day. She climbed into the car and George got into the driving seat. The journey was completed in silence – even her mother was quiet.

When they all gathered round for dinner – that is, everyone except Will, her mood lifted. The table looked splendid, but, of course, its central decoration and candle were down to Enid, who had felt well enough a day or so ago to go into the garden and pick some holly. The goose and trimmings had been her own responsibility and with Freddie carving, they soon set about demolishing it. The Christmas pudding, too, was scoffed down by the children and then everyone moved into the lounge to listen the King's speech which was to be broadcast on the wireless. It seemed strange without Will, she thought. When they visited him that morning she was so pleased to see he was still making progress, though it seemed there was no possibility of him coming home just yet. He was missing a very historical moment. The first ever wireless broadcast from Buckingham Palace or was it Sandringham? She settled on the latter and, having decided to clear the table after the speech, followed the others out of the dining room.

The boys sat beside the large Christmas tree which they had helped to decorate a day or so earlier. Amy was amused by the homemade newspaper angels from Canada which, much to Enid's disapproval, hung along the bottom of the tree. They had turned up in the trunk and she was wondering who had smuggled them into their packing, when Freddie appeared with a blanket which he draped around Enid's shoulders. He made sure she was comfortable before he went across to the wireless. She was impressed with the attention he lavished on her and hoped he wasn't still seeing the woman at the pub. If he was, George, who had been working at the garage for two weeks, would surely have said. Either way, she decided, Freddie deserved a pat on the back for the way he handled Enid, who was not an easy patient.

George sat in one of the easy chairs staring straight ahead as though he was in another world. She'd hoped so much that things would have improved since his stay with his family in London but, if anything, they seemed worse – far worse. Now he was convinced she and Charles were having some kind of affair. It was undeserved and untrue, of course, but she was beginning to think she might be tempted. She longed for George to hold her and love her. Oh, how much she needed the man she had married.

She glanced at her mother, who was asleep in the only upright chair Freddie could find. She did wish she wouldn't wear black. For goodness sake, it was Christmas – a time of celebration. Queen Victoria had a lot to answer for, she thought, and her mother looked most uncomfortable, with her head bent to one side. At least, with her asleep, they could all relax, but, even if her mother was forgetful and frail, she had been sharp enough to spot the look which had passed between her and Charles in church that morning.

She turned her attention to the children. 'Now you three, this is special, so you must be very quiet.'

Freddie twisted the knobs of the big wooden square box which stood resplendent on the cabinet he had bought specially. Bobbie insisted the wireless had a face. It made funny buzzing and squealing noises and Sam's giggle set the others off. She gave them a severe look.

'Shshsh,' she said and put her finger to her lips.

A moment later and they could hear the King's voice but it wasn't long before the boys became bored.

*"I speak now from my home and from my heart to you all ..."*

'It's very crackly -.' Bobbie said

'Shshshsh ...' George said.

Bobbie pulled a face at Jonathan who dissolved into more giggles.

'Shshsh ...' Freddie said.

The three boys sat squirming, giggling and pulling faces at each other but somehow managed their silence to the end of the broadcast.

'That was quite something, wasn't it? I think he made a damn good job of it, too. What about a toast to the King?' Freddie switched the wireless off and went to find a bottle of port and some glasses.

'Now how many of us?' He said when he returned. He pulled out the cork and began to fill the glasses.

Amy carried two glasses to where she and George were sitting.

Freddie looked across at his mother, who had slept through most of the broadcast. She was awake, so he placed a glass of port on the table beside her.

'The King.' He held up his glass.

'The King,' everyone responded.

Jonathan found the compendium of games he had unwrapped earlier and placed the box in the centre of the floor. Soon they were playing tiddlywinks with Amy, Freddie and the boys crawling around the floor pressing the larger squidgers onto the smaller ones to make them jump into the pot.

The sound of shattering glass interrupted the game and they turned to see Enid slumped in her chair.

'Good Lord.'

The glass, which had broken on impact with the parquet floor, had spilled its red content and Enid was slumped in her chair.

'She shouldn't be drinking that stuff - not with all that medication.' Freddie shook her gently. 'Enid, Enid talk to me.'

'She must have taken yours,' Amy said. 'Do think she should go to the hospital?'

'No – can't risk that. No, that's the last place.' He shook her again and she opened her eyes. 'She couldn't have drunk that much. We'll have to keep an eye on her and if need be, I'll call the doctor.'

'Hmm,' George said. 'He won't be too impressed on Christmas day.'

Christmas seemed right then to be as miserable as the rest of her life, Amy thought, as she watched George close his eyes. Peeved by his whole attitude, she went to the kitchen to wash the dishes.

\* \* \* \* \*

Freddie unlocked his mother's front door and helped her over the threshold. The servants had been given the rest of the day off, so he felt obliged to make sure she was safe before he left. She was very unsteady on her feet and her journey upstairs was slow. As he followed, he thought if someone had told him last Christmas that his wife would be on the verge of lunacy and his house would be occupied by his sister and her family, he would never have believed them. Sometimes he felt overwhelmed by the weight of responsibility. That was his life these days – taking care of people. His wife, his sister and his mother – all made demands. Sometimes he felt there was little left of himself – he'd given it all away.

'Nice and warm up here,' he said as he opened the bedroom door. As he helped her off with her overcoat, he was pleased to see the fire was still glowing.

'I can manage now.'

He placed her coat on a nearby chair and went to rake the fire, shovelled a few pieces of coal onto it and hoped it would stay in overnight.

'I have to get back now,' he said and bent to kiss her cheek. 'Maybe see you tomorrow,' he added, hoping that wouldn't be the case. He could do without a repeat of today.

'That'd be nice.'

'Oh, and Freddie -,' she said as he opened the door. 'It was nice to see you take such good care of Enid – don't think I don't notice things …' There was an emphasis on the word "things".

'Night, mother,' he said after a moment's thought. Safer to say nothing, he told himself as he closed the door behind him. He was left him wondering what exactly she had noticed. Not too much, he hoped, as he needed to have a chat with her about the state of the garage's finances which were strained now he had an extra employee. He had a feeling the bank manager might want a word or two in the new year about the size of his overdraft.

He hadn't intended to do anything but go straight home. Instead he found himself outside the pub which was still open. He supposed it was reaction to all the demands the women in his life made – except one, that is, and he hadn't seen her since George arrived on the scene. He shut his mind to Enid. It was only one glass of port after all and not all of it. She would survive. He needed Beth. Damn it. He'd purchased a silver bracelet and hadn't had the chance to call in to wish her a happy Christmas. If only he could find his brother-in-law some other employment – get him out from under his feet. It was so restricting having him there all the time.

He could hear the jovial crowd and smell the beer before he even reached the door. A chance to give Beth her present and have one for the road he told himself, and as he entered the pub. He looked into the Smoke Room, where the warmth and thick blue fug of smoke reminded him how desperate he was for a cigarette. He had restrained himself all day and, since Enid disapproved of him smoking in the house, had nipped outside only twice to light up. The crowd were having a bit of a singsong with a bawdy rendering of "Daisy, Daisy". Much as he fancied a smoke, Beth was not in this bar, so he went into the salon where he could see her pulling a pint. He pulled out a bar stool and knew she'd seen him.

At least in here it would be warm and bright and cheerful – most of all cheerful. Maybe this was meant to be the highlight of Christmas.

## Chapter Fifteen

It was near the end of January before Vi was allowed to come home with the baby. Her weakness was frustrating. For several days while she was in hospital whenever they allowed her out of bed, she felt dizzy and sick, so she knew it was going to be some while before she would be strong enough to look after her baby, let alone run a house. But staying with Ma was not an option since Harold had declared they could manage on their own and seemed to have taken great umbrage at the suggestion he wouldn't be able to cope.

'You've got to go to work,' Ma told him more than once when they were visiting her in hospital. 'A crying baby is a lot to cope with in the middle of the night.'

'Other people manage,' Harold said. 'And I'd appreciate you managing your own life and I'll look after ours.'

Vi was shocked by the tone of voice and knew Ma had been offended but it was more than she dared to argue, even if she had the strength. Now she was dreading her home coming. How exactly was she going to cope? It was all very well for Harold to say they'd manage. When he was away at work, it would be down to her.

As she dressed in the clothes Harold had brought in the previous evening, she felt very strange and supposed it was after living in nightdresses for so long. It was strange, too, because they were her pre-baby ones. She was surprised how much weight she had lost but then she hadn't eaten much for several weeks. Maybe that was the reason she felt light headed.

She sat on the edge of the bed and tried to think positive thoughts. At least she would be exchanging this metal framed monstrosity for the comfort of her own bed and the privacy of her own bedroom. What was more, she would be able to sit in her own comfy chair. She picked up a matinee jacket, one of several, and began to fold it ready to pack. She remembered knitting it, but the others were gifts – all hand knitted and so delicate. Lily looked gorgeous in them. Harold had chosen the name after his mother, saying the birth had to be registered within so many days. Of course, she had been too ill to be involved and, although she accepted what he told her, she begrudged the use of her mother-in-law's name, deciding she would choose a pet name.

'Lily,' she whispered and decided she was beginning to come round to his choice. 'I think I can get used to that.'

'Get used to what?' Harold's voice made her jump. He was much earlier than she expected.

'Oh – er – being a Mum, I s'pose.'

He ignored her answer and picked up the packed holdall.

'Don't take that yet. There's more to go in.'

He dumped it back on the bed.

'Don't take all day. Ray's waiting outside.'

'Ray?'

'Don't you remember anything I tell you these days? I told you only yesterday, Ray's offered to collect you from hospital.'

She remembered now. Harold's friend, the one with a car, was coming to collect her. She sighed, Harold was so impatient. She pushed the last of the baby clothes into the bag and thought she'd better get her shoes on. She looked down at her feet, remembering how they refused to go into most of her shoes when she was pregnant.

'Finished?'

She nodded, relieved the shoes fitted.

'Let's get Lily then,' Harold said and strode off to the nursery.

She felt herself hustled out of the ward, hardly having a chance to say "good-bye" or "thank you" and with the baby in her arms and unsteady on her feet, she walked towards the exit.

It was a peculiar feeling standing on the hospital steps in the fresh air. There was a giant universe out there and she felt small and vulnerable and nervous – very nervous. Being a mum was a whole new experience. Lily was an awesome responsibility and she was already doubting her ability to cope or at least to Harold's exacting standards. She looked down at the tiny bundle in her arms and realised she was going to be making decisions on everything which affected this little person. What a daunting thought.

'Come on, Vi,' Harold said. 'Can't keep Ray waiting.'

The car was right outside and she climbed into the back, careful to shield Lily's head. Harold banged the door shut and jumped in the front. He and Ray chatted about work, ignoring her for the whole of the journey. She leant back and closed her eyes. Even getting this far was exhausting. When the car stopped, she was hurried into the house with no chance of expressing her gratitude.

'The fire's alight, so you sit there,' Harold instructed. 'I'll bring you a cuppa in a minute, then I must get off to work.'

'But I thought -' She was certain today was his day off. He wasn't going to leave her alone on her first day home, surely not?

'Shift's changed,' Harold said and went to put the kettle on.

Lily began to stir and she glanced up at the clock. It was getting towards 1 pm and feeding time was an hour away but she had been instructed to keep to the routine – every four hours. She knew from experience that Harold would be leaving within the next ten minutes. He always liked to be early and, even her homecoming seemed unlikely to alter his habits. She sat down, wondering what had happened which could have changed his attitude to her. Once he was so caring. Surely, it couldn't be money? He'd said he paid into some insurance scheme and it was supposed to take care of all the hospital expenses. Apart from the arrival of Lily, she couldn't think of a single thing. Maybe Ma was right – some men had difficulty in accepting their role as a father or, possibly more importantly, accepting that she was now a mother first, then a wife.

She looked down at the sleeping child, lifting her tiny fingers so they curled around her own little one. Having Lily was a miracle but she was beginning to think the whole baby business, pregnancy and delivery had meant sacrificing her man in some way, though she was mystified as to why this should be. Hadn't he wanted a baby as much as she?

*****

George unhooked the boiler suit from the back of the door and struggled into it.

'Are you sure about this, Freddie?' he said. The suit was a spare and the sleeves too long. He rolled them up.

'Yeah, yeah. You'll be fine. Just crawl under it. The sump's pretty obvious. Take the plug out but make sure the oil drains into that pan I showed you. Then screw it up again and bob's your uncle. Fill it up. You know where the filler is? Nothing could be simpler. Oh, and don't forget to change the filter. Now where's that stupid piece of paper.'

As George did his buttons up, he wondered if he should tell Freddie about his experience with oil – or lack of it.

Then decided not to – maybe it was better he didn't know he'd already succeeded in seizing an engine up. In any case he needed to learn something about motor cars if he was ever to get another job and, the truth was, he was desperate to make the move. He'd had quite enough of Freddie. He never got away from him and it was beginning to set his nerves on edge. It was more than his patience could cope with some days but there seemed no way out and, as Amy was at great pains to remind him, it was a job. And a roof over their head.

Freddie might be good at selling motor cars but he hadn't a clue how to run an office. He watched as he turned over the mass of paperwork which was on the desk and which he himself had spent a long time trying to put into some kind of order. What was the point of all his efforts when Freddie tossed them across the desk like that? There had been over a year's worth of bank statements scattered amongst invoices and letters, some of which should have been answered months ago. He wanted to file them but the filing cabinets were full of spare parts and it had taken all his powers of persuasion to make Freddie realise that at least one of the filing cabinets needed to be used for paperwork. Then he thought of the two overdue accounts somewhere on the desk – the two he knew of – he suspected there were others. Yes, Amy might say it was a job but he had serious doubts as to how long the garage could remain viable before there was a call from the bank manager.

'I'll get on then.' He opened the door and felt the drop in the temperature. The workshop was warmer than outside, but the office was cosy. No wonder Freddie preferred to stay in there.

The car's front wheels were up on ramps and he checked the back wheels were chocked. He didn't want the thing coming down on his head. He pushed an old rug into position, placed the oil pan where he could reach it and, lying on his back, slid under the car.

In one respect Freddie was right, he mused. The sump was obvious but getting the plug out proved more difficult. His hands were blue with cold and he'd acquired a cut to the back of one of them by the time he'd succeeded. Whilst it drained into the pan, he went to fetch the replacement oil.

'This what you're looking for?' Freddie, who had come out of the office, lifted a one gallon oil can down from the shelf. 'I have to go to the bank. Shouldn't be too long.'

George stared after him for a moment. Donnie was out on another job. So this was well and truly down to him – there was no one to consult if he had any doubts. He found a funnel, unscrewed the cap and in his haste to refill the oil, almost forgot to replace the sump plug. Phew! That was a close call, he told himself as he remembered he also needed to replace the filter. Half an hour later, the job was complete, the car off the ramps and parked ready for collection and he felt a little smug. It hadn't been that difficult after all. He returned to the office. He'd earned a cup of tea.

He cleaned up the gash on the back of his hand with his handkerchief which, by the time he'd finished, was covered in grease and blood. Amy wasn't going to be impressed with that, he thought. He was warming his fingers around a cup of milky tea, when Freddie stormed into the office.

'That Austin,' he cocked his head. 'What the hell are you playing at? Why's it parked out there? Shouldn't it be in the workshop and didn't I tell you to put a pan under it?'

Taken aback by Freddie's anger, George put his cup down.

'I did put a pan under it and, what's more, I did the whole job. Put the new oil in, just like you said.'

'Bloody hell. That's fresh oil? Didn't you see it?'

'See what?'

Freddie ignored his question and returned to the workshop. He picked up an old oil can which had been cut open along one side.

George followed him outside, expecting to see a large pool of oil but until he squatted, he couldn't see any sign of a leak. Then, as he looked under the vehicle, he identified a drip of oil. Damn it, Freddie had gone out of his way to check up on him and be critical. Anger surged through him. He was determined to find fault and, yes, the oil had made a slight mess but it wasn't exactly pouring out. And it was true he'd almost forgotten the plug – but he hadn't.

Freddie slid the can under the car, watching for a second to make sure the leaking oil was going where he wanted.

'Can't you do anything right? Sending a car out with an oil leak is the surest way of losing a customer.' He stood up. 'Just as well this isn't being collected until tomorrow. And I'll be furious if I've messed this lot up,' he added, inspecting his jacket and trousers.

'But I did exactly as you said -'

'Really? So why the oil leak? Can't I trust you to do anything properly?' Freddie glowered at him.

George clenched his fists. He itched to wallop him and he had half a mind to walk out. The only reason he didn't was he knew it would hurt him and Amy more than Freddie. That thought intensified his anger. He'd done exactly as instructed and Freddie was unreasonable. It wasn't his fault the stupid car had sprung a leak. He didn't argue. Whatever he said, he was going to be in the wrong.

'I'll get Donnie to look at it in the morning. At least I've got someone I can rely on.' Freddie banged the office door behind him.

There was a difficult atmosphere in the garage for the remainder of the afternoon and when it came to closing time, the journey home was completed in silence. George was relieved when the car turned onto the drive but instead of waiting for him to open the garage door, as had become their routine, Freddie reversed at high speed back up the drive and shot off down the road.

'Don't know what's got into Freddie,' George said later as he sat in the kitchen watching Amy preparing the evening meal. 'He picks holes in everything I do and it wasn't my fault the blasted car developed an oil leak.'

'Didn't he say where he was going?' She put the finishing touches to a pie.

'Not a word.'

'That shouldn't take too long.' She opened the oven door and put the pie on the top shelf. 'Is he coming back for supper?'

'How should I know? This so called job really isn't working out. I came near to punching him this afternoon – that's how bad things are.'

'Oh? They can't be that difficult, surely?'

'Amy, you've no idea. He's bloody impossible.'

'Shshsh. The children –'

'Blast the children. Can't you see, this isn't working?'

'Calm down. Please, calm down. We should count our blessings. We're luckier than a lot of people. Remember all those men you told me about in London? We should be grateful.'

His mind conjured up the vision of men sitting on their doorsteps in the East End of London, the hopelessness in their eyes, but far from soothing him, the words exasperated him.

'Godamn it, Amy. Count our blessings? Can't I get through to you? Freddie and I are going to come to blows if I don't get out from under his feet.'

'Shshsh. I know. I know and I do understand.'

'I don't think you do. Look, I never get away from him – even when I'm home – it's his bloody home.'

'Shshsh. Something'll come along soon, you mark my words.'

He sighed. His life was jinxed. Didn't he deserve some luck? He'd given his best shot in Canada and it wasn't his fault he'd failed. There were days when he wasn't sure where he belonged – in Canada or in England? He felt a stranger in his own homeland. He felt himself descending into the depths of black gloom once more. Sometimes it felt as if he'd fallen down a manhole – plenty of sewage down there and most of the shit had been piled on him – and whenever it seemed the cover might be removed and he could see a scrap of blue sky, godamn it, someone replaced it.

Sometimes in church, he'd found himself questioning whether there was a God. And if there was, would he ever notice that they needed just a little bit of help?

'At least there is some good news today.' Amy said, lifting up the saucepan lid and poking the potatoes to see if they were cooked. 'The doctor said that if he was really good, Will could come home at the end of the week.' She turned to face him. 'Isn't that wonderful?'

Even that bit of news somehow failed to cheer him. Yes, he was immensely relieved his son would walk again and grateful they had been lucky enough to have such a gifted surgeon but how was he going to pay for it?

'Yes, sure is good news,' he agreed with a sigh. 'But how the hell are we going to pay the hospital bill?'

'For goodness sake, George, don't let's worry about that now. I'm grateful he's coming home. It's the best bit of news we've had in a long while.'

'There's still the money …'

'Something will come along.'

He frowned at her. She was always so damned optimistic. Didn't she realise it was only adding to the money they already owed? And he'd probably spend the rest of his life paying it all back.

'It's wonderful news. Come on, do cheer up.'

He knew she was right and, if he was honest, it lifted his spirits – a little.

'He can't go to school and he'll have to use crutches but at least he'll be home. Do you think you could borrow the car so we can go and collect him?'

'Borrow the car? Sure don't think Freddie'll be too keen on that, 'specially after this afternoon's little episode. He's in one hell of a temper. Maybe you'd better do the asking.'

Freddie's mood was no better the following morning and even Donnie suffered his sharp tongue, so George was relieved when he announced he was going out, leaving him the task of sorting out the registration and tax documents for the two new arrivals on the forecourt. There were "For Sale" boards to be put inside both of them.

Several telephone calls interrupted him, followed by two customers calling to collect cars. He was relieved to see the Austin owner drive off. The oil stain on the forecourt was the only evidence of his mistake and Donnie had shown him that he'd fitted the seal for the filter incorrectly, causing the leak. He supposed he'd have to apologise.

Customers queuing at the petrol pump also kept him busy and with Donnie stripping down a complete engine, it was down to him to serve them. He was taking the money from the last customer when he saw Freddie's Vauxhall appear from behind the pub. He stared in disbelief, then disgust. It was way past afternoon closing time and he knew Freddie was there for one reason only and it wasn't for a drink. He was seeing that barmaid – even when his wife was seriously ill – he was still seeing her.

He returned to the office to finish the paperwork, still wondering whether to tell Amy, when Freddie drove into the forecourt. Seconds later, he stuck his head round the door.

'Got those papers?'

'What papers?'

'Don't arse about. The papers for the Ford. Got a buyer for it.' He held his hand out and George scrabbled around on the desk, trying to locate them.

'They were here a few minutes ago.' He picked up a wad of bills, looking for the round disc which had a thick red bar across its centre. Tax discs didn't exist in Canada and he remembered examining it with interest before attaching it with a paperclip to the buff logbook.

'Don't tell me you've lost it.'

'For Christ's sake give me a chance, Freddie. I know you're doing me a huge favour employing me -'

'Damn right, I am. I must be mad. You're worse than useless.'

'At least I'm not unfaithful to my wife -'

Freddie stared at him and, for several seconds, he stared back. The silence was broken by Donnie, who came in from the workshop.

'Sorry.' He looked from one to the other. 'Am I interrupting?'

'No,' Freddie said. 'George was looking for some paperwork. Did you want something?'

'It's gone four. You did say I could finish early?'

'Er, yes.' Freddie said in a distracted way as George handed him the papers.

'I'll see you in the morning, then.'

As Donnie closed the door behind him, Freddie pulled up a chair and sat opposite George.

'Let me make this quite clear. You say a word to anyone about me – and you know exactly what I mean – you can expect your marching orders. And, even if you're married to my sister, don't think you'll be welcome in my house either.'

George stared at him for a second.

'I don't need to tell anyone, Freddie. If you're that blatant, I can't be the only one who knows.'

Freddie stood up and leant across the desk so his face was inches from his own.

'What I do is my business. Remember that.'

## Chapter Sixteen

With Sam and Jonathan back at school and Bobbie having joined them, Amy found she had some free time but that meant she had time to think and the more she thought the more despondent she became. She felt trapped looking after Enid. There seemed no end in sight and, far from having a female companion of her own age, at times it was like having an overgrown child around. But there were days when Enid was normal and she tried to console herself that the better days were more frequent.

None of this would have been so hard to endure if she had felt secure in her relationship with George but too often, he was an enigma. He was convinced she'd been unfaithful to him and it hurt. It was one thing his being sharp with her but she often found herself acting as unofficial referee between him and Freddie. Living under the same roof was putting a strain on them all. It would be easy to get as depressed as George over their predicament but she had to keep going. The boys needed her and so did George. The cost of Will's hospital treatment was a major concern. She tried to put a cheerful face on things and, even though she knew he would disapprove, she felt compelled to do something.

The following afternoon, when Doris was busy cleaning and Enid was having one of her better days and was sitting in the lounge with a book, she decided to visit her mother. It was a sunny afternoon and she enjoyed the walk, arriving in time for afternoon tea. The maid brought in a tray of dainty sandwiches and delicate cakes all served on bone china.

A cucumber sandwich was something she hadn't tasted in years and they were just the way she liked them, with a little hint of pepper. The habit of taking tea was a peculiarly English upper class habit and one in which she had never had the time to indulge when they were farming in Canada. She could already imagine what George would say – he would regard this as prissy.

She watched her mother sip her tea and tried to muster the courage to bring the conversation round to money. Will would be home tomorrow and somehow they had to pay the hospital bill.

'Amy. Amy. You've not been listening to a word I've been saying.'

'Oh, er, sorry, mother.'

'You were miles away. Whatever were you thinking about?'

'Money,' she said without hesitation. This was likely to be the best opportunity, so she plunged on. 'You see, I'm a bit worried. Actually, I'm very worried.'

'For goodness sake, child. Do stop beating about the bush.'

'We have to pay Will's hospital bill and the fact is, I don't know where we are going to find the money.'

Her mother frowned at her.

'George is being paid, isn't he? Freddie told me, it's putting an extra burden on the garage.'

'Mother, it's a pittance. Oh, I know we don't pay for our keep but the money George gets each week is hardly enough to buy Bobbie a new pair of shoes which is something I have to do this week.'

'Oh.'

There was a moment's silence whilst Amy let the information sink in. She knew from experience there was no hurrying her mother – not if she wanted a favourable decision.

'I wondered if you could … I know it's a lot to ask but is there any chance you could lend us the money.'

'Good gracious,' her mother almost choked on her tea. 'I can't believe both of you need a loan and in the same week.'

The word "both" grated but it was a second or two before Amy realised the significance of the word. George had been saying for some time the garage was in financial difficulty but she thought he'd been exaggerating.

'I'm already bankrolling you by helping Freddie. I don't believe I can do any more. No, Amy, you will have to find the money yourselves. George should ask for a pay rise.'

The fact that Freddie had asked for a loan occupied her mind, so it was several seconds before it registered her mother had refused. The unfairness struck home.

'Why is it you're always willing to help Freddie but never us?'

'But I am helping you. By helping Freddie, I'm helping all of you. And in any case, are you really suggesting I've never helped you? Amy, you are being wholly unfair and very forgetful. It wasn't only a shilling to get you all back from Canada, you know. It was a large sum of money. Then you expected to stay here without as much as a word and before you protest, I know Freddie had his reasons. I accept Enid was being very difficult at the time but none the less, it all costs money.' She paused long enough to pick up her cup and saucer before adding, 'In any case, as I see it, by injecting some money into the garage I'm making an investment in all your futures.'

'I know you've never approved of George but he is at least faithful to me.' The anger boiled over and there, the words were out. It was about time her mother knew exactly how Freddie really behaved.

Mrs Attwood stared at daughter for several seconds as though trying to assess what she really knew. So Amy went further. She wanted to make sure her mother knew all about Freddie's affair.

'Freddie is seeing that woman at the pub.'

'Yes.'

'You know.'

'Oh, it's all rumour. But, in any case, you should know by now, men are allowed to have their little dalliances.'

Amy was horrified.

'Mother, how can you ... approve of such behaviour?'

'I didn't say I approved.' She glanced up at the clock and Amy knew she was going to be dismissed. It was characteristic of her mother to conclude any conversation when she'd had enough. 'My dear girl, look at the time. Shouldn't you be going? The children will be home from school soon.'

She was still thinking about this conversation as she sat next to George in the car, on their way to the hospital. She hadn't dared to tell him she'd been to see her mother because she knew he'd be furious. Now she was dreading finding out the exact amount of money which was owed.

'Go and get Will organised. I'd better go and see the Almoner,' George said as they walked along the hospital corridor.

She wanted to go with him to learn how bad the debt was but his face was set. There was no point in suggesting it, so she left him at the office door and went on to the ward.

Will was dressed and sitting in a chair, his crutches leaning against the wall behind him.

'Can't wait to get home, Mum,' he said and she noticed he used the English pronunciation. "Mom" was being banished from his vocabulary. She was sad but didn't make any comment. He was trying to lose his accent and, if that made him happy, then so be it.

'Will mustn't put any weight on that foot. The Doctor says it needs at least another week or two of complete rest but he's very capable on the crutches now,' the nurse said. 'His next appointment,' she added and handed Amy a white card.

The nurse turned to Will. 'Now you, young man, mustn't undo all our good work. Use the crutches. No walking on that foot until the Doctor has given you permission. You understand?'

Will nodded.

'What about school?' Amy asked.

'No. Definitely not. The Doctor doesn't want any risks to be taken. It's very pioneering stuff, you know and we're all very proud of Will. Maybe in a couple of months. Better safe than sorry.'

The nurse handed Will his crutches.

'Off you go, young man. And remember, you mustn't use that foot yet.'

As they walked along the corridor, George appeared from the Almoner's office.

'Wow! Will. You are doing well,' he said after giving Amy a look which said "don't ask".

It was much later as they were in bed, that she summoned up the courage to put the question into words. He was lying on his back.

'Tell me the worst?' she asked and turned to face him.

'I can't make sense of it.'

'Is it a huge amount?' she said, dreading the answer.

'I don't know.'

'What do you mean, you don't know?' Now she was becoming impatient.

'Exactly that.'

'George?'

'Somebody, who wishes to remain anonymous, paid it.'

'What? Are you serious? Who on earth would do that?'

'I was told a rich benefactor of the hospital.'

She was silent. Could that rich benefactor be Charles? If that was the case, there would be ructions if George found out. She tried to snuggle up to him but he turned on to his side.

'Night,' she said and rubbed his back hoping for some kind of favourable reaction. She was disappointed when the reply was a grunt. She turned her back to him and spent a restless night listening to his regular breathing. A tear dropped onto the pillow. Yes, Charles, we've both made a mess of our lives …

* * * * *

Vi had been washing dirty nappies when Ma arrived and she took over the task, hanging the washing out in the back yard. The baby began to cry and Vi lifted her up, wrapping her securely in a shawl. She rocked her in her arms and went to sit at the dining room table where she had been looking through the Christmas cards. She picked up and re-read a letter, which had arrived with Amy and George's card. Harold had brought most of the cards into the hospital but her memory was vague. What a relief to know George was safe. She spotted a telephone number at the top of the page. She hadn't noticed that before. She heard Ma come in from the garden and put the kettle on. It wasn't long before she appeared with two cups of tea.

'There we are,' Ma said and sat beside her.

'Thanks.' She felt guilty Ma was doing all the work – her work – but the arrival of her latest grandchild seemed to have re-invigorated her and there was no sign of the arthritis of which she had complained in recent years.

'I've hung the washing out but we'll have to keep an eye on that weather. Now is there any shopping you want? Do you need any veg?'

'Ma, it's very sweet of you to do all this but it's time I got out and about. I've been home for nearly a week now and

I feel so much better. I want to start doing some of this for myself. What about if we go together?'

'If you're sure ...'

'Yes. Tomorrow, as soon as I've got Lily ready, I'll call round. Harold's on earlies tomorrow so there won't be any lie in. I can't wait to try out the pram. Oh, and did I tell you we've fixed a date for the Christening?'

'No. When?'

'Harold called on the Vicar yesterday evening. It's all agreed. Two o'clock, second Sunday in March. I was wondering ... Amy's letter.' She held it out for Ma to see. 'There's a telephone number. I've only just noticed. At the top. I think that must be Freddie's number. Wouldn't it be nice to invite them to the Christening?'

'Do you think they'd come?'

'Given half a chance, I'm sure Amy will. It's a long way though and it would be nice for them to stay over but it's more than my life's worth to ask Harold if they can stay here ...'

'If that's what's worrying you, I'm sure we can fit them in somewhere. Lizzie might have the boys. I'll see what I can arrange.'

'Would you? I want to try and telephone them. Maybe we could do that tomorrow?'

\* \* \* \* \*

Freddie heard the screech of brakes followed by a loud crash from where he was sitting inside the pub. He'd told George he was going for some lunch but he had every intention of making it a long one. He needed a drink but most of all he needed to share his troubles. His recent visit to the bank manager revealed how inadequate his management was and he didn't like being shown up. The pub made money and, even if running a pub was quite a different business, at least Beth would offer a sympathetic ear.

'To start with,' she told him. 'You shouldn't be in here. You should be back at the garage working. Long lunches shouldn't be a feature of your life until things are much better. There isn't any easy road – being in business is hard work and what's more, even if it's doing me out of trade, you should cut back on that.' She pointed to the pint of beer in his hand. 'At least until you're solvent again.'

He stared at her in astonishment. He'd expected empathy not criticism and condemnation. He'd had an earful from his mother and knew, just by being in the pub, he was breaking the terms of her loan. 'End the affair or no money' – that was the deal but he wasn't ready to do that – he needed Beth. How else would he cope with his life?

'Looks like the dog got off better than the cars,' a customer, sitting by the window, remarked.

'Sounds like, there's some business out there waiting for you.' Beth stood up and took his half empty glass.

'Hey!' He needed that pint to help him get through the rest of the afternoon.

'Go and see to your garage, Freddie. If things are that bad, you don't need this. Come and see me after you've closed and tell me what happened. Till then, I'll look after this. I might treat you to a fresh one if you clinch a deal.'

He left the pub and as he crossed the road, he could see there was indeed some business waiting to be done. Judging by the pool of water appearing under the Morris, it was possible the radiator had been damaged. He ambled round to where the two drivers were exchanging details – one of them was Charles.

'Think I'll need your help, Freddie,' Charles said with a grin.

He didn't smile back. Charles was the last person he wanted to assist and, if it wasn't for the lecture he'd received from Beth, he wouldn't even consider offering help now. He glanced towards the pub and there she was watching him through the window. There would be no excuses.

'Er, yes. Bit of a mess.' He nodded towards the car.

'Other chap swerved to avoid a dog. Damn nearly took me off the road in the process. Ah, well. At least it'll mend,' Charles said.

He could see Charles was shaken by the accident and, before their fall out, he wouldn't have hesitated to take him into the office. Now he dithered but Beth was watching.

'Why don't you come into the office and I'll fix some tea or something stronger if you want. We'll shift your car onto the forecourt and we can talk about a repair.' There, he'd extended the hand of friendship and, he hoped, secured some business. He looked across at the pub but Beth had left the window. He would have to tell her all about it later.

'What about the other fellow?'

The cars were blocking the road and Freddie spotted a policeman on a bicycle heading in their direction. He yelled at George and Donnie, who had joined the other lookers-on.

'Shift these cars, will you?' He pointed to the forecourt but didn't wait to see if the other man agreed. The road was blocked and he was pretty sure he'd rather have his car moved onto his forecourt than have a policeman breathing down his neck. He followed Charles into the office.

'Have a seat,' he said and pulled a chair out then he fished around in the office desk and found a hip flask.

'Needs must.' Even if Charles didn't need a drink, he did. He unscrewed the top and poured whisky into two silver cups, handing one to Charles.

'Get that inside you. You'll feel better then.'

'Bit like old times, eh, Freddie?' Charles downed his in one gulp.

Freddie wasn't sure he could agree but he gulped back his whisky and decided to talk business.

'Looks like you might need a new radiator. I can get the boys to look at it – maybe possible to repair it.'

'I'll run with that. I see you've got your brother-in-law working for you.'

'Huh. Yeah, until something better comes along.'

'You don't sound too happy about it,' Charles said.

'Between you me and the gatepost, we don't exactly get on.'

'But I thought - ? You always seemed to be good friends and didn't you give Amy away at their wedding?'

'Yes, but I never expected to have them living with me. The situation is difficult to say the least.' Freddie stopped. He'd said more than he intended.

'Ah, I get it. Living and working together.' Charles pulled a face. 'Probably not conducive to good brother-in-law relations.'

Freddie poured out more whisky. Beth was right, he did drink too much. But what the heck. Right then, he needed it.

'Not a bad place, you've got here,' Charles said. His eyes scanned the office. 'Remember how we talked about setting up together? I often regret that we didn't. Can I see the workshop?'

'Yes. We've got a Ford stripped down for a decoke. Donnie's the man for that. Come on I'll show you and while we're at it, we'll see what the boys have done with your car.'

It was over an hour later when they shut the workshop door and, as Charles said, it was a bit like old times. They both shared a passion for cars and, as long as the subject stayed on that, it was as though all animosities were forgotten.

Charles glanced at his watch.

'Guess I'd better get myself a taxi.'

'I'll run you back if you like,' Freddie said.

'That'd be good, Freddie. That'd be good.'

## Chapter Seventeen

'You'll never guess who telephoned this morning,' Amy said when George got home. She finished rolling out the pastry and rinsed her hands under the tap. She was sick of making pies but with three hungry boys and two hungry men, it was the best way of satisfying them.

'No idea. Tell me,' he said without enthusiasm.

'Vi. Isn't the telephone wonderful?' She picked up the kettle, filled it and placed it on the stove. 'She said it was the first time she'd been out since she came home from hospital. She and Ma, I think, were on their way to the market. The baby's going to be Christened and she wants us all to come.'

George sat down and proceeded to unlace his shoes.

Amy frowned at his lack of response.

'I thought you'd want to go. I said yes or at least we'll try.'

'I don't know about that. How are we going to afford it?'

'Oh, it's a Christening, for goodness sake. Nothing formal.'

'We still have to get there – all five of us. And then you'll say you have nothing to wear and then there's a Christening present.'

Amy turned back to the job of tea making. She put out three cups and spooned tea into the pot.

'Don't be so grumpy.'

'I'm being practical. Where's the money going to come from?'

As she made the tea, her mind went back to the time they were invited to their first Halloween party in Canada. George had been difficult then – prickly and gloomy. Nothing had changed and there was little point in discussing it further. His mind was made up. She placed a cup of tea in front of him and returned to the pie, filling it with the steak and kidney she'd cooked earlier.

'It's very quiet. What are the boys doing?' George said. 'I hope Will's keeping off that foot.'

'That reminds me. I've got to take him to the hospital tomorrow.' She scraped the saucepan clean and placed it in the sink, before turning to face him, rubbing her hands clean on the gingham apron she had borrowed from Enid. 'He's desperate to start walking but the muscles in that leg are very weak. Did I hear Freddie come in? I made him some tea.'

'I walked. He drove your old flame home.'

The last few words riled her but it was the tone of his voice and the unspoken inference which maddened her more. When would he understand it was him she loved?

'How do you mean – drove him home? I didn't think they were speaking and in any case I haven't seen "my old flame" as you put it since Christmas morning in church and you know perfectly well there's nothing between us.'

'Did I say there was?'

Infuriated by the words, she turned her back on him and continued working in silence. He was so unfair. Sometimes she wished they had stayed in Canada even if they were all starving. Then, at least, George was the man she'd married. He had been determined no matter what. He would have taken on the world but now he was morose and … crushed. The thought disheartened her. Would she ever find the George she loved again? And, of course, if they had stayed in Canada, the temptation of Charles would be thousands of miles away, a little voice reminded her.

'Just to let you know …' Freddie burst into the kitchen. He stopped mid-sentence when he saw their faces. 'What's the matter with you two?'

When neither of them answered, Freddie shrugged.

'Where's Enid? We're going out tonight. We're going to dinner at Home Farm,' he announced.

'Enid's in the lounge,' Amy answered. 'But I'm not sure …' She was going to add that she wasn't sure whether Enid was up to socialising but he didn't wait to hear.

'Home Farm is Charles' place. How did all this happen?' she asked George, determined not to miss out on the news. If he wouldn't tell her, then she would ask Freddie.

'I thought he lived at The Grange?'

'Not any more.'

'Of course, you'd know that.'

She ignored the insinuation, repeating her question as to how it was Freddie was socialising with Charles.

'There was an accident right outside the garage,' George said. 'One of the cars belonged to Charles.'

'Anyone hurt?'

'No. A car skidded into him trying to miss a dog. A copper came along, made a few notes and left us to it. We've got both cars for repair.'

'Good for business, then.' Amy giggled, trying to lighten their conversation.

'Yep and those two have been thick as thieves ever since.'

She stared at him and knew he was as uncomfortable about this development as she was. It could only mean one thing. They would see a lot more of Charles.

* * * * *

It had been a successful evening and Freddie longed to go and tell Beth all about it. He'd earned that pint but he would have to wait until tomorrow to claim it.

He helped Enid into the car, wrapping the blanket around her as it was quite cold.

'Nice evening, wasn't it?' He looked across at her. With Amy's help, she had chosen a deep maroon dress which suited her and he wondered if Amy was responsible for the jewellery and lipstick, not to mention the hairstyle. He had half dreaded taking her in case she had one of her outbursts. He could have gone alone but Charles was insistent. For once, Enid had joined in the conversation and there had even been a spark of her old self.

Sylvia was charming – a voluptuous, stunning blonde and he could see why Charles had fallen for her. He found her quite attractive, too but he had been careful not to flirt. He had to be on his best behaviour because Charles had invited him to discuss investing in the garage and he didn't want to risk losing that opportunity. Anything to get his mother off his back. Sylvia had been very understanding about the loss of their baby and within minutes had put Enid at ease. What an incredible day it had been with him and Charles managing to put their past disagreement behind them. In fact, he couldn't remember now exactly what it was they had fallen out over.

'Get that showroom built. Stock some new cars. That's the way forward," Charles said once Enid and Sylvia had gone into the lounge, leaving the men to linger over a smoke and some port.

Freddie reached into his pocket for his cigarettes. He offered one to Charles who pushed the silver table lighter across towards him. He lit up, took a puff and exhaled.

'It's always been in my mind to do that and I'm sure there are plenty of potential customers. Gerrards Cross is never short of money and these days, there are all those film stars. And there's money to be made servicing the cars we sell but we would need to improve the workshop facilities. An inspection pit would make a huge improvement.'

'We need to do our homework, Freddie. I'll leave you to do the research into what's likely to sell and I'll get on to my architect fellow. Get him to draw up some plans.'

Charles said he hadn't felt so upbeat in years and, he thought, as they drove home, neither had he.

'You looked wonderful tonight, darling,' he said.

'Did I?' She sounded surprised and he realised it was a very long time since he'd paid her a compliment and even longer since they had been out together as man and wife. His mother would be very pleased they were keeping up appearances.

It was almost a week later before Charles arrived to collect his car.

'I've got some sketches for you,' he said.

Freddie closed the office door behind him and removed a box of spark plugs onto a nearby chair. Charles placed two foolscap pages of sketches on the desk.

'These are some of my ideas. Take a good look and tell me what you think. I'd like to get on with this as soon as we can. I think we should go to the Motor Show – meet the manufacturers – see what sort of deal we can strike. What do you say?'

'That's a good idea. Olympia, isn't it?'

'You think it's a good plan then?'

'I think we should drink to success,' Freddie said and reached for his hip flask. He shook it. 'Damn. It's empty.'

'Why don't we discuss this over some lunch? We need to think about setting up a partnership. Look, let me settle for the repairs to my Morris and then I'll stand you a drink in the pub.'

'Deal,' Freddie said and thought Beth would be surprised to see him with a business partner.

Lunch consisted of a sandwich and a beer. They sat at a corner table, discussing their ideas and Freddie caught Beth's look of approval on several occasions.

'I'll set up a meeting with my solicitor. Then we'll be official,' Charles said.

'You've covered everything and solved all my problems,' he said with a smile – except two, he thought.

There were two complications in his life and he felt powerless to do anything about them. The prospects for the garage might have improved but there was precious little he could do about his private life. Maybe he and Enid might come to some arrangement which satisfied them both but what on earth was he going to do about George? He wanted his home back. Having his sister had been a godsend when Enid was really ill, but now it was slowly driving him mad. No wonder he'd taken to drink.

Charles grinned at him.

'Glad to be of service. You know we were fools, you and I. We should have done this years ago.' He held his glass up. 'Let's drink to the success of our new venture.'

'Cheers.'

\* \* \* \* \*

Amy was cleaning the oven. Beside her was a bucket of hot water mixed with Borax. Since she had taken over the daily preparation of meals, the cooker had seen much more use and she felt guilty about the state of it. She could have asked Doris to do it but Freddie had cut her hours, saying it would do Enid good to try to do some of the jobs around the house. She had to agree but, in practice, this never happened. She didn't hear the knock at the front door and was scouring the bottom of the oven when the kitchen door opened.

'Visitor for you,' Enid said.

She leant back on her knees and looked up at her sister-in-law who recently had taken to treating her much like Doris. It rankled a bit – no a lot. She felt like an unpaid skivvy. Enid was wearing an expensive silk blouse and the toning cardigan looked equally lavish. These days she spent most of her time reading what she described as cultured novels and when the boys returned from school, she would go to bed, saying there was too much noise that she was tired and needed a rest.

'I only want a quick word with Amy.'

She recognized the voice. Oh, my Lord. Her first thought was how did she look with her hair all tied up in a scarf and in her scruffiest clothes but then she wondered what George would have to say when he heard Charles had called to see her.

Before she could say anything, the door opened wider and Charles came into the room.

'Charles, what are you doing here?' she said still holding a cloth in her hand.

'I came to see you but – what are you doing?'

She dropped the cloth in the bucket and pulled the scarf off her head, hoping she hadn't got dirt on her face.

'What does it look like I'm doing?' She laughed. 'Don't look so horrified. I'm not afraid of getting my hands dirty.'

'I – er – you never cease to surprise me.'

She went to the sink to rinse her hands.

'You called for a reason?' she said over her shoulder.

'Do I need one to call on my favourite girl?'

'Shshsh. Please don't say that,' she said, shaking the water off her hands before reaching for the towel.

When she turned round, he gave her a long, meaningful look – a look which made her anxious. She had a feeling Enid was listening and decided that whatever it was Charles wanted, he should say it in front of her but, more importantly, she had to get him out of the house before George got home.

'As a matter of fact, I have a very good reason to want to see you.' He came right into the kitchen and stood only a few feet away from her. 'Oh, I do wish I could take you away from all of this.'

'You make me feel like Cinderella,' she said with a laugh.

'It makes me feel so sad to see you like this. You deserve better. I wish – '

'Why don't you go into the lounge,' she said, cutting across him. She didn't want to hear whatever it was he was going to say and certainly not with an eavesdropper. 'Go and see Enid, while I make some tea,' she suggested. It would be much safer than being alone with him. Enid was bound to make some dramatic announcement about their visitor over dinner and she could guarantee George would choose to misunderstand. She could see the scene and the minute

Charles' name was mentioned, George would become irrational and angry.

'I came to tell you about an opportunity George might be interested in. I've was visiting an old friend. Of course, I did think of going to the garage but I know what his response will be. He won't allow himself to be interested on principle. He probably won't listen to what I have to say, though, now I'm going to be a partner in the business, he'll have to start getting used to that.'

'Partner?' That was news to her. So that was why Freddie was anxious Enid should look the glamorous wife when they went to dinner at Home Farm. She was the one who had helped Enid dress. She'd even spent some time doing her hair – not that she got much thanks for any of that. Now she felt left out. Freddie hadn't said a word and nor had George. She really was beginning to feel like Cinderella. 'When did all this happen? I knew you must have sorted your disagreement out but a partnership?'

'We've put all our disagreements behind us and I think we'll do very well together.'

Over tea in the lounge, Charles explained that a friend of his had sacked his driver and was looking for a chauffeur.

'What made you think of George?' Amy wanted to know.

'Oh, something Freddie said. I got the impression this isn't the ideal situation for you all.'

'You're quite right, Charles. Amy has been wonderful while I've been sick but I think she needs a place of her own, don't you Amy, dear?' Enid said in her sweetest voice.

She was silent. She wanted to hurl something sarcastic and insulting back at Enid but, for the life of her, couldn't think what. Why was it she could only think of the appropriate reply long after the event?

'And there's a house?' she asked, checking she'd heard right.

'Just outside Chesham. Not too far away,' Charles said.

'That's exactly what they need,' Enid said.

Enid's voice had an edge to it but Amy knew it would be better for them all. If only George would agree.

'It's down to George, of course,' she said.

\* \* \* \* \*

'Freddie tells me, Charles has organised an interview for next week, is that right?' Amy said as she got ready for bed a few nights later.

'I'm not going.' George half grunted.

She stared at him in disbelief.

'Why ever not? It's a perfect opportunity. For goodness sake, I thought you were desperate to leave the garage and not only that, we'll have a place of our own.' She couldn't understand him. It wasn't often a second opportunity came along. Surely he didn't intend turning it down?

'If Charles is involved, I want nothing to do with it.' George turned onto his side.

She turned the light off and climbed into bed.

'Hmm. I can't believe you. You missed out on that last job because of your stubbornness. As your mother would say, you're cutting off your nose to spite your face. And, if it's because of me, for the hundredth time there is absolutely nothing between Charles and me.'

George didn't answer and she yanked the covers up in irritation.

'Has it never occurred to you that he could be doing it for Freddie? Now Enid is so much better, don't you think he'd like us out of his house just as much as we want to leave?'

She turned on her side and knew her anger would keep her awake for the rest of the night.

## Chapter Eighteen

'They're here.' Vi stood at the window with Lily, who was asleep, in her arms. She watched the car pull up outside the house. 'And if that's Freddie's car, he isn't short of a bob or two.'

Harold's reply was a grunt. He was reading the previous day's Daily Sketch and didn't bother looking up.

'Please don't say anything about the gas money,' she pleaded. 'I don't want anything to spoil Lily's Christening.' When he didn't answer, she said a mental prayer that he wouldn't ruin the day. Only yesterday, they had had a very heated argument and she knew Harold was still convinced George had taken the money.

'Who else would have taken it? How else could he afford to go to the pub? And how did he pay for his journey home? He had every opportunity and as far as I can see, there is no one else.'

'In case you've forgotten, Ma gave him some money,' she'd retaliated but Harold got more irate and banged his fist on the table. Lily had screamed and she had crept into the kitchen. He hadn't only frightened Lily. She had to face the fact that Harold was never going to get on with George and today was going to be difficult.

She went into the dining room and put the sleeping baby in her pram, tucking her in with a blanket before adding the white satin quilt Lizzie had given her. She couldn't resist a quick check of the table – the third time in half an hour. The sandwiches she had made earlier were covered in a tea cloth to prevent them drying out and she had got their best china out. Everything was ready.

The knock at the door made her scurry down the passageway and fling open the front door.

'It's so good to see you,' Vi said and threw her arms around Amy. 'I'm so pleased you made it.'

She still couldn't believe they were here. After all these years, Amy and George were both here. She had spoken to Amy on the telephone the previous day but she had said there was a possibility Freddie wouldn't lend them the car or, even worse, George would refuse to drive. The pips had interrupted their conversation twice before her money had run out and she knew she would have to wait until today to see if they would come.

'Come in. Come in.'

'You do look lovely, Vi,' Amy said. 'That pink suits you and so, it seems, does motherhood.'

Vi laughed and thought time hadn't been so kind to Amy. She could see a few grey hairs sprouting from the crown of her head and she was so thin.

'I – er – we thought it'd never happen and we are so lucky to have Lily.' She stared at the three boys, anxious Will would manage the step into the hall on his crutches. 'And I can't get over the size of the boys.'

She went to give Sam a hug but he shrunk back.

'Boys don't do hugs.' Amy laughed. 'Or at least not at that age.'

She was relieved to see Harold making some effort. He had taken charge of Will, and, having realised it would be easier for him to sit in a higher chair, brought one in from the dining room. He took Will's crutches and leant them against the wall beside the fireplace.

'How's Will?' Vi asked in a low voice as she took Amy's coat from her and hung it on one of the hooks in the hall. 'How much longer is he going to be on crutches?'

'Until he's stronger, I suppose but he's doing really well – manages a bit without his crutches but his leg aches and the muscles are very wasted. We are so relieved and thankful he's going to make a full recovery.'

'Yes, I think we all are.' Vi turned to George who had appeared in the hall carrying a bunch of flowers. 'So brother, here you are and am I pleased to see you. We were all very worried when you disappeared.'

George's face expressed his remorse and he handed the flowers to Vi, who gave him a hug.

'I guess I ought to apologise …' he began.

'Shshsh. You're not to worry about it. Not another word,' Vi said. 'Oh, come here.' She gave him another hug. 'It's so good to see you all. Now come on into the front room and I'll get the kettle on.'

'Harold,' she said when he failed to greet their guests. There was sharpness in her voice and he gave her a resentful look.

'George.' He held his hand out.

George shook it and there was an uneasy silence.

'Come on, none of this formality. Sit down everyone and I'll make some tea,' Vi said. Amy followed her out of the room.

'This is a lovely house. I wish we had somewhere like this,' Amy said. She stopped by the pram and pulled down the covers a little, so she could admire the baby.

'Ah, she's gorgeous and you both must be very proud.'

Vi grinned.

'I think George is envious. He wanted a daughter but every time they turned out to be boys.'

'Have another one,' Vi said.

'Three's enough. Anyway, we're struggling as it is. I don't think a fourth child would exactly help.'

Vi hesitated to comment. She wanted to be sympathetic but she didn't want to discuss the fact that George had come first to London, thereby losing a job. Amy might accuse her of making him feel too comfortable – that is until Harold and he almost came to blows. It was safer to change the subject.

'Did you have a good journey?' She lit the gas under the kettle. 'And I'm so glad Freddie let you have the car. Do you think George would take me out for a ride. I've never been out in a motor car and it looks such fun.'

'I'm not sure about that.' Amy pushed the door to. 'George is being a bit difficult,' she said in a half whisper. 'In fact I wasn't sure we were going to come at all. It was very much last minute. Now Enid's feeling better, she can be quite poisonous at times and Freddie said she wanted him to take her over to her parents'.'

'Whatever do you mean - poisonous?'

'Makes it plain we're living in her house and I emphasise her house and that attitude extends pretty much to the car, too. Just lately, she's made my life a misery. I know she didn't want us living with them in the first place but it was she who was the one who was ill and it was she who needed me to look after her.'

'Not much gratitude then?'

Amy laughed.

'In a way, I can understand why she's making life so difficult. You see, there's the possibility of a job for George but he's refused point blank to have anything to do with it.'

'What? But why?' Vi placed cups and saucers onto a tray. 'I don't understand I wouldn't have thought he could be choosy.'

Amy didn't answer and Vi stopped what she was doing and stared at Amy.

'Is there something wrong with this job?'

Amy pulled a face.

'It was Charles who told us – me about it.'

'Charles?' Vi took a moment to think why the name should be familiar. Then it all came tumbling back. 'Not the Charles?'

Amy nodded.

'I see.' She paused for a moment's reflection and thought about George's stubborn behaviour. 'My brother's a proud man but sometimes that pride gets in the way of doing the sensible thing …'

'Like going to my mother's. If he'd not rushed off here, then we might not be in this mess now.' Amy sighed. 'I'm at my wits end. There's a house with the job and it's over Chesham way and miles from Charles but he won't even discuss it.'

'There's nothing between you and this Charles, is there?' Vi couldn't help ask the question, then horrified, apologised. She had never ever doubted Amy's love for George before.

'There's nothing to apologise for but you're not the only one who has their suspicions …'

'George?'

Amy nodded.

There was a gurgling sound and Amy went across to the pram.

'But we're here for a Christening and I haven't caught more than a glimpse of the baby yet.' She pulled back the covers. 'Say I can pick her up?'

'Of course you can.'

The kettle was boiling and Vi poured the water into the tea pot and covered it with the cosy. Why was life so complicated? Even her own life was complex – or at least Harold was. Before Lily's arrival everything had been so wonderful – so straightforward. Now each day was filled with problems.

After a lunch of corn beef sandwiches and pickles with homemade fruit cake to finish, Amy cleared the table while Vi changed Lily and dressed her in the Christening dress which Ma had specially washed and ironed.

'Doesn't she look gorgeous?' Vi held the baby up for everyone to see.

There was a murmuring of approval and Vi went off to get herself ready before they all walked the short distance to the church for the two o'clock service. The rest of the family were there already and Vi watched as they all greeted George and Amy and marvelled at the size of their three boys. She put her arm through Harold's, aware there was no one from his side of the family present.

Lily was asleep and only stirred a little when the Vicar made the mark of a cross with the cold water from the font on her forehead. Soon they were all crowding into Ma's house to enjoy the tea she and Lizzie had prepared.

'No job yet then, George?' Ma asked.

'Amy tells me there's the possibility of one and it's got a house,' Vi said and realised her mistake by the look of thunder which crossed George's face.

'I'm sure George can speak for himself,' Ma said in a stern voice. 'George?'

'There is, Ma but it isn't suitable,' George replied.

'Suitable? I shouldn't think you're in any position to be fussy,' Ma said.

'I have a job, Ma and we've got a roof over our head and there's nothing else to be said.'

At that point and much to Vi's relief, Lily decided to strike up in her hungry voice and she went to sort out nappies and a bottle. Amy followed her into the scullery.

'You tread dangerous ground,' Amy said.

Vi tested the milk on the inside of her wrist before she replied.

'Someone has to say something and if Ma isn't seeing the whole picture, then I am and I'm going to give George a jolly good talking to. It's about time he shook himself out of this mood. It hangs over him like a black cloud.'

'You've noticed?'

'He lived here for several weeks, Amy. How couldn't I not notice? Somebody needs to knock some sense into him and I can see that he's not listening to you. How can he be so stupid as to think you were … well, seeing this Charles.'

'Do be careful. I don't want things made any worse and, in any case, he'll accuse me of asking you to talk to him.'

'Don't you worry. I'll make sure I put him straight on that while I'm about it. Now, how about you feed Lily? I'm going to get George to go back to the house with me and collect his belongings. Remember he left a few things when he did his disappearing act. I think he still owes me an explanation even if I don't want an apology.'

\* \* \* \* \*

'Damn it,' George said shoving a few clothes into an old holdall. 'It's none of your business and if Amy thinks she can get you to persuade me, then she sure is wrong. I won't take the job.'

'Don't be so obstinate. This is your second opportunity, so don't waste it. You might not get another chance and in any case, I don't understand why you're so dead set against it. And, before you say a word, Amy was completely against me speaking to you. Somebody has to talk some sense into that head of yours.'

'I don't want in any way to be in debt to that man.'

'What makes you think you would be.'

George stopped what he was doing.

'I'm already in debt to him, damn it. Who do you think paid for Will's hospital treatment?'

Vi stared at him in astonishment.

'What ..? But … Are you sure?'

'Oh, Amy thinks I'm stupid but I know she's been seeing him. She also thinks I don't know who paid the hospital bill. It wasn't just any rich benefactor. It was Charles bloody Ashby.'

'But are you sure?'

'The Almoner didn't say as much but I'm not stupid. In any case, I read it in the notes.' He laughed. 'Had a bit of practise reading things upside down.'

'Look, I am certain Amy doesn't know that,' Vi said after a moment's pause. 'And, what's more, I am equally certain she is not "seeing him" as you put it.'

'What would you know about it?'

'Amy told me about your accusations. For God's sake, George, can't you see what you're doing? You are doing your best to drive her to him and I, for one, wouldn't blame her for going, the way you're behaving.'

It was George's turn to stare at her.

'Yes, even if you can't see it, I can. You've had this black mood for months and she's borne the brunt of it. She's the one who's had to cope with her brother's stupid, mad wife, who, I now understand, is well enough to make her life hell and she's the one who has taken care of Will and the boys. You don't deserve her, George.'

He pushed the rest of his belongings into his bag in silence.

'I'll drive you back,' he said when he'd finished. 'Then we'll get on the road home. Amy said you wanted a ride, so here's your chance.'

'I thought you were a man who believed in providing for his family? By that I mean putting a roof over their heads – not your brother-in-law's.'

'That's enough, Vi. You've said enough.'

She followed him to the door and knew she'd failed in her task. Poor Amy. Things were not going to improve just yet.

'Come on or you can walk.' George held the door for her and she grabbed her handbag.

\* \* \* \* \*

'It's been wonderful seeing you all and such a pity you couldn't stay the night,' Vi said as she followed Amy and the boys out of Ma's house.

'Judging by the black look I got, it's probably for the best. I guess George hasn't been persuaded?'

'No, sorry. I tried. I hope I haven't made things worse. I did tell him a few home truths and I did say you didn't want me to talk to him. Oh, Amy, I do hope it all works out for you both soon.'

Amy bit her lip and Vi could see tears appearing in her eyes. They hugged and she watched as Amy climbed into the front of the car beside George then she turned and went back to join the rest of the family.

\* \* \* \* \*

George didn't talk much on the drive home. It was dark and he concentrated on the road. But he did do a lot of thinking. Some of what Vi said hit home. It was true he had been depressed and, if he was honest, he had been difficult but had he been completely unreasonable and was he pushing Amy into Charles' arms? And was he being foolish turning down this job? The truth was he didn't want to owe anyone anything and especially not Amy's former fiancé. He'd racked up a debt to his mother-in-law for their fare home. Now there was a bill for Will's hospital treatment and he resented Charles' interference. When he had walked into the Almoner's office, he had been confident he would come to some arrangement whereby he could have paid it in instalments but the matter had been taken out of his hands.

Despite the fact the wages he earned at the garage were a pittance and that there was no way he was going to ask Freddie for a rise, when it came to the job Charles had dangled in front of Amy, his pride always got in the way. Why hadn't Charles asked to see him at the garage? He had been in the office with Freddie on several occasions. No, it was an excuse for the man to call and see her.

His mind churned over and over. He glanced at Amy, thinking she was asleep but she was staring straight ahead. He wanted to reach out to her – to talk to her but somehow Charles was always in the way.

\* \* \* \* \*

'It's most unfair of you letting George have the car,' Enid said over breakfast. She glared at Freddie. 'I wanted to go to my mother's.'

Freddie looked up from the Sunday paper. He was reading an article on Edgar Wallace who had died recently and it took a second for Enid's remarks to sink in. He detested her petulant tone and he was becoming increasingly exasperated by the way she treated his sister. It was as if she was jealous but, for the life of him, he couldn't understand why.

'It was a Christening, for goodness sake. They don't happen every week and we can go and visit your mother tomorrow, if you like, when I get back from the garage.'

'Hmm.' Enid began to load up a tray with dirty plates and cutlery. 'I do think it's about time we had our house to ourselves. I am completely better, you know. There's no need for Amy to be here. I don't feel I'm in charge of my own household with her always in the kitchen. I'd like to get back to normal.'

Freddie's eyebrows rose at this. Enid must be jealous of Amy's cooking abilities. Previously, she had never spent more time than she needed in the kitchen. It was true, Amy had surprised him with repertoire of pies and stews as he knew she hadn't learnt to cook before she got married. He'd miss her appetising food when she and George moved out. Yet, much as he wanted his home and life back to normal, he wasn't convinced Enid had fully recovered. May be it was as well George refused to go for that job. He went back to his paper.

'It's all very well for you. You're not here all day. I'm the one who has to put up with her. She's always into this or that. You have no idea. There's never any privacy. Then all hell's let loose when the boys get home after school. And I can't tell you how nice it is not to have Will here today. The fights are horrendous.'

He wanted to say that their son was probably partly responsible for quite a few of the quarrels. Since Will had been out of hospital, Jonathan and he were forever arguing but all-out war had so far been avoided, though he'd caught Will being a bit too handy with his crutches on a couple of occasions. He folded the paper and placed it on the table.

He had lent George the car in the hope they would have a peaceful Sunday – just the three of them but it was going to be difficult with Enid in this frame of mind.

'It's not wonderful for me either.' He tried to reason with her even though he knew he would be wasting his time. 'You forget I work with George all day and it'd be really nice to come home and find it was only us. But Amy is my sister and, in spite of what I might say about George, I would never see her out on the street and you shouldn't forget that it's thanks to Amy, you are home and not in a mental institution.'

Enid dumped the plates into the sink with a louder than necessary clatter.

'She could go back to your mother's,' she said.

There are a lot of things they could do, he thought and it was true that if George wasn't so damn stubborn and went for that interview, then things might improve for them all. He'd hoped Amy would talk him round but he wasn't sure if they were talking about anything these days. There was always an atmosphere whenever he walked in on their conversations and he was choked off with George crawling about the place with a long face. Let's hope visiting his family would at least cheer them both up.

'Why don't we all go out for a walk?' He gave up reading the newspaper and tidied it up before re-folding it. 'The sun's out. It'd do you good to get some fresh air.'

'A walk? Some fresh air? Is that the only solution you've got on offer? And what if I don't want to go for a walk?' She began rinsing the dishes and piling them onto the wooden draining board. 'In any case we never have the chance to talk these days.'

'There's nothing stopping us talking while we walk.'

She pulled a face.

'If you don't want to go for a walk, then I'll go on my own. I might even go for a pint.'

'That's right. Go and see your lady friend. I'm not stupid. Don't think I don't know what goes on as does everyone else.' She stood with her hands on her hips, glaring at him.

He stared back. Beth was not in his thoughts but with Enid in her current frame of mind, the pub did offer more than one attraction.

'Coming for this walk?' He tried to overlook her remarks and sound conciliatory.

Enid turned her back on him so he went into the hall and found his overcoat. As he picked it up, he realised there was a roll of papers sticking out of the pocket. The sketches for the garage. He'd forgotten about those. He'd brought them home to show Enid and to see if they could be improved in any way before Charles got them drawn up properly by his architect. Now he'd show them to Beth and claim that pint.

\* \* \* \* \*

'I think I earned this,' Freddie said and took a large gulp of beer. 'By golly that's good. I've been on the wagon for twenty four hours. Enid's fault, of course.'

Beth raised her eyebrows.

'Maybe Enid is making you be sensible. You drink far too much but,' she pointed to the sketches, 'But, for once, I think you've earned it.'

'You like the design?'

'This Charles is a bit of an artist, isn't he? Yes. I think I can live with the view. Remember I'll be looking at this when I look out of the pub windows.'

'Good. I'm glad you approve. Now I can't wait for it all to happen.'

'It's good to see you cheerful and think what you'd have missed if you hadn't gone out looking for business that day.'

'You were right and thank you. When all this is over and my mother's no longer involved with the garage, I want to marry you.'

'Shshsh, Freddie,' Beth said hoping no one overheard. 'Divorce is not something to contemplate.'

'I want you as my wife and I'll do whatever it takes.'

Beth was silent for a moment.

'Divorce is considered a disgrace, Freddie,' she said eventually. 'You should think carefully before embarking on that. And, if it's me you're thinking of, then I should tell you I am happy as I am.'

She went to pour pints for waiting customers, leaving Freddie staring after her in disbelief.

## Chapter Nineteen

## May 1933

'Here she comes,' Amy said to Bobbie who was sitting astride George's shoulders.

'Wow! Oh, she looks like a bride,' Bobbie said. For a second Amy puzzled over how he knew about brides, then realised they had looked at some of Phoebe's wedding photos when they were last at Ma's.

'She's the May Queen,' she laughed.

It was George who suggested they all go to watch the May Day parade and it was the first time they had all gone out as a family since the Christening. How she had hoped that, by now, things might have improved but there was no prospect of any job or of moving out of Freddie's house. She consoled herself that, at least, George's mood had lifted in the last month. Looking back, it seemed this change followed their visit to London. Maybe it was something Vi said, though whatever it was, it hadn't made George changed his mind about that job.

The boys were so excited at the prospect of the funfair and even more about the fireworks later in the evening that they had arrived far too early. Their patience was rewarded by being at the front of the large crowd.

The May Queen, dressed in white, was sitting aloft on a make-shift throne, tied with ropes onto an old cart and disguised with a green tarpaulin which was covered with a profusion of handmade paper flowers. It was pulled by young lads who were wearing their school uniform trousers and white shirts. Following were her maids, also dressed in white, each carrying a basket of paper flowers or a large hoop decorated with pink ribbons and white crepe paper blossoms. The procession made its way to the common where she was to be crowned.

Amy wished she'd worn more sensible shoes for her feet already ached from the long wait but she could forgive the boys. They hadn't seen anything like it in their lives. Before they set off, Freddie gave each of the children sixpence, a fortune, she thought. He and Enid together with Jonathan planned to follow later. Excited children were darting about, trying to get the best view and she craned her neck but she couldn't spot her brother amongst the throng.

'I'm so glad the rain held off,' she said to George.

The dark clouds which had been a feature of the weather for the past few days had been replaced by less threatening ones. It was dull and not too warm but it was better than getting wet.

The crowning of the May Queen was followed by dancing about the Maypole. Brightly coloured ribbons attached to the top of the pole were held by the girls as they danced round and round until they formed a pretty pattern all the way down the pole. Then they danced back, unravelling them all.

'Can't we go to the fair?' Sam had already lost interest.

'It won't be open yet,' Amy said.

It wasn't long before Will and Bobbie wanted to do the same.

'I'll take them,' George said. 'You stay, if you like.'

'Where will I find you?'

'At the Big Wheel. Bobbie's desperate to get on that but I think he might be a bit of a coward when it comes to it.' He laughed and she realised it was a long time since she'd heard him do that.

'He doesn't have any fear – yet. I haven't seen Maypole dancing for years. Do you mind if I stay for another five minutes?'

'Of course not.'

'I'll meet you at the Big Wheel but please don't expect me to go on it.'

She watched the boys jumping about George in excitement. It was so good to see Will joining in the fun. The crutches were a thing of the past and he would be returning to school very soon. She turned back to watch the dancing and was soon engrossed in the complicated pattern the girls were making with the ribbons and didn't pay much attention to the movement of people around her.

'I wondered if you'd come.'

It was a second before it registered who was speaking.

'Hello, Charles.' She turned to face him. 'Have you brought your family, too?'

'Don't be silly. Sylvia would never be seen dead here.'

'Really?' she said in surprise. This Sylvia must be more sophisticated than herself or maybe more snobbish. The May Day celebrations were one of the highlights of the village year – fancy missing all the fun. 'It would have been nice to meet them.'

'Another time. You're on your own?'

'No. No, I'm not. George and the boys have gone to see the Big Wheel but I don't think they'll be brave enough to have a go. I haven't seen this sort of thing for years.' She indicated the dancers. 'I wanted to watch for a little longer.'

'They're very good.'

'They must have practised a lot,' Amy agreed. His proximity made her feel uncomfortable. 'But I have to find the boys now.'

'Don't hurry away.' He sounded disappointed. 'It isn't often I get a chance to spend some time with my favourite girl.'

'You mustn't say that.'

'As far as I know, there isn't a law stopping me and, in any case, I can't help it.' He caught hold of her hand. 'It was easier when you were in Canada ...'

She glanced up at him before withdrawing her hand.

'Please ... I don't want you to think ...' This was so dangerous. She needed to get away and she needed to make it clear that she had no intention of ever getting involved with him. 'I love George and I will never be unfaithful to him. You should know that.'

'Remember when I held you in my arms that day – I thought –'

'There was nothing to think,' she said too quickly.

'When you change your mind, I'll be waiting.'

'Charles,' she said as gently as she could. 'I will never leave George, no matter what. Please, you must accept that.'

He was quiet for a moment.

'We could have been so good together –you and I. You want me, you know you do. I've seen it in your eyes, so please don't pretend otherwise.'

She was speechless. Had her thoughts, her temptations been that obvious? And if so, what of George? No wonder he got so angry whenever Charles was near.

'You know in a week's time, I'll be one of the directors of this new company Freddie and I are forming. When the showrooms are built, I'll be running the office, leaving Freddie to what he's good at - sales. George's job could be on a much more secure footing with better wages but it's all in your hands, Amy. You could make life so much more pleasant for George if you really wanted.'

She listened, aghast at what he was implying. A memory of the conversation she'd overhead between him and Martha all those years ago flashed into her mind. Her decision to break their engagement had been right. He would never have been faithful. He hadn't changed at all.

He gripped her arm.

'You know you need me as much as I need you ...'

The girls finished their dance and there was loud applause. She watched, without seeing, as they skipped off in single file. She didn't want to believe what was happening.

'Let go, you're hurting.'

'Am I?' His grasp relaxed but his hold was still firm. 'I've tried so hard to put things right – to make things better for you. You have to believe me. That job. George was a fool.'

She was silent.

'And who do you think settled Will's hospital bill, Amy?'

The words stabbed her like a knife in the stomach.

'You?' She spat at him. 'What gave you the right?'

For a second he was taken aback and let go of her arm.

'I thought you'd be grateful ...'

The words turned the knife. She didn't want to feel grateful – not to anyone. All she wanted – George and she wanted – was a chance to stand on their own feet. Oh, God. Did George know about the hospital fees? Was that the reason for his difficult behaviour? He was never one for sharing his feelings. If only he would talk. If only.

'We could have managed,' she said. 'I have to go. Please excuse me.'

'I'll be waiting ...' His tone was menacing.

She almost ran towards the Big Will, half expecting him to follow, not daring to look round. Today was the first time George had climbed right out of his miserable mood. At last there was a glimmer of hope – a possibility he was recovering from the deep depression which had engulfed him since they had left the farm. She had no intention of extinguishing it.

They were standing in the queue for the Big Wheel and she slipped her hand into George's. He grinned at her.

'Come on. Be brave. We're all going on it.'

'Yes, Mum,' Will said, putting his arm through hers. 'And you have to come, too.'

## Chapter Twenty

When Vi's letter arrived asking Amy and the boys to come to stay for the weekend over Whitsun, she didn't think George would agree to them going and, even if George could be persuaded, she was sure they could never ever afford the fares.

She needed to get away – away from Charles. The previous week had been a nightmare. She was living on a knife edge, terrified Charles would confront George and equally terrified George would guess Charles' intentions. Two evenings running, Charles had appeared, allegedly with paperwork and the moment he arrived, George vanished upstairs and she would have followed but her brother always stopped her.

'Sis, please can you keep Enid off my back,' Freddie whispered in her ear. 'Charles and I need some peace and quiet.'

'What do you want me to do?' She couldn't imagine how exactly she was to keep Enid occupied.

'Oh, get her to discuss decorating our bedroom or something.'

She had hoped they would go into the dining room and was annoyed when she realised this was not their intention.

Freddie pulled the two armchairs closer together, leaving her no option but to sit with Enid on the settee. Whenever Freddie left the room to fetch something or to fix a whisky, Charles would try to strike up a conversation. She let Enid answer, keeping her eyes on her lap. Enid was bound to make her life even more difficult if she so much as suspected what was going on. But there was nothing going on, she told herself. Nothing at all. If only she could make Charles see that.

At about nine o'clock, she'd had enough. Freddie would have to manage Enid himself.

'It's been a long day,' she said to no one in particular. 'Good night all.' She closed the door behind her.

'Well?' George demanded as soon as she entered their bedroom. He was reading a book, propped up in bed.

'Well, what?' she said, knowing perfectly well what he wanted to know.

'Don't be so difficult. You know exactly what I mean.'

'If you want to know what they were discussing, you shouldn't have scuttled off. It was most unsociable of you.'

'You know I can't stand that man and I didn't scuttle off, as you put it. Isn't it bad enough me having to put up with him at work all day?'

For a second, she wondered how much better George's life would be if she allowed Charles to make love to her. She shut her mind to the thought.

'If you must know, there isn't much to tell. Freddie might have to go to London and they're going to start building very soon, I think.'

She started to undress. She felt so weary.

'Why would Freddie go to London?' George shut his book.

'Oh, I don't know,' she said in irritation and pulled her nightdress over her head. 'Something to do with new cars, I think.'

'I didn't miss much, then.'

'No, probably not.' She refrained from repeating that if he was interested, he should have stayed downstairs and climbed into bed.

'George, did you give any more thought to me going to stay with Vi?'

'We can't afford it.' He placed his book on the bedside cabinet and slid down under the covers.

'I've had an idea. What if Freddie took me and the boys when he went up to London? There'll be room in the car.'

'That's supposing he's going on his own.' He was lying on his back.

'I think that's the intention. Do say we can go. It would be like a mini holiday and I do so need a break from Enid's constant sniping. I feel like her slave these days.'

George didn't answer and when she looked he was asleep, leaving her wide awake. She plumped the pillow up and tried to get comfortable. She felt so mixed up. A sudden and incredible yearning for their life in Canada hit her with extraordinary force. There, life had been simpler and, although they hadn't been trouble-free times, whatever the difficulties, they got through them – together. If this was how George felt, no wonder he despaired. It was easy to look back and think it was all wonderful, but in truth Mother Nature had deemed otherwise. Now, while they weren't hungry and they had a roof over their head, nothing about her life was simple or satisfactory. She sighed. Whatever made her think things would be easier in England?

\* \* \* \* \*

With Amy in London, George found himself alone. It would have been nice to have gone with them but that would have meant losing the extra money he earned for working on a Saturday. Freddie had taken Jonathan and Enid to her mother's for lunch and for the first time since he'd left Canada, all he could hear was silence. No boys squabbling, no Enid complaining, no Freddie burying his head in the newspaper whenever there was trouble or getting angry when Enid was being unreasonable but, more disturbingly, no Amy.

His Sunday was usually occupied with the boys. Often they would all go out for a walk or take a ball and kick it about. 'To get out of Freddie's hair,' as Amy would say. He could concur with that. How he wished he could permanently get out of 'Freddie's hair'. If only he could find some other employment but the trouble was, any jobs on offer came with a wage insufficient to cover the cost of housing them all. Maybe he shouldn't have been so pig-headed about the position Charles had found but he detested the man and everything he stood for. It was insufferable enough being financially indebted to him and he couldn't bear to think of him with Amy.

All these thoughts occupied his mind as he wandered around the house. He looked out of the kitchen window, then the lounge and then he ambled up the stairs. He stood in the doorway of the boys' bedroom. There wasn't much space for the three of them but at least Jonathan had his own room. There would be even more squabbles and fights if he hadn't.

Going into his and Amy's room, he found his outdoor boots. He would go for that walk.

The sun was high in the sky, birds were busy feeding their young and the leaves on the trees were out but still retained their fresh green look. His walk took him down to the river which swirled by, swollen by the recent heavy rain. How could he feel depressed on a day such as this? It felt good to be alive and he felt invigorated by the wildlife about him yet he couldn't help but compare the scene with what he'd left in Canada. The countryside was so much … smaller, intimate with the Chiltern Hills folding and twisting about him as he followed the tiny lane into the valley. It was so green, too, whilst the prairie had been immense and either white in winter or, in summer, when the crop was up, golden, though, when they had left there had been nothing but black dust and sand. He shut his mind to that, preferring to remember the huge skies and an intense blue with amazing light. You could see for miles and in some places it was as though the track sloped off the curvature of the earth. The silence was extraordinary. Yes, it was quiet here but there was always the squawk or tweet of some bird such was the proximity of trees. In the prairies, where everything was big, a man really did feel small and insignificant – really did appreciate that Great Spirit which the Indians worshipped. He supposed the only place he would find the same peace would be in a church and he resolved to visit the little one he had just passed on his way home.

Such were his thoughts as the path widened out and he found himself walking alongside the river bank. He stopped to pass the time of the day with a solitary fisherman.

'Nice specimen,' George commented as the man showed him his catch.

'Plenty there, but they're not playing today.'

'Will you eat it?' George said.

'No, no. I'll put it back later. They taste of mud.' He adjusted his rod and cast again. 'I like the solitude. Gives me time away from my wife.'

'I suppose it is a cheap occupation. Maybe something I could take up. Quite fancy the solitude myself.'

The man looked up at him and for the first time he realised he wasn't just any countryman and the tackle and rod he was holding looked expensive. There was a tweed jacket abandoned on the grass behind him and he was wearing good quality waders.

'Mmm,' he said in an indifferent tone and shrugged his shoulders.

'Do you mind if I sit beside you and watch for a while?'

'So long as you're quiet. Don't want to scare the fish off.'

George sat down on the grassy bank, trying to see if he could spot any fish. The water was fast flowing on the bend but the river was wider at this point and as he strained his eyes, he spotted a fish in the reeds. It looked different to the one in the net and he wished he knew more about the different species but he hesitated to ask. He guessed the man beside him had come for some solitude and he understood how he must feel.

Half an hour drifted by and George found the whole scene soporific. He knew he ought to start heading home – he had several miles to walk.

'Sure is enough to calm you – this fishing,' he said as he scrambled up.

'You don't sound local.'

'Spent a bit of time in Canada. I suppose I've still got a bit of an accent.'

'What were you doing in Canada?'

George sat down again.

'Farming.'

'Farming?'

'Till it all went wrong.'

'How do you mean?'

George found he was soon unburdening the whole story.

'So what are you doing now?' The man propped his rod into its rest and his dark eyes stared straight at him.

George hesitated. He'd been very open about his difficulties in Canada but did he want to admit to those in England? Potentially, this man could be a customer of Freddie's or worse, a friend.

'This and that,' he said and clambered to his feet. 'Temporary work.' Except, he reminded himself, it had become pretty permanent.

The man reached into his waistcoat pocket and pulled out a business card. He found a pen and wrote on the back.

'I might have a job, if you're interested.'

'Could be.'

'If you're interested, come and see me at that address – the one I've written on the back.' He thought a moment. 'I'm there most Thursdays. Thursday afternoons – if you're interested.'

'Thanks,' George muttered. 'Good fishing,' he added and, slipping the card into his trouser pocket, set off home.

\* \* \* \* \*

'Oh, how wonderful,' Enid said as she walked into the hall and found the house was empty. 'No one here but us.'

'I wonder where George is,' Freddie said. He didn't like to show how much he agreed with Enid. Having the house to themselves was marvellous after all these months – if only it could become permanent. Friday had been the real test – Enid left alone in the kitchen for the first time since ... he didn't know when. Dinner hadn't been quite up to Amy's standards but she had tried and he gave her full marks for that. Even their trip to his mother-in-law's had been pleasant. With the garage re-development now going ahead, he could hardly believe how much better his life had become but he couldn't help wondering if it would be better still if Beth was his wife.

'Does it matter where George is? The place is ours and I, for one, just love it.'

He had planned to go to the pub but with Enid in such a decent mood, he changed his mind. He knew, if he had gone, he'd feel guilty. In any case, his conscience reminded him about the importance of being a good father and, seeing Jonathan kicking a ball around in the garden, he went to join in the fun.

\* \* \* \* \*

'Last day, tomorrow,' Amy said as she sat with Vi on the park bench. 'It's all gone too quickly but I can't say I'm looking forward to going back.'

Vi rocked the pram while they watched the boys who were attempting to play cricket. They were using Harold's bat which was far too big for them, especially for Bobbie who staggered about as he struggled to swing the bat at the ball in the way of his eldest brother, who Amy now realised, he idolised.

'I can't believe how quickly the time's gone,' Vi said. 'It's a shame Freddie can't collect you – save you going all that way on the train.'

'Cheaper too but at least the boys are happy. They're getting very excited about the train ride. They always enjoy that and, in any case, I couldn't expect Freddie to make the journey 'specially for me. I wonder if his business meeting was successful. He and Charles are as thick as thieves these days …'

'Not ideal – not after what you said happened on May Day. What a horrible man this Charles must be.'

'To think I nearly married him. I think I had a lucky escape but now I dread him making a scene in front of George. Oh, if only he could find another job. It isn't as if he hasn't tried. He scours the papers and he's called in on every business for miles around. I can't tell you how demoralising it is for him, not to mention that we'd both love a place of our own. I suspect Freddie would like the house back. He doesn't say as much but Enid makes it very obvious we've outstayed our welcome.'

Vi glanced at her watch and Amy realised she had only half listened.

'I think we'll have to get back. Harold will be home and he'll expect his dinner.'

'Perhaps I shouldn't say this but I do think Harold is a bit unreasonable at times.' Not a bit, Amy thought, but very unreasonable and very difficult. Look at what had happened the previous day. True it was his day off, but poor Vi had to do everything while he sat in his chair, giving his orders and reading his paper. And, looking back on their stay, he hadn't exactly made them feel welcome.

'He's gone through a difficult patch this past year what with that bang on the head and me being ill and don't forget it's not that long since his mother died. He's not so bad, really.' Vi stood up and Amy felt guilty that she had criticised him. Of course, Vi would defend him.

It was a warm and sunny afternoon with hardly a breeze and, as they walked along the streets towards home, the boys trailed behind. The houses had largely been built since the beginning of the century, Edwardian terraces with a variety of bay windows, all with a fashionable stained window in the front door and tiled paths which led to polished doorsteps. At least here, there were shrubs and bushes which cheered the place up, unlike where Ma lived which always seemed so drab with the front doors opening straight onto the street. But many of the roads looked similar and Amy found she easily mistook one for another and knew she'd probably get lost if she had been alone. At last they reached Vi's house and Amy ushered the boys in before following them into the house.

'Mrs Smith?' a deep voice called as she was about to shut the door. A uniformed policeman stood at the gate.

She thought later, as she made a pot of tea that her instinct had told her immediately something was wrong. It was strange how therapeutic it was – making tea. But nothing would take away from the dreadful news which the police officer had just broken to Vi.

'He collapsed at work,' he said. 'I'm so sorry but he never recovered.'

Vi stood rocking Lily in her arms, her face white with shock, she said nothing. It was as though she hadn't heard.

'Mrs Smith?' the police officer said gently.

'Come and sit down, Vi,' she had said and took Lily from her.

Vi sat in Harold's chair, then stood up as though she thought Harold was there in the room. Amy gently pushed her down again.

'I'll make some tea …' She took the baby with her into the scullery.

'They got an ambulance,' she could hear the police officer saying. 'They did their best but there was nothing they could do. I'm really sorry to have to break this news.'

Lily grabbed at her necklace and Amy clasped the little fingers endeavouring to unwind her little fingers. Poor child – now she would never know her father.

## Chapter Twenty One

'Okay, okay,' Freddie said, not disguising his annoyance. He needed George to be in the office to answer the telephone which seemed to ring constantly and to make out the invoices because that way the books were kept up-to-date, something he knew he had been very bad at. Some days he wished George would find another job – that he hadn't invited his sister and her family into his house. He tried to ignore the small voice reminding him he had been only too pleased to have Amy's help when Enid was sick. Now, increasingly, he had to admit, George had become very useful. Not only could he hold a sensible conversation with prospective customers, especially about repairs and servicing but he had got the office running smoothly with a filing system which actually worked and with the building works affecting so much of the garage, a functioning office was a godsend. He knew if it had been left to him, as Charles had pointed out on a number it occasions, it would have been chaos.

But this afternoon? Why did it have to be this afternoon? George had wanted the previous Thursday off, but with Donnie sick, it wasn't possible. It was the time he tried to keep exclusively for Beth but, even he had had to forgo that pleasure the previous week. Right then, there were plenty of punters interested in purchasing cars and, with quite a number still waiting to be sold, he didn't want to lose business because he was absent. As he glanced out of the window, yet another builder's truck pulled into the forecourt. The sooner the new show room was completed, the better. He turned his attention back to George, who stood in the open doorway.

'I suppose I could be back by around three. Will that do?'

'I suppose it'll have to. Thanks,' George muttered.

'Don't sound so grateful,' he said more to himself.

He turned his attention back to the manufacturer's specifications for Humber, a make for which the garage was now a distributor, but his mind wandered. Things had been difficult during the previous few days. Enid had the sulks because, with Amy staying in London for another week, she had been responsible for all the meals. She did nothing but complain and criticise and some days he found the dust and noise at work more bearable than the arguments and moods at home. That was why his time with Beth was so important – it was his only opportunity to relax.

And now there was to be a funeral. He could see George being absent again. It really was a damn nuisance but right then, he found himself wondering what George was up to. He hadn't said why he wanted to leave early.

'Good morning, Freddie,' Charles' voice cut through his thoughts.

He hadn't realised George had left the office door open. He looked up to see Charles grinning at him. At least somebody was cheerful.

'Morning,' he grunted.

'Don't sound so pleased to see me.' Charles dragged a chair over and sat opposite him.

'You don't have to deal with the staff or their problems.'

'You mean I don't have to deal with your family problems,' Charles said in a sharp voice. 'Couldn't help but overhear a bit of your conversation with George.'

'Hmm.'

'Cheer up, old man. It can't be that bad.'

Freddie gave him a withering look. Charles' house was sufficient in size for him to escape from any squabbling the children might do, whilst he had to suffer the arguments, the fights and the general hullabaloo. Sometimes he wanted nothing more than to move into the pub permanently.

'I came to discuss our grand opening.'

'Grand opening?' Freddie repeated. He shoved the car specifications he'd been studying to one side and pulled out his diary.

'There's no question about it. We have to have one and I thought we'd invite a few dignitaries – someone to cut the ribbon so to speak. The Rotary and the Vicar and Sylvia'll come. Of course you must bring Enid.'

Somehow Freddie didn't feel excited about holding a grand opening. It was one thing Sylvia being there but Enid ... With Beth opposite? It was going to be very awkward.

'Do we have to make it that big?'

'Of course we do. It'll drum up business and give us some publicity. We've, or rather, I've ploughed a lot of money into this and I don't want it going off like a damp squib. Yes, Freddie, I intend for it to be a very grand opening and we'll get one of those Humbers into the centre of the showroom,' he said and pointed to the booklet on the desk. 'Centre stage, so to speak and with the Prince of Wales driving one, they're going to be very popular.'

'Do you mean this Snipe?'

'Of course I do, Freddie. They'll be queueing up now the Royals are driving round in them. And,' Charles continued, 'we'll have cocktails – get a few of 'em tiddly. Make them part with their money.' He grinned. 'Now what about food? A buffet of some kind, do you think? What about getting the pub to do the catering? You seem to know the landlady quite well.'

Freddie felt himself colour up.

'As a matter of fact, I'm having lunch there. I'll make some enquiries.'

'Right then. I'll leave you to make the catering arrangements and I'll drum up the guest list and sort out the invitations. Oh, and I think we ought to place an ad in the paper. Half a page should do it. Now, when are we taking delivery of this beauty?' He reached across the desk for the pamphlet, flicking through it and reading some of the details. 'Isn't she magnificent? Let's look at your diary and sort out a date.'

* * * * *

Beth placed a kiss on Freddie's lips and slipped out of bed. He admired her naked beauty, catching her hand. They had foregone lunch and spent the entire afternoon in bed and now he was reluctant for their time together to end.

'Don't go.'

'Some of us have to earn a living and it's late. I need to sort out a few things before opening time.'

'Forget work. Come back to bed.' He tugged at the finger he had hooked with his own.

'Freddie, I thought you knew by now. You can't run a business by being absent.' She pulled her hand free, grabbed her dressing gown and headed for the bathroom. 'I need to cash up from lunch time, remember? I want to get sorted before we open for the evening,' she said as she reached the door.

'It can't be that late.' He reached for his cigarettes.

'I've got lots of jobs to do,' she said and closed the door behind her.

Freddie removed a cigarette, tapping it lightly on the packet before clicking the lighter and holding the flame to it. He puffed a few times then exhaled enjoying the moment and wishing, yet again, he could marry Beth. Quite forgetting Enid would be present on the Grand Opening day, he visualised moving into the pub – very quietly, of course, and when everyone's attention was on the garage. By the time the festivities had died down it would be a fait accomplit. Maybe then, she would agree to marry him.

'Come on, Freddie,' Beth said when she came back fully dressed. She sounded a little irritated. 'Stop day dreaming and get out of bed,' she urged. 'It's almost four o'clock.'

'Is it really?' He pretended ignorance and supposed he'd better get up before he outstayed his welcome. 'George'll be in a right huff when I get back. I said he could go as soon as I got back. I think I mentioned three o'clock.'

'That's no way to treat your staff.' She frowned in disapproval as she sat in front of the mirror to powder her nose. 'And, by the sound of it, you're going to miss that brother-in-law of yours when he finds another job.'

He didn't bother to reply but stubbed his cigarette out in the ashtray and searched for his underpants in the pile of clothes on the floor.

'You'd better let yourself out. I have to go down. And don't forget to give some thought to the sort of food you want. Oh, and numbers, of course. I'll need to know how many.'

He pulled his trousers on but, in spite of knowing George was not going to be too pleased with him, he didn't hurry. The afternoon had put him in good spirits and he decided he would try to make up for his absence by not being too grumpy about time off to go to London for a funeral. True, George hadn't asked yet but he would. Maybe he would be generous and allow him to use the car. That way he'd make sure Amy came back and he really did miss her steak and kidney pies.

*****

George set off at a fast pace, his anger dissipating with every step. He had felt like clouting Freddie but somehow had kept himself under control, drawing on the discipline he'd learnt as a soldier. Besides he knew it would have been futile losing his temper, he would only pay the penalty somewhere else along the way. And there was the funeral looming. He would want time off for that.

It was going to be a long walk to the address written on the card. He had no idea if the prospective job was going to be one he would want to do but he had to try. He thought back to the Saturday, two weeks earlier, when he'd shoved the card into his pocket. He hadn't given it another thought until the following morning when he was searching his pockets for his keys. He had stared at the words embossed on the card:

### Joshua Goldberg

### Importer and Supplier of Fine Cloth

The address was somewhere in the City of London, near St Paul's, he thought. It was quite a classy card – edged in gold with Olde English writing – very impressive. On the reverse was scribbled a local address. That had surprised him as he had thought the man had travelled out from London. He wasn't sure where the place was but Donnie was able to direct him. He hoped the guy would be there since he was a week later than he'd planned and now it was going to be more like early evening rather than afternoon by the time he arrived. He supposed he could have asked for a lift but he didn't want Freddie to know a thing about what he was doing and, if it worked out, he would enjoy the satisfaction of seeing Freddie's surprise when he gave in his notice.

Grateful for the lighter evenings, he arrived to find a very ordinary house at the end of a short drive. It was empty. He inspected the card again to check the address. Yes, this was the place. He peered through the windows but all he could see, beyond his own reflection, were bare floorboards. It was all very strange and he was more than disappointed his long walk had led him literally up a garden path. He turned round and began to walk back the way he'd come but he could hear banging as though someone was hammering nails. He ambled round to the back of the house to see whether that someone could tell him what had happened to the previous occupiers of the house.

He reached the corner as the hammering ceased.

'Blast it,' the man cursed and picked up a piece of wood to examine it.

'Mr Goldberg?' George said in astonishment at being fortunate enough to find him.

The man looked up, his face blank at first.

'Ah, I remember. We met … Fishing. Correct?'

'That's right, sir. You gave me this card. Said you might have a job for me.'

'Hmm. You're lucky I'm still here. Should have gone hours ago but I wanted to finish this.' He indicated the piece of wood. 'I was never any good with my hands. It's a sign for the house … Anyway, you want to know about this job?'

## Chapter Twenty Two

'George!' Amy said in surprise. He had arrived before breakfast and caught her still in her nightclothes. She opened the door fully, trying to hide behind it, not wanting the neighbours to see her state of undress.

'Don't I get a kiss?'

'Yes, yes. Oh, come on in.'

She closed the front door and watched him place the holdall he was carrying on the floor before allowing him to embrace her but their kiss was cool. When they separated, she stared at him, wondering how it was they had drifted so far apart. Did he still think she was seeing Charles? Or worse – had Charles said something while she'd been away? She wanted to find words to reassure him but before she could think of something, all three boys burst into the room.

'Daddy!'

'At least someone is pleased to see me,' he said and gave each of them a hug. 'How's Vi?' He whispered over the tops of their heads.

'All right – not really coping but what do you expect?' How did she explain Vi had been in a state of shock since the visit from the Police and spent most of the days wandering about in a daze – that she seemed to have forgotten little Lily, wasn't eating and apparently not sleeping.

'Where is she?'

'Upstairs. I've been trying to get her into something suitable for the funeral.'

'What do you mean, trying?'

'She's not functioning normally. I'm at my wits end, trying to cope with her and the baby and the boys.'

'I want you and the boys to come home with me,' he said. 'Tonight,' he emphasised.

'We – er – I can't do that,' she said feeling torn. It was true she had been in London for over two weeks and she didn't envy George having to live with Freddie and Enid by himself. But how could she leave Vi? She didn't know how well Harold had provided for her or how she was going to cope. Money had yet to be discussed. They had survived on the food in the pantry for several days. 'I can't leave Vi alone and what about Lily? Are these the clothes I asked you to bring?'

'Yes,' he said and handed her the holdall.

'Thanks.'

'Yes, but sweetheart, you've done enough. I need you now.'

Sweetheart? When was the last time he'd used that endearment? Certainly not since they had left the farm. She stared at him. And he needed her now? She hadn't felt needed since the day they left Canada. And as for her having done enough? What did he know? He hadn't been here these last two weeks, coping with a screaming baby and three boisterous children, not to mention getting Vi through the identification and the bureaucracy involved. And the funeral arrangements – that, too, had been far from easy. No, he most definitely hadn't "needed" her for some time so why should he now? She didn't understand why his words, far from pleasing, irked her.

'I've got a big enough family for God's sake. Why aren't they here? I'll talk to Lizzie after the funeral and Ted – he's head of the family. Now, get Vi down here. She needs to face reality.'

Amy took a deep breath and exhaled very slowly. He had only arrived a few moments ago so what gave him the right to order everyone about? It was true, his family had been absent for much of the previous week, except for the odd occasion when Ma popped in. Of course, Phoebe hadn't bothered to visit once but Vi had long ago explained how snobby she could be. But Lizzie? She was closest to Vi and maybe could have been here more. She had made excuses for them all and it rankled that George should feel he had the right to march in and take over.

'You –,' she spluttered, for a second lost for words. 'You waltz in here and give your orders. How do you know what's been happening? And things are pretty real here. How dare you suggest otherwise.'

George stared at her.

'Vi is in shock, that's all,' she moderated her tone. They didn't need to fall out. A funeral was difficult enough without quarrelling.

'Losing any life is tough and losing the person closest to you is the toughest of all. But, Amy, life goes on. Vi has got to get herself together. She has to for the sake of Lily. Every time a man was killed on the battlefield, do you think we gave up and wandered about in shock? We'd have been dead men if we had. We had to get on with things.'

She shook her head. He sounded so callous. She picked up the bag and left the room wondering why the man she loved so much had disappeared. Then she remember the first funeral they attended together – remembered how unfeeling he had seemed then. If this was the way he coped through the Great War – it had a lot to answer for and it had left a horrible scar.

'George is here,' she told Vi when she got upstairs. 'Come on, let's get you dressed then you can go downstairs to say hello.'

She coaxed Vi into a dark skirt and, rummaging amongst the clothes in the wardrobe, found a purple cardigan and a plain white blouse. As she helped her dress, she thought for the hundredth time, how they should have gone to the shops and bought something suitable but it wasn't possible with Vi in her present state. Besides, where was the money for such an outfit? It had been difficult enough getting her to choose the coffin and decide on the hymns and she had been grateful for the kindness of the undertaker. Thank God, Ma had offered to pay for the costs or it would have been a pauper's funeral.

With Vi's outfit sorted, she went back to her own room. She hoped George had remembered to put in her silk stockings and her black skirt. She needed to get dressed before she confronted George again. Confronted? Was that all there was to their relationship these days? Maybe, she conceded, she should go home if for no other reason than to try to save her marriage.

By mid-morning, the rest of the family were crowded into the darkened front room.

'They're here.' Ted was standing at the window, peeping through a crack in the curtains. He waited for the black horses to stop outside, then turned to face them.

'Time to go, Vi,' he said in a hushed voice, placing his hand under her arm and assisting her to her feet. The rest of the family were to follow for the short walk behind the horse-drawn hearse to the nearby church.

Amy placed Lily in Vi's arms, gathered the boys together and followed George outside where top-hatted undertakers were waiting for them. She gazed at the glass sided funeral coach with its polished brass lamps and black and gold fringed drapes which framed the windows. A beautiful spray of lilies had been placed on top of the coffin and several other floral tributes – one in the shape of a cushion – were lying beside it. As they moved off to make the slow journey to the church, neighbours joined the group of mourners and followed the cortège.

\* \* \* \* \*

'She looks like a ghost,' Lizzie whispered as she sipped her sherry. 'Did you see when Lily was crying? She didn't notice. Now when my babies were tiny, I could hear their cries everywhere. I don't understand ...'

It's time some of you took some notice, Amy thought staring down into the tea leaves which remained at the bottom of her cup and puzzling over why all George's relatives seemed to like Sherry. Somehow she'd never acquired the taste.

'Do you know if Harold left her ..? Well, you know ?'

'No, I don't. We haven't got round to the will. In fact, I don't even know if Harold made one but I think he's left her the house.' She didn't add that the funeral costs were not insignificant or that when she mentioned this to Vi, she was very vague, saying only that there was an insurance policy. As yet the policy, like the will, had not materialised.

'She'll need an income,' Lizzie continued. 'Maybe she should take a lodger. That's what a lot of widows do.'

They probably have little choice, Amy thought, but before she could say as much, Thomas was beside them offering sandwiches, followed by May who carried a tray with more glasses of sherry. George's youngest brother and sister had suddenly grown up but, from past experience, she knew not to discuss private matters in front of May – she was far too nosey. She watched Lizzie remove a glass from the tray, replacing it with her empty one and couldn't help noticing a tale tell splurge of pink in her cheeks.

'Yes, possibly she will need to take in a paying lodger,' Amy agreed once the youngsters had moved on with their refreshments. 'But I wouldn't know where to start and I'm not sure Vi will either.'

'I've seen lots of adverts in shop windows. That might be a good place to start.'

'I'm not sure I'd want a stranger in my house. Anyway, it's the meantime which worries me. Poor Lily. I suppose it's the shock but, as you say, Vi seems oblivious. George wants me to go home with him tonight and, to be honest, I really should go. It would save the cost of the train fares for a start and the boys are missing school. Will really can't afford to miss any more lessons. He was away for months when he had that accident.'

She hoped Lizzie would pick up the hint she'd dropped – that she would realise Vi would need lots of help and support once she left but with May joining them, the subject was changed and she was left wondering if any of the family were aware of how dire things really were.

By late afternoon most of the guests had departed with only Ma, Ted and George remaining.

'I'll make some more tea,' Amy said and went to put the kettle on. She was relieved to see Vi in the back room with

Lily and, for the first time in days, she was changing her. Maybe now the funeral was behind her, Vi would begin to recover. While she washed up, she could hear the murmuring of conversation from the other room. Sometimes there was a louder comment or two and she could tell they were discussing Vi.

'That's agreed then,' Ted announced as she returned with a tray of tea which she placed on the table.

'And what exactly have you agreed?' Amy couldn't keep the edge out of her voice as she passed the cups round. She went to sit beside George. Why was it men always made decisions without thinking of consulting those most involved?

'We think Vi should move into Ma's for the time being,' Ted said in a decisive tone and it made her think anything Vi might have to say about this would soon be over-ruled. 'That way, we'll know she's eating and that Lily is being looked after properly.'

'Yes,' Ma agreed. 'I think it'd be for the best right now. Ted's going to look into her finances over the next few days.'

'And we're going home,' George said.

Amy said nothing. No one had thought to discuss any of this with her or Vi, yet they were expected to fall into line. Men! They had decided and that was that.

## Chapter Twenty Three

'I'm exhausted,' George flopped on to the bed. They had been home long enough to tell Freddie all about the funeral and to get the boys off to bed and were now alone for the first time since his arrival in London earlier that day.

'It was a long day.' Amy shut the door. They could have stayed the night but, no, George was adamant about going back the same day.

He sat up and began to undo his tie.

As she undressed she thought he wasn't the only one who was exhausted. She thought of Enid who was already in bed – 'dead-beat' according to Freddie. Huh. What had she done to make her so tired? When she visited the bathroom a few minutes ago, there were dirty towels all over the place, a pile of Jonathan's filthy clothing on the floor, not to mention a line of scum round the basin. Doris had been on holiday for a few days and the house showed it. In the kitchen, the cooker had the evidence of fried food and, wherever she looked, there was a layer of dust. What exactly did Enid do to make her so worn out? Not much at all when compared to her own time in London. She had long got over any sympathy she might feel for Enid or Freddie, even, who had managed to annoy her the moment she arrived. It seemed she had hardly got her jacket off when he hinted she should make a steak and kidney pie especially for him. Right then, she had not been amused that he, apparently, had missed her cooking. One day, she promised herself, one day, he was going to have to get used to Enid's attempts in the kitchen because at the first opportunity they would be moving out.

She sat on the bed and pulled her petticoat up over her knees in order to undo her suspenders. She rolled the silky stockings down her legs with enormous care. They were her only pair and she was desperate not to snag them. She examined them for ladders and, with a sigh of relief that there were none, thought of the drawer full she once possessed. But any despair she might feel at her own situation could be nothing to what Vi must be feeling right then. She wished she could have stayed longer, that George hadn't been so insistent about returning Freddie's car. She hoped more than anything else that Vi would soon be able to make decisions for herself and her daughter.

'I've been offered a job,' George said over his shoulder.

It was a second before his announcement registered.

'What?' She turned to look at his back, not sure if she'd heard correctly.

'I've been offered a job,' he repeated.

'Really?' She knew she had squealed in delight but the news was so exciting. How had he kept this knowledge to himself all day when she would have been bursting to tell everyone?

'Shshsh.' He stood up and, placing his finger over his mouth, came round to the end of the bed to face her. He lowered his voice. 'I haven't accepted it yet so I don't want the whole world to know.'

'Why? Why on earth not? It's wonderful news. How did you manage to keep it to yourself all this time?'

'With difficulty.'

'I'd have thought you'd be shouting it from the roof tops.'

She thought of the journey home which had been completed mostly in silence. Following the squabbles between Will and Sam when George threatened to make them all walk, there had been an uneasy hush. Sometimes, she thought he was overly strict but to say anything was to court an argument and, as they had been so near to one on several occasions already during the day, she, too, was silent.

'I don't want Freddie to know – yet.'

'But I don't understand. Why not tell Freddie? He'll want to replace you and he'll need a bit of notice. Isn't he planning some kind of Grand Opening?'

'For goodness sake, keep your voice down. The official opening is Friday – next week.' He undid his trousers, took them off and began to fold them along the crease.

'Next week? Have the builders finished?'

'Yes. Just a massive amount of cleaning to do before we set up the displays. Freddie's got a guest list as long as your arm and we're all expected to be there.'

'All of us? Me?'

'Yes, all of us – boys, too.'

'This guest list …' she said, wondering who exactly was on it but not daring to ask.

'I think it'll be an interesting evening,' he continued. 'Enid's going but you'll never guess who's doing the catering.'

She shrugged. 'How would I know?'

'The pub and you know what that'll mean …'

She pulled a face. Freddie's mistress. She often thought Enid suspected Freddie was being unfaithful but the two of them actually meeting … George was right, things could indeed get very interesting. But she was impatient to know more about the possibility of employment.

'Never mind all that, do tell me about this job. Why on earth haven't you accepted it?'

'Because there's something I need to talk to you about first.'

'What? Oh, for goodness sake, George, stop talking in riddles.'

'Keep your voice down.' He frowned at her. 'It's a bit of a long story,' he began. 'That first weekend you were away, I went for a long walk – right along the river and I met this chap, Joshua Goldberg, and we started talking. He said he had a job which might interest me.' He opened the wardrobe and hung his trousers on the rail.

'And?' She wished he'd get to the point.

'He gave me his business card.' He struggled with his cufflinks. 'Damn stupid things. I never was any good with one hand.'

'Here, let me.'

He stood still while she removed the gold and mother-of-pearl cufflinks – almost the only luxury he possessed, she thought, as she placed them in the dish on top of the chest of drawers.

'Now do tell me about this job.' She couldn't hide her impatience.

'He said to go over and see him the following Thursday. That's when things got difficult.'

'Difficult?' she prompted.

'Freddie refused to let me have time off.'

'Didn't you tell him what it was for?'

'No, I didn't. I wasn't exactly sure what the job was and I didn't want to discuss it with him until I knew. Donnie often gets off early, so I thought he'd let me this once. But no.'

'Why not?' She stared at him in amazement. Then the thought that there had to be a reason why he hadn't accepted this mysterious job made her suspicious. 'What is this job? You do want to do it?'

'There's house ...'

'A house?' she almost shrieked.

'Shshsh.'

'A house?' she repeated in a lower voice. 'A house? Really? What sort of house?'

He nodded but there was a guilty look on his face.

'What's the catch?' Something wasn't right. She knew there had to be a drawback.

'George?'

He didn't answer but pulled his pyjamas from under the pillow and slipped on the jacket.

'There is a catch, I suppose?'

'Not really. Just that ...'

'George, I am not stupid.' Her frustration made her raise her voice. 'Please tell me. What is this job?'

'Shshsh. I don't want Freddie to know about any of this until – well, until you've agreed.'

'Agreed to what?' She said in exasperation.

'He's looking for someone to do some housework.'

'Who is? Stop talking in riddles.'

'Mr Goldberg.'

'I don't understand.'

'He wants me to be his chauffeur and you to help in the house.'

She was speechless. She thought of her red, rough hands and the hours of washing, ironing and housework she'd been doing over the previous months. First Enid, then Vi. She'd had enough.

'No. George, no,' she said in a measured tone. The thought of yet more cleaning horrified her.

'Think about it. And you'd get paid.'

'No,' she said and climbed into bed. 'I am not doing any more skivvying for anyone – not anyone, not even if I get paid for it.' She pulled the bedcovers up over her ears. She didn't want to hear any more.

*****

Freddie knew things were never going to go according to plan when Enid announced she wanted to be involved in the arrangements for the Grand Opening. It was one thing her attending the event but quite another contributing to its organisation.

'Sylvia and I could sort out the food,' she declared over breakfast the following morning.

Ever since he had taken her for dinner with Charles, she had talked about her 'doing' something with Sylvia but it was usually very vague and never amounted to anything. Freddie ignored her words and carried on reading the editorial of 'The Times'.

'Now Amy's back, I'll have more free time,' Enid said in a louder voice.

It was some seconds before he looked over the top of the newspaper in Amy's direction. She had stopped washing the dishes and was glaring at him, leaving him in no doubt that Enid was already overstepping the mark.

'There's no need to do a thing,' he said, anxious to prevent any meddling with his arrangements with Beth. 'We've placed an order at the pub.'

'The pub? We need something more upmarket than food from the pub. I thought the garage was trying to attract the more well-to-do clientele and if that's the case, we need proper caterers.'

He put his paper down. It was the first time she had shown any interest in the garage, so why now?

'There's no need for you to worry about a thing,' he said, almost adding, that since she had never stepped foot in the pub, she wouldn't know whether the food was good or not. 'Charles has seen the menu – tasted it, even,' he said.

'And he's very happy with things and that's good enough for me.'

'Oh,' Enid pouted. 'Can't I do anything?'

'Be there on the night and look your most glamourous. And speak to the punters, of course. I'm sure you'll charm them.' He picked up the paper, hoping he'd said enough to put her off. Her involvement was the last thing he wanted – or needed. On the evening, it would be difficult to keep her away from Beth who had said she would be there to supervise. In any case, he had sort of invited her.

'Now Amy's back, there's nothing much to do here, so I thought …'

Freddie pretended not to hear. Much to his relief, Jonathan caused a distraction by upsetting the honey pot.

'Oh, now look what you've done. Amy, dear, could you bring a cloth?'

In the ensuing commotion he escaped but not without observing Amy's angry expression and wondering how long before war broke out between the two women. Enid did take liberties.

\* \* \* \* \*

George spent the entire morning working on the coachwork of the newly delivered Humber Snipe, which was parked in the centre of the completed showroom. With four doors and shiny metal bumpers it looked the height of luxury.

He wrung the water out of his leather and began to dry off the black bodywork with great care. Next he took the polish and buffed it till it shone like a mirror. Charles was hoping to bring in another vehicle later that day but the plan was to leave the showroom with a fair amount of space for entertaining their guests. And in order to keep an element of surprise, Freddie had hung large white sheets at the windows. They were to stay there until the big day. Already promotional posters had been pasted outside the garage and a large advertisement was to appear in the local paper.

While he worked, he would often whistle but today his mind was occupied with Amy and how he was going to persuade her that he should take this job. A Chauffeur. The job of his dreams and he'd wanted to accept straight away but Mr Goldberg had insisted he discuss things with her first. He thought it'd be a formality and she, like him, would jump at the opportunity. Instead he'd been astonished when she flatly refused to consider it – wouldn't even discuss it. That night, he'd crawled into bed deadbeat but unable to sleep because he was so angry.

Maybe Enid would do the job for him, he consoled himself. He had witnessed the scene in the kitchen that morning. He had never seen Amy look so angry. Possibly, after a day or two, Mr Goldberg's offer would seem more attractive. He made up his mind, he would take Amy and the boys to see the house which could be theirs if only she'd see sense and he would take them all as soon as possible.

That evening, Amy produced one of her steak and kidney specials.

'Fantastic, sis,' Freddie said as he mashed his potato.

Enid picked at it and then threw her fork down.

'Maybe tomorrow we could have some fish?' she said. 'I think that's more to my taste.'

George tried to conceal his amusement. He concentrated on mopping up the delicious gravy with a slice of bread but couldn't help thinking how patronizing Enid was. He didn't need to look at Amy to know she was seething and was surprised when she said nothing. He knew exactly what he would say if she grumbled to him later. There was, at last, an alternative.

## Chapter Twenty Four

'You could have warned me.' Freddie yanked the sheet off his head.

'Oops, sorry,' George said, not concealing his amusement. It was mid-afternoon and he was up a ladder, unhitching the sheets which hung at the showroom windows. One by one he dropped them down to Freddie who was using them to conceal the two gleaming cars now parked in the showroom. Secretly, he thought anyone with a bit of savvy would know what was under wraps. After all there was a new metal sign over the entrance announcing the garage was now a distributor for Humber.

Freddie bundled the last sheet under his arm and marched over to the partly shrouded car and set about completing its disguise while George climbed down the wooden ladder.

'There, I think that should do it.' Freddie stood back to admire his handiwork. 'When the ribbon is cut tonight and everyone has a drink in their hands, we'll unveil these two babies.'

'I hope it doesn't rain or they'll all get wet,' George said, voicing his thoughts. When he had helped Freddie tie the ribbon across the entrance, it had been very overcast and he knew the guests were to wait outside until the big moment.

'There won't be any rain, you'll see.' Freddie disappeared into the office, leaving George to return the ladder to the workshop.

Visitors began to arrive twenty minutes before four o'clock which was the time set for cutting the ribbon and he and Donnie were called into the office.

'I want you to wear these.' Charles handed them each a parcel. 'Smart new overalls. Even got the Humber logo on them. You have to look the part.'

As he and Donnie slipped into the brown overalls, Freddie was standing at the window.

'There's quite a crowd outside already,' he said, turning to face them. 'and it looks a bit threatening. Not sure if we'll have to cut the ribbon a bit earlier. What do you think?'

'Can't cut the ribbon before Sir William arrives,' Charles said. 'Have we got any brollies?'

As George did his buttons up, he gave Donnie a look which said 'I told you so'. They had only been discussing the weather a few minutes earlier as he was concerned Amy would get wet but, according to Donnie, Enid was being collected by Sylvia, so he hoped they'd all come together.

A clap of thunder sent Freddie sprinting through the showroom and yanking the ribbon off its hook. He opened the door for the visitors to pile inside. Seconds later a deluge thundered on the roof and the windows began to steam up.

George and Donnie followed Charles out of the office and, as instructed, mingled with the crowd.

'So much for the ribbon.' George heard Freddie remark in a gloomy voice to Charles. 'I knew things would go wrong the moment Enid wanted to get involved.'

'Don't be so silly, old man,' Charles said. 'These things happen and anyway, Sir William will be here any minute. Just make sure everyone's got a drink and then we'll get him to unveil the Snipe. Might not be a ribbon but I think it'll be impressive enough. Now where's the lady with the drinks.' He turned to George and Donnie. 'Come on boys, lend a hand. By the time they've all got a glass in their hand, it'll be time to do some business.'

\* \* \* \* \*

'Hurry up,' Amy yelled at Sam who was splashing in all the puddles along the edge of the path. Sometimes she despaired at her middle son. If there was a way of doing something which was unconventional or would get him into trouble, he would find it. Right then they were in a hurry and he had his new shoes on. She knew what George would say if he arrived with them soggy or, worse still, scuffed. 'We're late and your father won't be pleased,' she told him as she held his hand. 'So no more jumping into puddles, we have to hurry.'

She glanced at her watch. It was nearly five o'clock and she knew both Freddie and George would be annoyed but it couldn't be helped. It wasn't her fault it had decided to rain. She had rushed about making sure the boys were clean and tidy and was still feeling peeved with Enid who had insisted Sylvia leave without them. Though, if she was honest, there wasn't room for them all in that little car.

'We need to be there early,' Enid said when, at the last moment, Will announced he needed the toilet. 'It'll be too much of a squash anyway,' she added and got into the open top Morris. Amy thought the car was the one which belonged to Charles, but, according to Enid, Sylvia had liked his car so much, he'd bought an identical one for her. She tried not to feel envious.

They had driven off, leaving her annoyed they hadn't taken at least one of the boys. She knew they would have to stride out if they were to arrive in time for the ribbon cutting ceremony Freddie was so anxious for them to witness. Then, before Will returned from his visit to the toilet, there was a deafening clap of thunder, followed by a heavy shower of rain which, as she stood by the open door, she could see bouncing off the path, the water forming rivulets and puddles. She thought of Enid and Sylvia in the open top car.

'What's so funny, Mum?' Will asked as he joined her.

'Oh, nothing. Just that we're going to be late and there's nothing we can do about it.'

They waited, impatient for the weather to pass but it was over half an hour before the storm eased to a fine drizzle. By the time they reached the village, they were damp but the rain had stopped. She was grateful when they spotted the garage roof and knew it wasn't much further.

She admired the new frontage – the latest design, according to Freddie. She hadn't seen how things were progressing for nearly a month and she had to admit, it was very impressive. She liked the fresh green lime paint so fashionable right then. The forecourt had new Macadam and an ornate chain marked the boundary to the road. It must have cost a fortune but she supposed Freddie didn't have to worry about that now he had a wealthy partner.

It was as if Charles was waiting for her. He was standing by the door and the moment he spotted her, threw it open.

'Amy, for the Lord's sake do come on in out of the wet. Come on, join the party.'

He held the door for her and she ushered the boys ahead – a bad mistake, she soon realised, as Charles put his arm around her. She watched the boys head towards the cars and disappear amongst the guests, leaving her on the periphery.

'You've been hiding from me,' he said in her ear. She could smell alcohol and wondered how much he'd had to drink.

'Where's George? Ah, I see him,' she said, wanting to get away but his hand tightened its grip around her waist.

'What's the hurry?'

'Is Sylvia here yet?' She was desperate to escape his hold. 'Did you get the storm? Enid was with her. They must have got wet.'

'Oh, er ... yes, you could say that. They've gone back to change.' He laughed and, distracted for a second, his hold loosened. 'They arrived like drowned rats. Sylvia will insist on driving about with that roof down.'

'Oh, dear,' she said and attempted to step away.

'Not so fast,' he said clutching her arm. 'We need to talk.'

'Oh? Can't imagine why,' she said, feigning ignorance.

'I hope you haven't forgotten our little conversation – the one we had on May Day?'

'Nothing's changed, Charles.'

'Now don't be so hasty. There's something you should know.'

She didn't want to hear any more but his grip had tightened on her arm.

'We've decided to appoint an office manager and while you've been away, George has been such a good chap ... such a good chap. Almost ideal, I could say but,' he said placing strong emphasis on the word 'but'. 'Well, to be honest, he is expendable, you know and I am sure there are lots of other suitable candidates.'

She didn't answer – didn't know how to answer.

'Amy,' he pulled her closer and whispered in her ear. 'Don't you see, you and I were meant for each other ...'

For a second she froze, unsure how to react.

'Of course,' he continued when she said nothing. 'I could tell him we met several times – you and I.' His tone was menacing. 'You see, I was in London, too and more than once last week. What do you think he'll make of that?'

She wrenched herself free.

'I will not be blackmailed,' she said and, seeing George close by, turned away before he had a chance to stop her.

'Think about it,' he said.

*****

'Seems to be going well,' Beth whispered in Freddie's ear as she stopped with a tray of drinks.

'Except for the cloudburst. Couldn't have happened at a worse moment.' Freddie took a glass from the tray and thought how sexy she looked in a maid's outfit. 'You should wear that getup to bed.'

'You shouldn't drink so much.'

'Maybe not,' he said with a shrug. 'But you do look ... Oh, dear, here comes trouble.' He'd seen Enid and Sylvia returning and neither of them looked exactly happy. He sighed. He'd been enjoying the party up till then. 'I suppose I'd better go and make my peace.'

'Peace?'

'Enid made such a fuss – I'm surprised you didn't notice. I think everybody else did.'

'I did. She was er – a little wet.'

'Yes and she thought I should drive her home. How could I do that? Not with all these customers lined up. Not good for business at all and you'd be the first to tell me that.'

'Freddie!' Enid's voice shrieked across the room and before either of them could move she had edged her way and stood between them.

'Are you planning to purchase a car?' Enid said in her most superior voice.

'That's enough, Enid. Beth is in charge of the food and we were discussing requirements, weren't we?'

'Yes, yes and I'd better get on. Nice to meet you at last, Mrs Attwood,' Beth said with a smile and took her tray to the next group.

Freddie, who was determined any arguments Enid might like to pick should happen later when they were alone, spotted Amy. She was preventing Sam from getting into the Snipe and he wondered what else the boy had been up to. Maybe it should have been an adult only event but he'd wanted to show off to everyone. Pity his mother had declined the invitation, but she was very frail these days. At least there were only Amy's three, he thought with relief. It could have been far worse but Jonathan had gone to stay with a friend – Enid had insisted and Charles' two were at boarding school.

'Amy,' he shouted over the din. 'Come and meet a friend of mine.' He turned to Enid. 'Do me a big favour. Save the rows for later. Please. And be a nice girl, mingle. You were always good at that.'

'This is Rodney,' he said the second Amy was by his side. He tapped a middle-aged man in a dark suit on the arm and interrupted his conversation. 'All his friends call him .. er … maybe, I won't tell you what we call him.' Freddie winked. 'He and I go back a long way,' he continued by way of an introduction. He grabbed a drink from Beth's tray as she passed and placed it in Amy's hands. Out of the corner of his eye, he could see Enid who, far from mixing with the guests had stopped Beth. The expression on her face horrified him. Oh, my God! Did she know?

He turned to Amy, who being polite, had struck up a conversation with Rodney.

'I need your help. Now,' he said in an urgent tone. As he watched Beth smiled at Enid. Were things going to be all right? They seemed to be having a very earnest conversation about something and he hoped it wasn't him.

'Please,' he whispered.

'What is it?'

'Enid. Can't you see?'

'She's having a conversation. So?'

'With Beth. Oh, you know. Don't act dim. Please … I need your help.'

* * * * *

Sipping the wine, Amy decided it wasn't only sherry she didn't much like. She would abandon her glass as soon as possible. With a certain amount of embarrassment, she witnessed Freddie excuse himself in as abrupt a manner, as he'd interrupted Rodney's conversation in the first place. Now she found herself guided across the room. The place was jam-packed and they had to ease themselves between drinks, food and people. She could see Enid and Beth and knew there was nothing she was prepared to say or do. Freddie deserved it. He'd been the one to play around all these years. Now it seemed he would have to pay the consequences and she had no doubt that George, for one, would find the whole situation comical. If it wasn't so tragic, she might, too.

They passed Will who was peering into a car. Bobbie standing on tiptoe was behind him but she couldn't see Sam and hoped he wasn't into mischief.

'It was terribly funny,' Enid said to Beth as they reached them.

Beth laughed but it seemed whatever was amusing them was not for her and Freddie's ears as the subject was very obviously changed on their approach.

'I thought you were mingling,' Freddie said in a disapproving tone of voice.

'She was,' Beth said. 'I stopped her because I wanted to know if there were any guests who would prefer a non-alcoholic drink.'

'Ooh, yes. I would,' Amy said and thought Beth had been very quick on the uptake. Why had she chosen to defend Enid? She placed her glass on the tray. 'Is that water?'

'Lemonade,' Beth said.

'Thanks.' Amy picked up a glass. Whatever the crisis, it seemed it was over, for the moment. In fact, it very much looked as if Beth and Enid had hit it off – otherwise why would they be laughing. In her experience Enid only laughed when it was at Freddie's expense. She studied each of the women's faces and her instinct told her that the joke had indeed been on Freddie and they were in this together. But, she thought with a wry smile, she wasn't sure Freddie had realised yet.

\* \* \* \* \*

'You're late,' George said. 'I thought you said you'd be here by four.'

He was annoyed and didn't bother to hide it from her.

'We got here as quickly as we could.' she said not bothering to expand – there didn't seem any point in saying they had been there sometime and George never did make allowances for getting three children organised or, now she thought, for the weather. Since the evening they returned from London, they had hardly talked and she knew she hadn't been forgiven for refusing to take on the housework for his prospective employer. But, couldn't he, for once, look at things from her point of view. Yes, she wanted nothing more than to move out of Freddie's house and away from Enid but only to be at the beck and call of another household? She remembered how sometimes in Canada she had considered running away. Then it had been impossible, especially in winter, when to do so would be like committing suicide but now ..?

Then, there was Charles. If she didn't give in to his demands, would George's job become impossible? Would he have a job, even? She half thought of telling him everything – the whole sordid tale, but what was the use? He already didn't trust her and probably wouldn't believe anything she said and, if Charles carried out his threat to imply they were in London together, it was obvious who he would believe. It was all very depressing.

'You missed the Grand Opening – one of Charles' cronies – Lord something or other.' His words interrupted her thoughts. 'It didn't go quite to plan – the ribbon cutting had to be abandoned as it rained. I knew it would.'

'I didn't miss much, then,' she said and thought he sounded a little pleased it hadn't worked out as Freddie hoped.

'Where are the boys? Didn't you bring them?'

'Of course, I did.' She said irritated that he had yet to enquire whether she had been caught in the rain. She felt taken for granted – not just by him but by Freddie too – and Enid.

'They're new,' she said, noting his posh brown overalls and wondering how much they cost. There had hardly been enough money to buy Sam's shoes.

'Charles dished them out this afternoon. Got the Humber logo on them.' He pointed to his top pocket.

'Very nice,' she said, realising he hadn't had to pay for them.

'Where are those boys? I hope Will isn't getting into mischief.'

'Stop worrying. Anyway, it's Sam who needs the watching.'

'Make sure they don't do anything they shouldn't. I'm supposed to be mixing with the guests. Freddie's anxious to take some orders and he wants me to take them out for a test drive.'

'Not tonight, surely? And not in these cars?' she said meaning the ones in the showroom.

'No, of course not. There's a couple lined up outside. You probably saw them.'

There were lots of cars outside so how would she know which were which?

'Damn stupid idea if you ask me,' he continued. 'But that's what he's expecting me to do. They'll all be drunk, of course.'

'Maybe that's the idea. Get them to purchase a car before they sober up.'

'Most of them can afford it,' he said and, seeing Freddie beckon, headed across to the other side of the room.

She watched him go wondering how it was one could feel so alone amidst a crowd. She tried to reassure herself she wasn't unique and wasn't the only one in the room with problems but, whichever way she looked, there didn't seem to be a solution.

'There you are.' Enid's voice broke into her thoughts. 'We need some help to clear up some of these glasses.'

Too weary to argue, she took the tray Enid held out to her. There were lots of abandoned glasses, not all empty, on the nearby window ledge and she began to stack them.

'Not those, silly.' Enid snatched the tray. Two glasses toppled and smashed on the floor. 'Now look what you've done. Get a bucket and clear the glass up before somebody treads in it.'

'Don't you dare to talk to me like I'm some kind of servant. You might treat Doris like dirt at times but I am not your home help. I'm - '

'Is there a problem?' Beth cut across the remainder of her sentence.

'Enid seems to forget I am her sister-in-law and not her unpaid skivvy – running here, doing this, doing that,' Amy found herself snapping. Damn them. It all was too much.

'I'm not suggesting you should,' Enid said, her manner caustic and mocking. 'But it would be nice to have some help.'

'Look, you may be my brother's wife,' Amy's voice got louder. She turned to Beth. 'And you may be my brother's mistress but I am not his or anyone else's slave.'

She was aware of a hush as everyone stopped talking and stared at them.

'That's right, you heard,' she said in a louder voice. 'And I don't suppose for one minute the rest of you can claim to be white than white.'

Then she spotted Sylvia and she couldn't stop.

'And your husband,' she said pointing to Charles. 'Is the worst of them all. Not only does he indulge in extra marital affairs but I expect you already know that. But did you know he's a blackmailer too? Yes and he's doing his best to blackmail me.'

She grabbed hold of Bobbie who was close by and flounced out of the showroom.

## Chapter Twenty Five

George brought the car to a standstill relieved to arrive back without an accident. His passenger had been very annoying, leaning across and inspecting the dials and even once grabbing hold of the steering wheel. Freddie should have booked them all in for tests drives at a later date. He hopped out in order to hold open the passenger door.

'I'm sure Mr Attwood will be happy to discuss figures with you, sir,' he said helping the man to get out of the car. He steadied him on his feet and shutting the car door, watched him zigzag towards the showroom – one drunken customer, he concluded. As he watched, the door was flung open straight into the man's face, knocking him sideways, as Amy charged out.

'What the dickens …' he said to himself. 'God damn it, Amy,' he said in a louder voice. 'What the hell do you think you're doing?' All his efforts to be pleasant and which had, he thought, resulted in the man wanting to buy the car were now probably wasted. It was a wonder he was still standing. 'That was a potential purchaser you almost knocked over.'

Amy ignored him and dragging Bobbie along, fury etched across her face, marched past him.

'Hey, where do you think you're going?' He grabbed her arm and pulled her to a stop.

'Away from here. Oh, I don't know.' Tears welled in her eyes. 'I've had enough – enough of you all.'

Seeing the man make it into the showroom, he pulled her back against the car, preventing her from going anywhere. He opened the driver's door.

'In you get, Bobbie. You can play at being a driver.' He turned to Amy. 'We need to talk.' He opened the rear passenger door and indicated for her to get in and for a second, thought she was going to refuse. Then she climbed in and he got in beside her.

'What's happened,' he said after a long silence during which he'd handed her his handkerchief.

'I've …' Amy dabbed her eyes. 'I've done something awful.'

'It can't be that bad …' he said and knew immediately he'd said the wrong thing as more tears streamed down her cheeks. Lost for words, he held her hand. It was a long time since they had held hands, he thought. They seemed so distant from each other these days. Not surprising considering what they'd been through. His mind went back over the nightmare which had been the last few years. Everything was such a struggle and now he questioned whether there was any point to it all.

'Take me home.'

'How can I do that?'

'I can't go back in there, George. Please.'

'What am I supposed to say?'

'Tell them I'm not well. I can't face them – any of them – not right now.'

He stared at her for several seconds. What would Freddie have to say about him driving her home? He sighed. He really ought to ask permission, but what the heck.

'All right but I'll have to come back and in any case there's Will and Sam. And, when we get home, you'd better tell me exactly what's been going on.' He got out of the back of the car and, pushing Sam across into the passenger seat, got in beside him and started the engine.

He focussed on driving them home, determined that once they were there, she would tell him exactly what all the fuss was about. He hoped it was something trivial and that he could get back before they missed him.

'You have to take that job,' Amy said the moment the front door closed behind them.

He gazed at her in surprise, for a second dumbstruck.

'Are you serious?'

'Never more so.'

* * * * *

'Well, what do you think?' George asked as they stood together in the garden.

There was a pause before she answered as she gazed about her, analysing the plants in the unkempt borders. There were lots of overgrown shrubs and she knew precisely what she would do with it all, though she knew George would insist on a vegetable plot. Beyond was a small orchard with a couple of rows of apple trees. She could hear the boys squealing and laughing and knew they were rolling in the long grass. There was the gentle hum of insects and bees as they harvested nectar. It was tranquil – so calm and so different to their lives. Right then, it seemed as though they were at war with Freddie and Enid and she longed for peace.

'It's amazing,' she said not liking to admit he'd been right all along.

'Look what I've got.' He held up a bunch of keys. 'Come and see round the house.'

'You didn't tell me …'

'Wanted to surprise you. I collected them this morning. Mr Goldberg said he'd be here about four and he wants to meet you. You are still sure about this?'

She nodded and they retraced their steps, going round to the front of the house. George turned the key and the door swung open.

'It's quite a modern house isn't it? Maybe not as new as Freddie's but it can't be that old. Why doesn't Mr Goldberg want to live here?'

'Fancies himself a new house,' he said.

'A new house? What's wrong with this?'

'I think he's quite well off. From what I can gather, he's earned a fortune selling cloth to the rag trade in the East End. He's had some architect design a house – a pretty large house. You can see it from the end of the orchard. There's enough land here and you've heard of the saying, an Englishman's castle? I think that's what he's planning.'

'A castle?'

'No. No, don't be silly. We'll walk to the end of the orchard and have a look but, first, let's a have look round the house.'

It was almost an hour later, when the boys voices echoed around the empty hall, announcing their arrival.

'In here,' Amy called out to them. They were standing in what they had decided would be their dining room. It was the smaller of the two living rooms and had a sandy-brown tiled fireplace and French doors which looked out onto a small lawn. Their tour had taken them through three bedrooms, a small bathroom with separate toilet and had finished with a discussion on how they were to furnish the house with so little money.

As the boys came running in, out of breath from their romp in the garden, it reminded her so much of when they arrived at their last house. What a contrast. Whilst in Canada it had been incredibly hot with everything scorched brown, dead or shrivelled, here, despite the sun shining for most of the day it was lush green and moist – a garden of Eden by comparison

'What do you think?' George asked the boys.

'When can we move in?' Will wanted to know.

'I think that's a yes, then,' he said and smiled at Amy.

She hadn't seen him smile much in recent months but now there really was something to smile about and she made up her mind.

'I don't need to meet Mr Goldberg. I know I'll like him and I think I can manage two mornings of housework.'

George hugged her.

'We'll make it work, won't we?'

'Yes,' she said. 'We'll make it work.' She hugged him back and knew they had come home.

## About the Author

Born in Kent and raised in London, the author has always loved the countryside. Ann is married, has two sons and six grandchildren and writes from her Norfolk home. She has travelled extensively across Canada, Australia, India and Europe and in March 2015, was featured in one of India's national papers, The Hindu.

Visit her at: www.annbowyer.com

Follow her on Facebook or Twitter

If you enjoyed this book, you may like to read the first book in this series, 'A Token of Love'.

Made in the USA
Charleston, SC
29 June 2015